AN ENGLISH MADE IN INDIA

HOW A FOREIGN LANGUAGE BECAME LOCAL

KALPANA MOHAN

AN ENGLISH MADE IN INDIA

Books by Kalpana Mohan

Daddykins: A Memoir of My Father and I

AN ENGLISH MADE IN INDIA

How a Foreign Language Became Local

KALPANA MOHAN

ALEPH

ALEPH

ALEPH BOOK COMPANY
An independent publishing firm
promoted by *Rupa Publications India*

First published in India in 2019
by Aleph Book Company
7/16 Ansari Road, Daryaganj
New Delhi 110 002

ISBN: 978-93-88292-87-0

1 3 5 7 9 10 8 6 4 2

Printed by Parksons Graphics Pvt. Ltd., Mumbai

CONTENTS

INTRODUCTION: A KILLER LANGUAGE

This is my ocean, but it is speaking
Another language, since its accent changes around
Different islands.

—Derek Walcott, 'Tropic Zone'[1]

I was introduced to the beauty of the world around me through the prism of English. As a child, I felt sorry for my mother. She had never ventured beyond the hallowed gates into the exclusive club of the English language. My mother attended four years of elementary school in the late 1930s in Kerala's North Paravur where she learned to read and write Malayalam. In 1944, she was married, at fourteen years of age, to a man she had never set eyes on, as was customary in conservative Brahmin families in the early part of the twentieth century.

My mother never savoured the kinks and clefts of the English language or fretted, as I did, over English words—their spelling, pronunciation, texture and usage. Nor did she travel by Enid Blyton's fictional train, along with Darrell Rivers, to a school in Cornwall called Malory Towers. In her imagination, my mother had never flung open picnic baskets stocked with cucumber sandwiches and lemonade, or bitten into scones served with clotted cream and jam. She had never chortled upon reading how one morning Wooster actually defied Jeeves, his man Friday, because, as Wooster said, 'You can't be a serf to your valet'.[2] I suppose my mother would never have given old P. G. Wodehouse a dekko, even if he'd lounged, pipe in mouth, on the teak sofa of her drawing room in Chennai. It follows that my mother had never quoted Milton or Pope or Tennyson the way many educated people of the day often did in India. Until the day she died, 'lipstick' was 'liftick' and 'briefcase' was 'briescafe' and that, really, was that. In her world view, the universe of English was hardly a paradise lost. English was merely a cold planet in an alternate universe filled with people who had a crick in their neck.

I had never believed that I would string together words in English until one day in the year 1972, when, as an eleven-year-old, I discovered, to my complete amazement, that I could actually speak the language. Thrust into a new environment in Dar es Salaam, Tanzania, where my father had begun work as an accountant with the government, I began cobbling together perfectly grammatical English sentences—under duress. A muckle of English words had been hiding there all along, right under my tongue, pullulating under a heap of Tamil and Malayalam.

I'd imbibed English by osmosis in the 'English-medium' school I attended, hearing the way my Indian teachers spoke it, with interjections of Tamil between sentences. My 'library English' seemed sufficient only for homework, yet I'd picked up on the mounting importance of English, reading voraciously the volumes of *Encyclopaedia Britannica* that my father kept under lock and key in our almirah, as well as literary classics and American comics borrowed from our local lending library. Early on, I realized that Hamid Sayani, the first anchor of *Bournvita Quiz Contest* on All India Radio, sounded different from my teachers at school who pronounced the letter 'M' as 'Yem' and 'F' as 'Yef'. I also heard the difference between the way Sayani wielded the language and the way my father spoke it. I gleaned other things as well. My paternal grandfather, the principal at a school in Gujarat's Dahod district for three decades, read and wrote in Malayalam, Tamil, Hindi and Gujarati and had a vast understanding of Sanskrit. However, what seemed to give him a great sense of accomplishment was his felicity in English. To my father, his father and all my uncles and aunts, the English language was a prized possession whose mastery in both speech and writing was a testament to good breeding.

Over the decades, this awe of and aspiration for English diffused into every section of society in India. In *City of Djinns: A Year in Delhi* (1993), inside a den of eunuchs in old Delhi the reader meets Panna, a large yet gentle hijra, with a 'light stubble' and 'a huge protruding belly' who has adopted an infant. She has dreams for the child: 'When she is older I will send the child to a good girls' school and see that she is taught English. Maybe one day she will be beautiful and become a model or film star.'[3] In the eyes of this transgender woman who has faced the censure of society from birth, English remains the holy grail that will ensure a good life for her child. In the lowest strata of life, too, English held its sway. In her memoir, *Karukku* (2012), Dalit writer Bama tells us about a woman who says 'bycket' instead of 'bucket' and ends up becoming the laughing stock among a pack of illiterate women.

Undoubtedly the way one pronounced a word was a giveaway. In Tanzania in the seventies, I discovered that I spoke English with a different accent from what I heard around me. Local Tanzanians spoke it with a lilt of Swahili. My Goan friend, Berny, who was born and raised in Dar, and was fluent in both English and Swahili, spoke English in a style shorn of regional intonation or any affectation. Berny, my self-appointed tutor, corrected my English, hammering and buffing my pronunciation as needed. 'Say No-vem-ber,' she said to me, telling me to enunciate all the syllables in the word. 'It's not Naumber.' When I referred to the 'Nobel' Prize as the 'Noble' prize, Berny tweaked that too. Then she dragged me into her world of 'English music' on the radio. A spanking new gadget of the times, the cassette tape recorder became my lifeline as I chased pop, rock, blues and country music. I crooned alongside Donny and Marie Osmond, The Carpenters, Tom Jones, Donna Summer, Cliff Richard, the Bee Gees, Santana, Abba, Jim Reeves, Boney M., Harry Belafonte, among many others. My gift for mimicry, a natural extension of my ear for music, helped smooth out the rough edges of my once Tamil-inflected English. At the time, I didn't realize that a friend, my ear and my love of reading would hone my accent enough that I would soon begin to speak an English that had lost any whiff of my South Indian roots. By the time I left Tanzania, my accent when I spoke English was clinical, bereft of Indian regional cadences, even though it lacked the flourish of the Etonian English of those who had attended elite schools in India.

Indeed speech was a marker for those who lived in British-ruled India (both Britons and Indians). When I read *Sun in the Morning*, M. M. Kaye's memoir, I realized how much English families stationed in India during the Raj worried about preserving pedigree. One afternoon when Kaye returned home from school imitating the accent of her Eurasian friends, her mother was horrified that her daughter had picked up the appalling Anglo-Indian 'chi-chi' (pronounced 'chee-chee', not 'she-she') accent. Kaye was pulled out of school that very day; a few weeks later she was packed off to boarding school in Britain.

As writer Jerry Pinto pointed out to me one evening in Mumbai, the spit and polish of the Etonian accent still had its place and its advantages in India. He believed that only those who had that posh accent knew the value of it. I too was painfully aware, over a half-century after Kaye's experience, that the voice of elite lettered people opened doors everywhere and this class awareness engendered in speech had been handed down through the generations. It was only in East Africa, when I was old enough to grasp the gravity of it all, that this notion of 'them' and 'us,' of an unspoken pecking order in a complicated, striated world first crossed my mind.

I figured out soon enough that there were as many English accents as there were colours of skin and that there were as many Englishes as there were places in the world. There was American English, Australian English, the English of the Caribbean, the English of parts of Africa, and I grew conscious of this other kind, Indian English, of which I was a part, that was spoken by probably the largest number of people in the world. Ironically, it was also in Africa that the full force of this variety of Indian English accosted me. In one middle-class enclave of Dar, our family was surrounded by an expatriate community from many different states in India. In Sherbanu Mansion, our apartment building in Dar, I could place all the people by region merely by hearing them speak a word or two in English. I recalled Professor Henry Higgins's tall claim from *Pygmalion*: 'I can place any man within six miles. I can place him within two miles in London. Sometimes within two streets.'[4] Of all the Indian languages—23 official languages and more than 19,000 dialects[5]—English was that telltale tongue that tom-tommed a fellow Indian's origins.

There was Nigam Uncle, from next door, who could never say the word 'school'. He said 'ischool' and 'istate' in the style of a person typically from Uttar Pradesh, just as the gentleman in the flat to our left spoke an English stained by Bengali. He spoke excellent English but he could not say the word 'very' without it sounding like 'bheri'. Mr Rao, our neighbour on the second floor, wielded an English from which dangled so many tassels of Telugu that many of his sentences closed with the 'u' or 'lu' sound, and in the privacy of our home, my father had begun to refer to him as 'Waterloo-Paperlu'. There was also good old Balu Uncle down the road; when he spoke Tamil it sounded like Malayalam; when he spoke English, it too sounded like Malayalam. My father's sanctimonious stance about the English of our neighbours made him the butt of my ridicule at home. I poked fun at his English because, as I reminded him, his was also tainted by our mother tongue, Tamil.

I'd picked up on other differences in the world of English. When I was growing up, I'd wondered why English books and magazines looked and smelt nicer. The paper was glossier. They felt superior and this subliminal message was not lost on my generation. In the homes of upper-crust Indians, it became fashionable to learn English and communicate in English, the fallout of which is heard even today in India, with the result that English has become the marker of education, culture and sophistication. Regrettably, over the decades, English became this measure of intellect, an unpleasant consequence that in recent times led award-winning actor Nawazuddin Siddiqui to lament that in India the English language—which should merely have been a means of communication—denoted not only intelligence but also prowess in a chosen career.

I began to see how India had been split by English. I learned how deep in the Indian Civil Services, too, the divisions in the ranks between the English speakers and those who were mother tongue specialists were stark. English had divided us 'into two nations—the 10 percent elite who learned English and shut out the 90 percent who did not',[6] in the opinion of writer Gurcharan Das. But the greatest paradox of India's English was that while it divided, it also linguistically united the country, and the pre-eminence of English became a self-fulfilling prophecy among the educated classes. As more people with lower income aspired to have their children educated in 'English-medium' systems, English reinforced its position as the cornerstone for advancement.

'English makes you tall,' wrote Kiran Nagarkar who straddles the worlds of both Marathi and English in his prose. In *Ravan and Eddie* (1995), Nagarkar remarked that English was an 'open sesame' that doesn't open mere doors, 'it opens up new worlds and allows you to cross over from one universe to another'. In the world painted by Nagarkar, a pre-#MeToo era when sexual harassment lawsuits were not a thing, presumably, English would also help score with the fairer sex. Because 'There are only two kinds of people in the world. Those who have English and those who don't. Those who have English are the haves, and those who don't are the have-nots. If you know English, you can ask a girl for a dance. You can lean Eileen Alva against the locked door of the terrace and press against her, squeeze her boobs and kiss her on the mouth, put your tongue inside it while slipping your hand under her dress.'[7]

◆

In 1784, more than a century after the British East India Company had established trading posts in several ports across India, Sir William Jones, among the most famous of Britain's Orientalists appointed by the British government to study Indian culture, presented his seminal theories on Sanskrit. Jones and other scholars had been commissioned by the British government to investigate ancient Sanskrit legal texts to help interpret Hindu and Muslim law in the colony. Addressing a gathering of members of the Asiatic Society, Jones declared that Sanskrit, Latin and Greek had descended from a common Proto Indo-European language. In a series of lectures, Jones also extolled the logic and intricacy of Sanskrit grammar and the theories of Ayurveda, while expounding on the richness of the subcontinent's history and civilization.

However, half a century later, in 1835, Jones's findings became inconsequential as the British East India Company changed its strategy in India. By the late eighteenth century, Britain had racked up losses in a prolonged war with France and lost thirteen colonies in North America. The Seven Years' War in Europe had involved overseas colonial struggles between Great Britain and France as they fought for control in North America and India. The British East India Company teetered on the edge of bankruptcy. Its only trump card was its vast dominions in India, which, as time went on, it was wagered, could become the last bastion of British imperial power, one rife with potential despite it being a belligerent assemblage of states. The British government debated financial policy and the funds that must be disbursed and, furthermore, what exactly was deemed a 'useful' education. A traditional Indian education, according to the British government, did not translate to gainful employment for the individual or, more importantly in this case, line the coffers of the Raj. The English language was brandished as the cure for all ills. In February 1835, politician and essayist Thomas Babington Macaulay, who had claimed that 'a single shelf of a good European library was worth the whole native literature of India and Arabia', made a case for why Indians needed to be educated in English. Macaulay's 'Minute on Indian Education' described the ultimate objective of teaching English to Indians:

> We must at present do our best to form a class who may be interpreters between us and the millions whom we govern,—a class of persons, Indian in blood and colour, but English in tastes, in opinions, in morals,

and in intellect. To that class we may leave it to refine the vernacular dialects of the country, to enrich those dialects with terms of science borrowed from the Western nomenclature, and to render them by degrees fit vehicles for conveying knowledge to the great mass of the population.[8]

By 1837, Persian was discontinued as the official language of the Indian dominions and the provinces. By 1844, those with English education were given preference for entry into government jobs. By the middle of the nineteenth century, universities had been opened in Bombay, Madras and Calcutta, the three important provinces that now saw the rise of native elites schooled in English and keen on social reform. While poor uneducated natives were carted off, like sardines in a can, to build railways and sugar plantations in the Caribbean and colonies of the empire, a whole tier of privileged Indians sailed to Great Britain for an education, crossing the forbidden kaala pani (black waters). In line with Macaulay's injunctions, the empire began cloning 'brown sahibs' to mimic the English who, after a period of training at Oxford and Cambridge, were recruited for the Indian Civil Services where they excelled in administration. In the words of the late novelist R. K. Narayan, such men 'were also educated to carry about them an air of superiority at all times and were expected to keep other Indians at a distance'.[9]

The turning point came in the year 1857 when Indians rose up in revolt. The segregation between the ruler and the native had become more pronounced as the relationship soured further even as the nineteenth century wound to a close. In 1924, matters came to a head when a young student who needed urgent medical help was refused admission to the General Hospital in Madras. The young man died due to negligence; there was a vacancy only in the European ward and none in the Indian ward. This incident provoked a furore among the people.

The tension had been escalating over the decades as Britons in India adopted a supercilious tone. Railways had carriages for 'Europeans Only', while some shops in the army cantonment catered exclusively to white people; theatre entrances and seats were marked 'Europeans Only'. Despite this friction between the people, the flow of words between the languages could not be checked. Words from Hindustani and other regional languages coursed through the fissures between the people.

Language had an uncanny way of emerging into the white man's tongue just as Indian moustaches had a profound effect on British facial hair among the members of the British Army who, until then, had mostly been clean shaven. Just as moustaches became fashion statements on the faces of civilians in Great Britain, words such as 'shampoo' (from Hindi champna to knead) entered daily parlance in Britain. In a similar vein, Victorian prudishness informed the sari blouses worn by high society women in Bombay and Calcutta. English preferences in music would begin to impale conservative arts in South India; temple dancers, the devadasis, noticed the changing patronage of the arts and they learned to render 'God Save the Queen' in impeccable English. The violin, today an integral instrument in an Indian classical concert, entered the stage during the Raj. One classical dance composition titled 'Oh My Lovely Lalana' described the plea of a man trying to convince his lover of his feelings for her and in one of the stanzas, the lyrics are in both Telugu and in English thus: 'iTUvaNTi step—is it fit to take, sit a while here, let me convince you.' Even the gods were not spared from the new influences. At Chennai's Kapaleeswarar Temple, the resplendent festival celebrating Lord Brahma has always featured 'For He's a Jolly Good Fellow', a popular folk tune that originated in France. Inspired by Scottish and Irish tunes, legendary Carnatic composer Muthuswami Dikshitar wrote a collection of European airs in the early nineteenth century proving that it was impossible, in art, to not be influenced and, in turn, to not inspire.

The collision of two cultures invariably planted seeds for change. Shaped by English minds, Indians began to wield the weapon of the master. When the aforementioned young man died at General Hospital, a brilliant orator, S. Satyamurti, raged against the racism of the Raj in the English language. Thus, in a grand irony, the legacy of the empire became the language of India's independence struggle. Over time, the very people that the British educated would return home to fight for Indian independence and oust their rulers.

English education altered the cultural and political history of the Indian subcontinent. India's men and women were forever changed by it. In many communities, to learn English was considered a sign of being effeminate; even so men were encouraged to learn the language. In a way, English also became a route for those who learned it to prove something to those who pilloried them for learning the language of the master. Men armed themselves with English to show that learning it opened doors for them not just in their careers but also in the matrimonial market.

For most women in India in the early part of the twentieth century, English was that rare benediction afforded by the benevolence of the men in their family. While it was often educated menfolk who pushed to bring English-medium education into schools, convinced that their women needed to learn the language, there was always a certain dread that an English education would create a society of 'English educated, piano playing, singing and dancing women, Grace Darlings and Elizabeths'[10] who would cease to be good homemakers and spurn their own mother tongue. Then there was an undertone, too, that the knowledge of English would lead Indian women to imitate the alleged wantonness of Western women. Germane to the many evils believed to have been unleashed by the English language was the idea of what English symbolized—knowledge, literature, desire, fashion, virtue, labour and sex—starkly highlighting the contrasts between 'indigenous and foreign, feminine and masculine, labour and knowledge'.

Eighteen years after India's independence, India's relationship with the English language brought new challenges. It had been mandated that from 26 January 1965—fifteen years after the passing of the Constitution—only Hindi would be used in all communication between the government and the states. In the early sixties, as the date for the transition from English to Hindi loomed and the centre's plan to make Hindi the official language galvanized, the South ricocheted with protests and riots. Some people in the Madras Presidency killed themselves over the possible invasion of Hindi. In the most inconceivable way, this was a watershed moment for English in India. Suddenly, it appeared that English was indeed one of India's own languages.

Statesman C. Rajagopalachari's appeal to let English continue was critical to this decision. His appeal was forthright and persuasive. He believed that English was key to progress in science. Hindi was not the mother tongue for several Indian states, he wrote, warning that English would be the only means to preserve India's unity. In the decades that followed, English sank into our consciousness and became a part of our inheritance. The words of Hindi poet Kunwar Narain evoke this ambivalence in those of us who hail from the colonies.

I have a strange problem these days—
The power to hate with all my heart
Is ebbing by the day

I want to hate the English
(They ruled us for two centuries)
But Shakespeare sidles up
To whom I owe so much...

And this Kamban, this Thyagaraja, this Muthuswamy...
A hundred thousand times I tell myself
They are not mine
They're from some place far South
But the heart does not rest
Till they are made mine[11]

Writing a thoughtful series of essays in the eighties, Narayan wished that India would build its own 'Bharat brand of English' that would reach the marketplace and the village green. Narayan was never apologetic about the English language adopting an Indian avatar in India. In an essay titled 'Toasted English', he pointed to the Americans who had soldered and mended the English language to suit their purpose and 'achieved directness and unambiguity in expression'.[12] Like the magnificent 500-year-old banyan tree in Chennai's Adyar, English did send down roots, after all, as Narayan had hoped, its canopy stretching far and wide into the remotest parts of India, the fascination for it evergreen.

In the latter part of the nineteenth century, many Indian writers began to weave together their Indian and Western sensibilities, starting with Bankim Chandra Chatterjee in his novel *Rajmohan's Wife* (1864). English writers shaped the language, too, reaching into their stockpile of Indian words. I discovered how efficaciously E. M. Forster, Rudyard Kipling and Kaye used Indian words in their narratives. In Forster's *A Passage to India* (1924), Ronny tells his mother, Mrs Moore, that the young Doctor Aziz was not different from all of the natives, and 'if nothing else he's trying to increase his *izzat*—in plain Anglo-Saxon, to score'.[13] Thus the creation of Indian English, the branding of it as an 'English Made in India', happened over many decades and was the confluence of a myriad of currents.

In Kolkata, Ananda Lal, a soft-spoken professor of comparative literature at Jadavpur University, told me he made it very clear to his freshman students that contradictory to popular belief, Salman Rushdie was not the first writer to change English in India. While Rushdie put contemporary Indian writing on the map in the early eighties following his international success, he was hardly the first one to transform the language with an Indian ethos. Lal conveyed the spirit of this 'Inglish' succinctly: 'He was one step in the continuum of the evolution of English which began the day the first Englishman stepped into Indian soil.'

◆

For centuries now, India had taken an English expression and treated it with its 'teekshe-midshe-godshe' (or spicy-salty-sweet as Konkani speakers from Mangalore might say) seasoning. It was as if we had kneaded an English word, added a little salt, sprinkled some chilli powder, tossed in cumin and a pinch of jaggery, and then pulled and twisted it, and squeezed it out through the pen of our mother tongue.

Years ago while reading a collection of short stories by Rohinton Mistry, I discovered that all old people from the Parsi community in Bombay (as Mumbai was called) had co-opted English in some way and made their own private language of it. 'Old *bai* took English words and made them Parsi words.

Easy chair was *igeechur*, French beans was *ferach beech*, and Jacqueline became *Jaakaylee*.'[14]

I saw this sense of entitlement to own and take liberties with English at Chennai's fanciest movie theatre where, in the middle of a Tamil movie, the English subtitle accompanying a romantic song had a rhyme with no reason.

> Just one look was all it took, I fell sinker, line and hook!
> I bite my tongue, I smile excitedly. I'm drama queen—
> unexpectedly

'Hook, line, and sinker', an English language idiom that was used to emphasize how someone was completely deceived, was not just used incorrectly in the context of falling in love; the idiom itself had been chopped up and misused for the sake of metre and rhyme. In India this cannibalization was par for the course. Expressions and idioms could be pulled and twisted to suit any situation and I saw the fluidity of words and their malleability in that instance. In a paper on the future of language, David Graddol, a British linguist, stated that the fast growing urban areas of the world were breeding grounds for new hybrid languages.

Whether I was in front of a movie screen or out on the road in the country of my birth, the extensive reach of the language of the erstwhile colonial masters was obvious and so, too, the hybridization of which my late father's man Friday, Vinayagam, was a fine specimen. His education, in Tamil medium, had ended at the tenth standard, yet he communicated in a Tamil peppered generously with English words (such as 'night', 'tension', 'powder', 'noodles', 'gate', 'care', 'car', 'licence') which he assumed were as native as he was. A significant component of his daily repertoire was his favourite expression—'Aiyo!'—which has now entered the Oxford English Dictionary.

I'd also noticed a preponderance of Hindustani words in British and American literature of the nineteenth and early twentieth centuries. Sometimes, the origin of a word or expression was long forgotten and buried in the pages of history. The phrase 'big cheese' had wormed its way into American life in a peculiar manner. 'Cheez' means 'thing' in Hindi and was slang for anything first-rate in quality. The phrase alluded to the most influential or important person in a group. It is believed to be an offshoot of 'the real chiz' (the real thing, 'chiz' being an Urdu word). Returnees from India started to use it in Britain, and the unfamiliar, foreign *chiz* is thought to have become the more familiar *cheese*. The expression was popular among Eurasians and is believed to have first been noticed in American literature in 1910. As in the case of the 'big cheese', Indianisms were often corruptions of Indian words such as the phrase 'owhson-jhowson' that writer Farrukh Dhondy had heard his grandmother use often. Alluding to a noisy gathering of people, the term was a variant of 'Hobson-Jobson'—the eponymous dictionary of Indo-British words and phrases compiled by Henry Yule and Arthur C. Burnell in 1886—which was a play on the phrase uttered during the Shia Muslim Muharram procession in which people mourned the death of their martyrs, Hassan-ibn-Ali and Hussein-ibn-Ali, by walking through the streets beating their chests and backs crying, 'Ya Hassan! Ya Hussein!'

There is little doubt that Indian English is powerful—and temperamental. One might even say that it resembles the car steered by James Bond. It looks and drives like any other car but its fire can be seen only with use. Indian English may convey surprise, irritation, accusation and dismay where a garden variety English may implode, like an unpuffed roti. For instance, this sentence in 'Inglish'—'He's like that only!'—conveys a certain hopelessness and vexation. It means: 'the person in question is incorrigible and even if the world wants him to change and change is good for him, well, it's just too bad, he will not'. See how it takes two dozen words to convey something in proper English that Indian English articulates in four precise words? That is the latent might of Indian English. Rohinton Mistry employs 'only' masterfully in a line in his short story where he conveys the maid Jaakaylee's frustration at her Parsi boss and his wife. They were so highhanded that 'they thought they were like British only, ruling India side by side'.[15] The way Mistry uses 'only' in this sentence nails one of the most oft-heard Indianisms still in use in Indian English.

Consider the following sentence: 'I want to be in James Bond's bed.' The placement of the word 'only' in different positions in this sentence changes its import. In Indian English, the word 'only' is plastered on to the end of the sentence and it modifies the word that is most emphasized in the enunciating of it. 'I want to be in James Bond's bed only' can mean one of several things: I want to be only in his bed, nowhere else; I want to be only in his bed, not anyone else's; I want to only 'be' in the bed, not dance or sing or anything else; no one else but I shall be in that bed.

The word 'only' was a tricky part of speech for the savviest practitioner of the language. Grammar Nazis insist that 'only' must be placed as close as possible to the word or the phrase it modifies. However, this still does not eliminate ambiguity. A foreigner who lived in Bangalore observed that in some instances in India, 'only' was uttered in a rising dramatic cadence in such a way that it was not clear what exactly the 'only' was modifying. You had to rely on context, and if the context didn't clarify the meaning, it needed a clever rephrasing and a rapier of a tongue, something that might even have flummoxed 007.

The latent power of Indian English also lay in the

Indianisms that rose organically from the way of life in India. In pre-Independence India, the East India Company used to post its officers to particular stations. When they used to be out from their duty stations, the officers were said to be 'out of station' where 'station' referred to a place where English officials of a district or a garrison resided. Military terms have had a strong influence on the way non-military persons speak because everyone knows someone in the military who is always 'stationed' somewhere and it's easy to imagine how the term entered daily parlance in India. Strangely enough, after spending two formative decades in India and in East Africa, the American expression 'out of town' felt unsavoury on my tongue the first time I used it upon my arrival in the Silicon Valley. But my husband was out of station so often that I soon fell in step with that Americanism. The use of language is so much a part of the culture and psyche of a place that it seems our tongues yearn to capture that as closely as they possibly can.

An American journalist observed how the vagueness and timelessness of Indian English contained inside it 'the notion of death and rebirth' that time could be stretched at will.[16] In my experience, the use of the word 'would' was also a classic example of the elasticity of time in the country of my birth. A cousin wrote me an email thus: 'I would be coming to Chennai next week. While I would not trouble you or your driver, it would be extremely gracious of you to spare him if I would ever need him. I would be sending you the particulars as and when I get them.' Another expression in Indian English—'timepass'—evolved as an expression that meant 'passing the time' but the word was actually ascribed to the peanuts sold on Bombay city commuter trains. The peanut vendors had actually invented a name for their product. The very act of eating those monkey nuts (neatly wrapped in paper cones) was a 'timepass' and as vendors flowed through the train compartments shouting 'timepass!' the term seeped into Indian consciousness.

The idea of time as eternal manifests itself in the present continuous of India's English. In my view, this is not different from the Chinese tendency to not use tenses when speaking English because there is no concept of tense in Chinese. In India, a friend might say of another, in a direct translation from the vernacular: 'You must be knowing him', I encountered this usage often in R. K. Narayan's work and I'd often heard my father and his friends use it. In a delightful satirical poem 'The Professor', Nissim Ezekiel shows how the notion of eternity is encapsulated in an English riddled with typical prepositional and idiomatic errors while also demonstrating the Indian's preference for the present continuous tense over the simple present tense.

> You won't believe but I have eleven grandchildren.
> How many issues you have? Three?
> That is good. These are days of family planning.
> I am not against. We have to change with times.
> Whole world is changing. In India also
> We are keeping up. Our progressing is progressing.
> Old values are going, new values are coming.
> Everything is happening with leaps and bounds.[17]

In my own experience, the logic and concision of Indian English was often both creative and illuminating. For example, if we could postpone why couldn't we 'prepone'? Inside an aircraft bound for Delhi, a flight attendant in a red skirt and a matching blazer marched up and down the aircraft's aisle minutes before we landed at Delhi's airport, warning us all to please 'upright' our seatbacks. Noun-verb combinations such as 'air-dash', 'lathi charge' and 'gheraoed' were once unknown; today, they're on the front pages of newspapers. At Jaipur Airport in Terminal 2, a toilet declared itself to be a 'Physically Challenged Toilet' with a sign to that effect on the door of the stall.

Today, a subliminal language thrives in the pages of India's matrimonial classifieds where the need to be stingy with space and money has birthed a whole other vocabulary. Some words are now a part of daily life such as 'well-settled', 'wheatish', 'convented', 'status family', 'presentable' and so on. The language is arcane and coded. It's loaded with societal beliefs. 'VB' means very beautiful; 'bhp' stands for details such as birth, horoscope and photograph; the word 'issues' alludes to children (from a previous marriage, for instance). 'Convented' refers to someone who has attended an English-medium convent school; a 'status family' hints at an upper-caste family; a 'homely' girl is not a plain Jane but a woman who might be an excellent homemaker.

In the company of non-Indians, I've often had to explain how there are also more nuanced words for family relationships in Indian languages and how these have flowed into Indian English. A brother-in-law is a co-brother to a gentleman who has married that man's wife's sister. Likewise, co-sister. 'Aunty' and 'uncle' are generic terms of address for all members of a previous generation who deserved respectful address. Hence, one day, every woman becomes an 'aunty' and every man an 'uncle' to a new coterie of Indian children.

In Indian languages, many words were often said twice for emphasis and for lyricism. This feature too we have transported into our style of English. An Indian friend pointed out that Indians often turned a statement into a question. 'You are finished with your lunch, no?' What defines it as a question is the tag at the end and also the inflexion with which something is said. The question tag is often incorrect or non-existent or the general purpose 'isn't it?'.

Steven R. Weisman in his essay 'On Language', described what he called a 'rococo euphemism, courtesy or indirection' in Indian English and he pointed out how people who died met with an 'untimely demise', and their families are 'condoled' by friends, just as they had been 'felicitated' on happier occasions.

In the remote corner of Bihar, on the road to Gaya, where no one cared about anything but death and sin, I saw signs for 'Spoken English' lessons, and minutes from Mahavira's water temple in Pawapuri, I happened upon an advertisement for an English school called Shakespear's English School with an 'e' fixed under the apostrophe as an afterthought. It did not inspire confidence, rather like the 'Toe-away Zone' right by a busy thoroughfare in the middle of Patna.

Proper nouns often fall prey to misspelling and mispronunciation. Many stories abound on how a bridge in Chennai got its strange name. According to one account, the British put up a bridge over the reeking Cooum River and called it Hamilton Bridge. The inhabitants of Chennai had trouble pronouncing 'Hamilton', and the word ended up sounding like Hummulton. To the ear, the word resembled the Tamil word 'ambattan', meaning barber, which is why Hamilton Bridge now goes by the name Barber's Bridge. A similar story revolves around Kennedy Street in the heart of Chennai's Mylapore. Named after the settler tribe called 'Kannadian' whose specialty was making and selling of yogurt, the word morphed into 'kannadi' from which it evolved into Kennedy Street which, to the eyes of those who lived in the shadow of the queen, seemed just right. This is what colonialism often looked like. A second culture dominated the first, orchestrating how it must think about itself. In India, this reset of culture happened yet again in the nineties when India opened itself up for foreign investment and the tentacles of American hegemony ensnared people and informed their language.

In my late father's home in Chennai, his valet and chauffeur, Vinayagam, too, had succumbed to American colloquialisms even though he did not speak English. When something was doable, he looked at me and wobbled his head up and down in a succession of quick nods and said, 'Sounds good!'

As Indians built lives in America, Indian English began morphing yet again, adopting Americanisms that were once only experienced on the silver screen. In the opening chapter of *English, August* (1988), Upamanyu Chatterjee fixates on this Americanization of India's English. Its story opens with two friends, Dhrubo and Agastya (nicknamed August), shooting the breeze inside a car, pondering Agastya's future in a dreary town called Madna where Agastya will soon report for duty as an officer in the Indian Administrative Services. Chatterjee ferries us inside the car where the two men are smoking pot. 'Dhrubo exhaled richly out of the window, and said, "I've a feeling, August, you're going to get hazaar fucked in Madna."' Like me, Dhrubo reflects upon the potency of India's strange English. '"Amazing mix, the English we speak. Hazaar fucked. Urdu and American," Agastya laughed. "A thousand fucked, really fucked. I'm sure nowhere else could languages be mixed and spoken with such ease."' With the universality of English largely a result of American global dominance, Indians have now begun to say 'elevator' and 'apartment' rather than 'lift' and 'flat'. We prefer to eat 'cookies' instead of 'biscuits' and we stand in a line rather than in a queue. Or, as it happens more often than not, we don't stand in a line.

This melding was inevitable, according to linguist David Crystal. Just as Great Britain was the juggernaut of the Industrial Age, India had considerable heft in the age of high technology and Indian English had begun to matter because Indians had begun to matter on the world stage. Thus English itself was being redefined every day by global forces. In 2017, Crystal estimated that there were now around 2,000 Indian words or expressions in the English lexicon. That number is only growing.

◆

Each book published by Writers Workshop is handbound in a handloom sari and embossed with the late Purushottama Lal's beautiful calligraphy. In 1958, Lal and a coterie of writers founded this organization in Calcutta with the credo that English would play a creative role in Indian literature through original writing and translation. 'I cannot imagine a Punjabi writing Bengali poetry, or a Maharashtrian writing Hindi poetry, but there are Tamilians, Bengalis, Punjabis, Gujaratis, Jews, Goans, Sikkimese—all Indians writing in English on Indian themes for Indian readers.'[18] Lal believed that English expressed the 'pan-Indian' psyche, symbolizing the cultural and sociopolitical aspirations of all Indians. English was the only conduit, as Sanskrit once was, of dialogue between Indian intellectuals across India in spite of 'political pressures and regional language loyalty'.

Although English may not be the dominant language of the future in the world any longer, Graddol says it plays a crucial role in shaping the new linguistic order and that its real impact will be 'in creating new generation of bilingual and multilingual speakers across the world'[19] even as we continue to lose a language every fourteen days.[20] The language had 'lost armies of linguistic gatekeepers who used to ensure that only the language of a social elite—sanitized by copy editors— reached public consumption'.[21]

English had gone through cleansing and fortification in past centuries. The National Language Project in English began in the sixteenth century at a time when interest in scientific thought and the humanities had exploded in Europe.

Intrigued by the founding of the language academy in France, poet John Dryden clamoured for the English language also to be structured by a committee. Over a century later, eager to protect English from 'barbarism',[22] writer Jonathan Swift proposed the standardization of the English language but his efforts too did not bear fruit. A half-century later, on a mission to fix the language, Samuel Johnson would build the English dictionary and reign in spelling. Two hundred years later, the Internet and the thrust of globalization would lead to democratization of the language and, ultimately, to a tossing out of established etiquettes. In the end, the lack of institutional fetters allowed English to borrow freely from other tongues and grow in whimsical ways.

Lexicographer Kory Stamper observed that the English language was much more like a river; every dialect of English was its own current and 'every one of those currents is integral to the direction of English'.[23] That implied also that the force was impossible to contain. The French people had begun to realize how impossible it was to fence their national language. The young people of France preferred 'now' to 'maintenant' while texting because of the sheer convenience of it. The most intransigent of all languages with standards developed by the Institut Française, French had begun opening the gates to let in English words. Now, 'email', 'weekend', 'jogging', 'brainstorming' and 'marketing' were as French as they were English.

As in France, in an India touted to be the youngest nation in the world, the nature of the English language would be determined by the country's youth, now nearly half its population.[24] They were writing more than ever before and writing on their own terms. In the new India, English was fast becoming just another Indian language of convenience.

In an interview, writer Chetan Bhagat decried the elitism

around the English language in India and observed that India's pedagogy in English was outmoded and impractical. '...And we tell children to make sentences with "dexterous". What is the point? What is the point of making a sentence using a word?'* Bhagat felt that explaining the meaning of a word by using it in a sentence was a pointless exercise because one could always formulate a worthless sentence that threw no light on the meaning of the word. To drive the point home to his teacher, Bhagat simply wrote the following feeble sentence on his paper: 'When I grow up I want to be dexterous.'

Following the publication of Bhagat's books, the world of publishing noticed how, for the first time, an Indian-born writer was hogging the limelight and the bestseller charts. A home-grown non-literary writer was receiving huge advances and selling over 800,000 copies of each book, a figure until then unheard of even for the literary giants in India. It was obvious that the people who determined the market were the youth of the day. They were reading books whose language was accessible to many who were first-generation English learners. With Bhagat's success, the element of fear and awe around the English language seemed to have sloughed off. The young people of the day didn't care about the pretensions that had dogged the older generation of Indians who had learned English.

Written language mirrored speech more and more now. Years after India gained independence, Rajaji had insisted that English would fulfil an important role as a link language between states. With changing mores, however, in many

---

*'Chetan Bhagat speaks on what English language means to him (Part V)', *British Council India*, 1 December 2009 <https://www.youtube.com/watch?v=rBZXhd17FjY&t=218s>. Go to 2.00 to listen to this part of the conversation.

families across India, English is now a link language between husband and wife or children and parents as more couples marry outside of state and national borders. All of a sudden, India is becoming fraught with linguistic challenges with English assuming a central role.

The new English speakers are often born out of necessity and convenience than out of a need to speak a particular kind of elitist English. The push for English medium from kindergarten is taking the country towards monolingualism. It is entirely possible that in a few decades, English or a particular version of it, will overtake Hindi to become the most popular language in India. Most of the advertising budget catered to English language consumers because of their spending power. The government paid more attention to English media, too. With rising literacy boosting the number of publications, by 2016, India boasted over a 100,000 publications across all its languages, including English, which claimed about 14 per cent of the total.[25]

English has moved from being the gatekeeper of the elite to being a ladder up for the masses, or as Sir Mark Tully said to me: 'from being the language of status to being the language of opportunity'. James Tooley, a professor at the University of Newcastle in England who has studied the growth of private schools in the slums of Hyderabad, India, said interviews with parents suggested that the desire for English as the language of instruction was by far the strongest reason for seeking out such schools. The English language had thus lost all its connotations with the British Raj. Now it was only viewed as the language of jobs and progress.

That's why my father's man Friday, Vinayagam, was frustrated that he couldn't cobble together a sentence in English even if his life depended on it. He knew how to set up a smartphone in minutes. He repaired most of the computer problems in our home, paid bills online, fixed all electronic kinks in the house—with a tenth grade education in the vernacular. Yet, his greatest longing was to acquire the English language. If he only knew English, he said, his earning potential even as a driver would have tripled.

If Vinayagam is in awe of English for its market potential, savvy English speakers are in love with the language and its vocabulary. It seems like every town now holds literary festivals with a focus on English books. With every tweet, literary swashbucklers like politician Shashi Tharoor make national headlines for having used an English word that few humans could understand.

In some ways, India's relationship with English is similar to the plight of Bernard Shaw's Eliza and Alfred Doolittle. With aspiration comes certain expectations of comportment. 'I have to live for others and not for myself,' says Alfred Doolittle to his Mrs Higgins. 'Middle class morality… That's the tragedy of it, ma'am. It's easy to say chuck it, but I haven't the nerve.'[26] For India, too, as its middle class rose into wealth and affluence, there was no going back to the way things were.

India felt it was judged by the English it spoke and wrote and felt an obligation to the English-speaking world. This expectation or standard had hurt the country in the world of translation. 'The minute I publish in English, it gets translated right away into twelve languages,' Sudha Murthy, one of the country's bestselling writers, said to me. Bhagat. Mrs Murthy discovered that writing in English catapulted her into greater visibility. Yet, as writer and translator Arunava Sinha explained to me, something precious had been lost in translation. Allowing herself to write in English when she was a writer in Kannada altered a text. When translations worked their way from English, they were watered down to such a point that they were 'like the copy of a copy of a photocopy of an original'.

Yet, like Bhagat, Lal, Narayan, Raja Rao and many others, Mrs Murthy is free to speak in a voice she chooses. Who was I to wonder why she chose to write in English? Poet Arundhathi Subramaniam captures the hypocrisy and the arrogance of those who lord over others on issues of identity, language and belonging:

> This business about language,
> how much of it is mine,
> how much yours,
> how much from the mind,
> how much from the gut,
> how much is too little,
> how much too much,
> how much from the salon,
> how much from the slum,
> how I say verisimilitude,
> how I say Brihadaranyaka,
> how I say vaazhapazham –
> it's all yours to measure,
> the pathology of my breath,
> the halitosis of gender,
> my homogenised plosives
> about as rustic
> as a mouth-freshened global village.[27]

In 1940, while addressing a conference of English scholars, Dr A. N. Jha wondered why India was ashamed of its version of English. 'Must we condemn the following sentence because it does not conform to English idiom, even though it is a literal translation of our own idiom? *I shall not pay a pice what to say of a rupee.* Is there any rational ground for objecting to *family members* and adhering to *members of the family*?... A little courage, some determination, a wholesome respect for our own idioms, and we shall before long have a virile, vigorous *Indian English*.'[28]

It seemed that Jha's dream was coming true. In the dusty town of Kanchipuram, just about 70 kilometres east of where the British were challenged in 1806 by Indian soldiers in Vellore's majestic fort, I came upon the most symbolic representation yet of India's brand of English. Inside the legendary Ekambaranathar Temple stood an uncommon tree that was as Indian as the neem and the coconut. This unique specimen sought the sun, its branches wide and long, and it bore a different variety of a fruit on each branch. Its leaves, too, seemed different in appearance. Yet, it was feted as a whole entity and accepted as India's own distinct species and at its core, this strange hybrid was a mango tree, India's evocative, fragrant and juicy national fruit.

ONE

'JUST TEACH HER ENGLISH'

In a place called Chamba Valley in the Dhauladhar range of mountains in Himachal Pradesh, on a court where green and orange flags flapped in the breeze, a dozen boys shouted over a game of volleyball. I watched the boys from the balcony of the home of the president of Dalhousie Hilltop School. As they played, they yelled to each other in a language that they had grown up with, their mother tongue. It was the argot spoken by friends when they were tossing a ball on the field, the bhasha of soul mates. It was not English.

In a moment of frenzied focus, I heard the real India speak. 'Game shuru karo. Chalo. Run!' It was a simple command. 'Begin the game. Let's go. Run!' If the president, Poonam Dhawan, were watching them, they'd be in trouble. But this was after school hours when most people, the president included, let their hair down. When the boys paused in their game, for those one or two breathless seconds, all I could hear up at 8,000 feet above sea level was the quiet murmur of the creatures of the forest.

To get to Dalhousie, I had rented a car that ferried me from Amritsar and wended its way past haystacks and fields towards Pathankot, about 30 kilometres from the fragile border between India and Pakistan. The road skirted past endless fields of sugar cane, wheat and rice. Every few miles, kilns flanked by Jenga stacks of red bricks poked out from the soil.

It was October. The days had begun to shrink. Sikh men zipped by on bikes, their orange and yellow and pink and purple turbans, a parade of colour in a sombre sky. In the distance, farmworkers loaded hay onto a truck that seemed about ready to keel over. Chennai Express, a dhaba that opened after the eponymous movie became a hit, was now a popular pit stop for travellers although their aloo paratha outflanked their masala dosa. New apartments were coming up. Giant billboards urged people to book now, promising a flat in a land known as India's granary, its bread basket. Between acres of grass burnished to a mustard green, white Sikh gurdwaras and Hindu mandirs dotted land that had once soaked in the blood of Muslims, Hindus and Sikhs during India's partition in 1947.

Ahead of us a van called itself 'Milk Van'. A line below the sign told me a little more about the milk: 'Ice Mixed Milk'. Most vehicles sported warning messages on their bumpers— most often 'BLOWHORN' or 'Pleasesoundhorn'—reminding me of the green and yellow autos of Kolkata that often had messages painted in blue ink with no spaces between the words: 'obeythetrafficrules'. Sometimes, the pithy lyricism of Indian roads could take me by surprise—'Safety is no accident'—but the one that deserved the prize was a simple gory rhyme I had seen on the velvety highway connecting Bangalore and Chennai: 'Speed thrills but kills.'

After Pathankot, we began the ascent into the hills. Groves of eucalyptus and beech lined the narrow mountain road. A farmer carried feed on his bikes for his animals. The signposts for English-medium schools dotted the scene. Badhani School was at the foothills within easy access of the highway. As we climbed towards the peaks of Dalhousie, we passed clusters of upscale schools whose hoardings paid homage to India's leaders and visionaries. As we pushed upwards, the road narrowed some more and the car now snaked up the thin ledge on the mountainside.

Named after Lord Dalhousie, the governor general of India from 1847 to 1856, the hill station is in the Chamba District. Located on the western edge of the Dhauladhar mountain range of the Himalayas, Dalhousie is surrounded by snow-capped peaks. I found out that in this rarefied atmosphere where good teachers were as hard to come by as oxygen, schools watched each other like hawks, poaching both excellent teachers and wealthy children.

It was unclear, in this valley of sudden slopes, where the mountains ended and where a school began. Yet, it seemed that if there were a place in the world where one wished to make something of oneself, it must be here between the deodar cedars, blessed by the power of Shiva who resided at Mount Kailash, in direct view of Dalhousie from Dainkund Peak a steep climb away.

The driver revved up some more as we passed a mile of signs announcing Dalhousie Public School. Soon a billboard proclaimed 'The Hilltopians Spirit' alongside the photograph of Nobel laureate Rabindranath Tagore and his message: 'Everything comes to us that belongs to us if we create the capacity to receive it.'

Then the driver roared upwards for a few more minutes when, in a manoeuvre that made my hair stand on end, he lurched into a hairpin turn and up the ramp leading towards a building where, plastered in white letters on an orange backdrop was the name of what could have been a chalet in Switzerland: Dalhousie Hilltop School. From its courtyard, students and teachers looked out every day into the valley which looped about for miles and where nature's drama played out from sunrise to sunset. Most boarding schools up in the hills of India are attended by the children of the rich. They are seen as elitist educational institutions. Attending many of these schools sets up students for life as connections made here can take them far. But I was discovering, thanks to Poonam Dhawan, that many of the students at Dalhousie hailed from less privileged backgrounds and were often the first English speakers in the family. India's burgeoning middle class had put elitism within reach of many families. Hedged in by railings with the logo of the school—an orange sun rising from green hills—the school had been Poonam's father-in-law's dream in 1979 when he built it between the apple orchards and pine trees on his ancestral property.

◆

'Fifty lines, each of you!' the president of Dalhousie Hilltop School yelled, rushing out of her office into the courtyard where three uniformed boys in brown blazers dribbled a ball. 'You were talking right outside my office. Don't think I didn't hear you!' This was a few days later; the boys had been speaking in Punjabi while playing ball and Poonam, whose antennae caught every infraction, had heard them.

Sometimes, as on the first day I was in school with Poonam, a child walked up to her first thing in the morning with her book open. 'Imposition,' Poonam said to me, with a laugh, 'for speaking in Hindi during school hours.' Poonam had left behind a husband, children, grandchildren and a cushy life in Austin, Texas, to assume the leadership role at the school started by her father-in-law. But she had traded peace for chaos. For sure as the bell in her school rang every forty minutes, Poonam fought fires almost every hour. She swore she would never resort to corporal punishment, a feature of the bad old days that was still employed in some schools. 'But I do believe that children need to learn that there are consequences to their actions.' Hence, 2,000 times in all, the child had had to write the following most unforgettable line of her elementary years: 'I will speak only in English in school.'

The imposition was severe by most standards. But the head of a first-rate boarding school had to make children squirm now and then. In contrast to Hilltop's approach, the sisters who ran Sacred Hearts Convent 2,000 feet below preferred another mode of punishment. If a child was caught not speaking English, he would have to go to the dictionary and write out 500 English words and their meanings. There was a rumour floating about the school that some of the children had words and meanings ready in advance, so the sisters devised a solution for that, too. They made the students work on their punishment right under their very noses inside their office.

Sacred Hearts Convent, the first residential school of Chamba Valley, was built in 1901 on the Potreyn Hill, and was once accessible only by a palanquin or a tonga, a horse-drawn two-wheeled vehicle. With its manicured spaces, its chapel and its old wood-panelled library, the school reminded me of Cornwall's fictitious Malory Towers where, as a pre-teen, I had followed Darrell Rivers around on her adventures. Like me, every fan of an Enid Blyton story had vicariously lived life inside a boarding school. Schools like Sacred Hearts were once the British empire's preferred institutions for grooming its children. English children were not allowed to mingle with Indians lest they pick up their language and manners. Hence they were shipped off to institutions like these in the 'hill stations', far away from the heat of the plains, for an education that mimicked that of Eton. Often, these schools were the training grounds for entry into the British Army or Navy.

By the mid-nineteenth century, following Macaulay's decree, the British empire was also interested in grooming Indian mediators, those who would be 'sahibs' and were 'Indians in blood and colour but English in taste, in opinions and morals and intellect'.[29] The missionaries arrived in the early nineteenth century and set up base in many parts of the subcontinent to impart an education untethered to caste, creed, gender and culture from which they would teach English and, innocuously, it seemed, preach religion. An upshot of colonization was, of course, the attempt to pry pagans free from their ancient practices. By the middle of the nineteenth century, an English education was a requirement for admission into the first universities set up in Bombay, Madras and Calcutta, which also established that an education in English-medium schools would be an advantage. And when the Raj ended many schools that had once been the exclusive purvey of Englishmen and Eurasians opened up to the upper crust of Indians. What was good for the white man had to be superlative for the native.

A university education naturally led to jobs in the government and the civil services. After a period of training at Oxford and Cambridge, these brown Englishmen were recruited for the Indian Civil Services, where they excelled. An ecosystem was thus established whereby the English language became the means to rise through the ranks of government; it was the lingua franca, a link language between people, which also improved access to objects of desire. What normally should have been labelled a mere skill—the command of the English language—now assumed an aura of intellect and enlightenment. Through most of the twentieth century, the term 'convent-educated' was a loaded expression in India's social scene, implying pedigree in education, career and even matrimony. Every man wanted to marry a girl who could speak English, whether or not she could speak her mother tongue.

'Just teach my child English' is a refrain Poonam hears often from parents as far away as Amritsar, Ludhiana and Jammu when they drop off their children at her boarding school.

While the country of my birth was home to a plethora of languages and dialects, the English that parents actively sought was the speech—and, it follows, the comportment and self-confidence—of the typical convent-educated child, a speech shorn of any allusion to mother tongue, place of birth, caste, or creed.

Unfortunately, the very divisions the best English tried to dispel began to build steep walls between groups of people. An upscale 'public' education patterned after Eton that offered English at a high level, along with horse riding and polo, catered to a group that would never identify with the poorest strata of society or even the middle classes. The plea to Poonam from Hilltopian parents reminded me of a piece of writing by journalist P. Sainath—'the biggest growth sector in India today is the inequality sector'[30]—and I understood his vexation towards gated schools and gated communities that had now become the norm, physically demarcating one India from another.

Among the many journalists writing on the subject of education was one gentleman who was a product of the gated school system. Now he wrote regularly about his philosophy on government-funded education. While making India his home, the former Bureau Chief of the BBC, Sir Mark Tully, travelled extensively in India's rural areas. He saw that there was one solution, however daunting its implementation. He believed that English needed to percolate to every student in India and that government schools needed to improve their teaching of English as a link language while *not* making their schools English medium. The craze for private schools, he maintained, would end only when government schools offered English at such a high level that it became *more* than a 'library language'—good enough for research and also for conversation and business transactions. Tully's beliefs mirrored Mahatma

Gandhi's ideas and on one campus, in the most unexpected setting for a school, I saw that it had been put into practice by a visionary and her dedicated pack of teachers. The first batch of children were about to graduate from such a school. In many of his speeches and his writings, Tully emphasized that English needed to be taught well enough that it was a solid second language and that it could be learned without establishing it as the medium of education. In his view, too many poor people continued to 'sacrifice money they can ill afford in the belief that private education will provide a better future for their children'.[31] Almost always, their sacrifice was in vain. They were let down by the educators.

Tully's suggestion would be a Sisyphean task to execute in an India where government schools struggled with many challenges besides the absenteeism of teachers. Until then, if such a day came at all, educators like Poonam wanted to be the answer. She went into the villages that were within a day's drive of the school to recruit children from families that could afford it. The lives of the farmers were so arduous that it was little wonder how much Hilltop seemed to be a promise for their future. An English education symbolized the liberation from a life of physical toil and drudgery for the next generation. 'Just give them English so they can go to Keneda,' some parents said to Poonam as if going to Canada would adjust the sails of their lives. But I understood their sentiments. Following the election of Donald Trump to the presidency of the United States, many of my fellow Americans dreamed of life in Canada. Some parents hit Poonam with another request during her recruiting mission: 'Also please help our child get PR—permanent residency—in Keneda.' The business of parent management, whether parents were unlettered or overly qualified, was a difficult task and I marveled at Poonam's resilience and cheer.

The morning I walked over with her to meet one of her classes, a few girls ran up to her as we approached the stairs.

'And how are you today?' Poonam asked, hugging one of them tight.

'As bright as the sun, ma'am,' the girl responded, beaming. 'Fantastic as a summer day!' said a short one in pigtails. 'Splendid!' said a third, her eyes flashing. 'And how are you, ma'am?' she asked, in turn, of Poonam who collapsed into a tinkle of laughter. 'Terrific, thank you!' their rotund principal responded and walked on ahead, a stack of papers in hand, her peach and cream complexion redolent of the side of a Hilltop apple in summer.

◆

In the sun-dappled courtyard one afternoon at Hilltop, a skinny boy flitted about between the chaotic groups just before the school assembly. Cupping his hands to his mouth, he shouted, 'Everyone! Speak in English!' He dove into huddled groups, splitting them up. Most likely, he was a monitor, worried about getting caught for not enforcing the rule in school, especially when an outsider from America was visiting. The students, all outfitted in brown blazers, cardigans and khaki-coloured trousers, soon lined up, grade-wise, shushing one another as they spotted Poonam leaving her office to preside over the assembly.

One of Poonam's missions was to get her students to speak fearlessly in public. Now she called on them to volunteer to talk about themselves in front of the crowd. The first boy began well enough. He introduced himself and stated his grade. 'My father is a farmer. I've taken commerce stream because I want to go abroad.'

As each child returned to his or her spot, Poonam asked their friends to evaluate the speaker. As she scanned the assembly to pounce on the next child to drag out to the front, I saw some of them hiding behind one another, desperate that they not be targeted. Between each presentation, Poonam spoke to the children about how to present themselves and their strengths and their failings. Behind her a row of orange pillars enumerated qualities she wanted in her kids. Painted in bold green letters, some words were nouns. Some were adjectives. Together they conveyed the values and guiding principles for the school: 'tolerant'; 'loyalty'; 'dignity'; 'compassion'; 'endurance'; 'positive'; 'diligent'; 'perseverance'; 'teamwork'.

A girl raised her hand to convey her feelings about the speaker who had just finished. 'He did not spoke properly,' she said tentatively.

'Speak!' Poonam interjected to correct the child, and listened as she tried to complete her thoughts.

I realized that the fearless speakers were those who could speak confidently in English. One boy admitted as much in his presentation. He talked about his felicity and fluency in English as being the reason for his confidence. He used words like 'enthused', 'traversed' and 'gregarious', applying himself just as I once used to when my own father challenged me to learn and use one new English word a day in order to improve my vocabulary. In this young man, Himanshu, I recognized my own aspiration, in the sixties and seventies, to be a player in the world of English.

Poonam alighted on another young man, Nikhil, and wondered if he would volunteer. He walked up to stand next to her.

'Hello, everyone! This is Nikhil. I'm a student of Class XI. I'm in non-medical. And I'm passionate to be a journalist because I'm gregarious and confident enough to be in this profession. And I love to watch tennis and Novak Djokovic is my favourite tennis player. I'm very helpful and I'm honest, hard-working, dedicated, relentless. But at the same time, I'm very shy and I don't talk to people much. I'm very introvert and this is the kind of habit I need to traverse over.'

Poonam thanked the young man and quizzed the assembled children about their feelings about his speech. 'What did you think about Nikhil on a scale of 1 to 10, with 1 being bad and 10 being excellent?'

'10!' they screamed.

'Absolutely a 10!' she shouted back, beaming and clapping along with the rest of them as Nikhil went back to join the line of his classmates. Poonam then explained how Nikhil had distinguished himself from the pack of speakers who went before him. 'It was different. Remember that you are a unique person and you have to introduce yourself in your own manner.' She said Nikhil revealed a lot of personal details about himself as well and that even if the kids didn't know him before, they certainly knew him now after he introduced himself to them.

'You know he's shy. He's an introvert. You know he's hard-working and helpful. But you also know he wants to change and wants to become more outgoing.' She looked at Nikhil seated on the floor in the line for his grade. 'It was fantastic. Thank you!'

Nikhil smiled. He had a light in his eyes. I sensed the other children withering. I imagined many heads brimming with ideas about what they could have said about themselves, words and feelings that would remain unborn in the mountain air because they didn't have the means to package them for delivery. To me, those children were Shreya Ghoshal with a sore throat at a world music competition. The notes were locked in a throat that had swollen itself shut. In contrast, I saw Nikhil pumped up with self-confidence. Earlier that week I'd noticed how he was the most fluent in English in his grade and Poonam often called on him as she taught his class. She asked if he were taking part in the annual day celebrations in school later that month. He responded in the negative. 'Why not?' she demanded. 'You'll make a natural anchor. You'd better take part!'

I felt that Poonam had been preparing, all her life, to run such a school up in the mountains. On one of the days that I visited, I stayed with her for over fourteen hours and her energy didn't flag. Another afternoon, she ignored her waiting lunch as teachers and children trooped in and out of the room. Between meetings, she finally decided to dig into her lunch, at 4 p.m. She had the fortitude, the vision—and the Marwaha family nose as she called it—to go after her dreams. She had one talent, a priceless one in an educator—the gift of the gab. Her way with words, in both English and Hindi, reminded me of the torrential outpouring of the Niagara Falls, its volume and power awe-inspiring. In her impeccable choice of words, I gleaned her own father's impossible standards for his daughter and her mortification at having made a mistake while talking with him and using an incorrect word—'elevating' instead of 'alienating'. When I listened to her, I heard the received pronunciation of Chandigarh's Presentation Convent and the American bullishness born of years in high technology. Stuck to the window of her office were two signs that attested to her drive. One of them—'Excuse limit 0'—she said, with a laugh, defined her spirit in everything she had done in her life. The second poster was the logo of the Texas Longhorns, the athletic team that represented the University of Texas at Austin, her alma mater. The Longhorns took their name from a breed of cattle known for their horns which could extend to over six feet tip to tip for bulls, and seven feet tip to tip for steers and exceptional cows.

Poonam's passions ran high. Once Poonam was arrested—

for her activism during the Union Carbide disaster in Bhopal.
But she was married to a man who didn't let anything ruffle
him. Poonam didn't get that. 'How can you be this way,
Sudhir?' She wanted him to take a stand. 'Have an opinion.
What is your opinion?' Even though Poonam bulldozed her
way through projects and got things done, there was one aspect
of school-building that confounded her despite her doggedness.
She found that it was difficult to hire—and retain—the best
teachers. A good English teacher was hard to find.

Ruchi Pradhan Datta, who headed the English department
at the Lawrence School in South India's Lovedale, understood
Poonam's predicament. 'The problem is the degrees do not
support quality in India.' Though Ruchi was a third-generation
English speaker who was also the product of one of India's
oldest public schools, La Martiniere at Lucknow, a degree
in journalism and her training in voice and accent had also
primed her for a career in English education.

Ruchi rattled off the hurdles. 'How do we preach to
children who watch American television and read Stephen
Fry? Should we pursue British spelling? Or American spelling?
What about accents? What about the many accents in India?'
Standardization was hard to achieve across regions, she said.
The rules of English pronunciation used to be a lot simpler.
Everybody aspired to have a specific accent stipulated by
'Received Pronunciation'. Ruchi said teachers now needed to
be trained in American, British as well as 'neutral' accents.
American grammar rules were different, too. 'Today's
generation is a very confused generation,' she said. There were
other choices to make: Was it 'privacy' said with the short 'i'
sound or 'privacy' with the long 'i' sound? Was it 'schedule'
said in the British way or the word enunciated with a 'k'
sound? Of course, challenges arose from the rules of grammar
in bhasha (regional language), too. It was hard to explain to a

child trained in a bhasha the notion of a preposition. There was no preposition in Hindi. Ruchi explained how first-generation speakers did not get that concept. 'They end up saying, "I'm listening music."'

English had thus become a beast that was impossible to tame. And what was English any more in a global world that dipped into a ragbag of Indian, British and American Englishes? From accent, to pronunciation, to spelling, the life of the English teacher in India was an intimidating prospect. I saw why Poonam, who was passionate about the subject herself, would find it hard to hire a qualified English teacher. At the time of my visit the position had been unfilled for a few months. Poonam showed me one of the applications she had received for the job. A master's degree holder in English had applied to teach at Hilltop but the applicant's letter was riddled with grammatical errors. I felt sorry for Poonam. I felt sorry for the students. In the meanwhile, Poonam also played the role of an English teacher.

On one of the evenings before dinner, as the television played on low volume in the background, Poonam sat in her home, cigarette in hand, her perfect Audrey Hepburn face pensive about the ceaseless legal imbroglios that had now pitted her and her husband against his relatives. 'This is the new India,' she said, exhaling smoke into the chilly air, fretting about having to contest her claim to the school her father-in-law had established, 'where most Punjabi families fight over property, where everything is only about money.' The state of her own world mirrored the fragmentation of the larger world. It was the state of declining value systems, of pacts broken, of new walls going up where old ones were razed to the ground, of families forgetting what brought them together in the first place, of progeny erasing the memories of their forebears.

Sometimes she wanted to give it all up and return to her

home, husband, children and grandchildren back in the States. 'But my kids at the school. They need me!' she signed. 'What will happen to my kids?' she asked, mopping her kohl-lined eyes with a Kleenex. For Poonam, of all the jobs she had ever pursued, this felt like her calling. She was sceptical of the motives of some other educators around her. 'Education is big business in India. We don't build schools here any more. We build groups of schools.'

Many of these groups advertised loftier goals as well. Satchidananda Jothi Nikethan International School at the foothills of the Nilgiris in Tamil Nadu claimed in its one-page colour advertisement that the fully residential school 'educated the mind and illuminated the soul'. Most humans, I suspected, needed to attend Satchidananda Jothi Nikethan before they exited from the world. In Dehradun, India's ground zero for elite schools, an all girls' residential school called Unison World School claimed it would help in 'realizing her potential'. Affiliated to 'CISCE and University of Cambridge CIE', this was a school with a difference. Mentioned in bold were the student exchange tie-ups with international schools in Hertfordshire in the UK, Christchurch in New Zealand, and Perthshire in Scotland.

In contrast, Poonam's vision for her school was simple and straightforward. And on that evening as I talked to her about her lonely life from March through early November every year, I understood her frustration. If all the stars would align, she could create a lasting haven that reflected her father-in-law's values and her own.

◆

Along the winding route from Coimbatore to Anaikatti where Kerala meets Tamil Nadu is a green board that people took seriously in these parts: 'Elephants Have The Right Of

Way'. Vinayagam was at the wheel and we were approaching a tribal school, Vidya Vanam. Here teachers and students were bussed to their homes before darkness rolled into the villages cloistered in these verdant ghats. Vidya Vanam educated children from kindergarten through high school. It was started in recognition of a simple fact that even as the elephant roamed the countryside, the ant too needed the sun and claimed its space.

The tribal villagers wanted their children to learn English because, unlike them, the first generation of learners in their families may one day have to forage for jobs in cities. Over 100 million tribal people live in the forests of India but as forests continue to get eroded, they have become marginalized and estranged from their resources. Now, many of the forest dwellers are day labourers working in the brick kilns around Anaikatti. Today, the school has grown to a strength of close to 300 students and 30 full-time teachers. The first batch was ready to graduate.

Inside Vidya Vanam's little office are black-and-white pictures of three thought leaders adorning a cream-coloured wall. Mahatma Gandhi, philosopher Jiddu Krishnamurti and Rabindranath Tagore embody the philosophy of education at the school. One of the ideas from Gandhi's *The Story of My Experiments with Truth* informed Vidya Vanam's director's attitude to learning. When I read Gandhi's memoir, I felt that practising one's beliefs to an extreme invariably led to hypocrisies in most of us. Gandhi, however, seemed to be able to veer so far in the practice of his principles that almost always he was able to avoid being labelled a hypocrite. Would I have found a friend in him? I'm not sure. Had he been my uncle, I may have avoided him like the plague. But as I read his work, I realized how clear he was in his perception of how deeply India's mind had been tuned by its masters. He believed that education itself was an indoctrination of sorts and detailed his own struggles with identifying the best strategy for the education of his children. Gandhi felt that people lost their liberty when they became enslaved to the citadels of education.[32] Specifically, he believed that children did not need English before Grade 6 and that the mother tongue was the language in which concepts had to be taught first. He felt that when Indian parents trained their children to think and talk in English 'from their infancy…they deprive them of the spiritual and social heritage of the nation'.[33]

T. Srikanth oversees the administration of the school and teaches math and physics. When Srikanth taught at a school in Chennai, he noticed a derision towards those students who were first-time learners of English. That bothered him because he realized that even when a child was talented in math and science, his inability to express himself cost him in the classroom.

Srikanth insists that English will happen naturally for all his students. The school formally introduces English only around the time the child is nine or ten, around fourth grade. In the meanwhile, the child hears both English and other Indian languages around him. The idea is to teach concepts as much as possible in the language he or she knows best. Teachers often reinforce concepts in two languages. More than the language of instruction, there are other pressing concerns, especially in these parts. How do you teach children that the future of the planet is important? And how does one teach a child who was born and raised in the hills to respect the elephant corridor? At the heart of it all is a fundamental question: What sort of education is right for him or her?

Vidya Vanam was started by Srikanth's mother, Prema Rangachary with this precept that every system of education had to do the following: teach respect, compassion, kindness, and curiosity to explore the world. The purpose of education was manifold but among the key values to impart to a student were optimism, curiosity, fearlessness, care and compassion.

One of the words I heard several times from Srikanth, and from his mother was this notion of 'fearlessness' in learning. From the outset, their idea was to build a classroom where children feel no fear while learning and exchanging ideas with others in the classroom. They are encouraged to talk about any topic. Vidya Vanam does not follow textbooks but culls out the curriculum from different resources and shapes learning around themes. One year, the focus was rice, so all their projects at school revolved around rice; a year-end debate, that was attended by journalists, focused on genetically modified rice. Recycling and the preservation of the environment is an important aspect of the programme, so the school has receptacles in the courtyard for recycling different materials. The playthings in Vidya Vanam were inspired by the Montessori system, yet their physical manifestation was local. There were painted logs representing the Fibonacci series that used wood from a coconut orchard that had been cut down.

The school brings out a newspaper in English and in Tamil every week and while the stories are different in each newspaper, the content is similar. Forest conservation and respect for the environment are a priority in the elephant corridor. 'Why are forests important?' was one of the feature stories in the edition of the English paper the week I visited. During the same week the Tamil version discussed 'Komban', a story about a tusker, the largest elephant in Asia, that enters villages in search of water and food. When I scanned the paper, I was struck by how city life insulated us from the struggles of the people in rural communities.

When we left Vidya Vanam, Vinayagam drove me across the border from Tamil Nadu into Kerala. We passed a few lottery shops and two bakeries right by the border. Nothing else existed for miles—just mountains, brick kilns, banana plantations, coconut, breadfruit trees, mango orchards, cows, and sheep. Just as I began to think that all civilization had ended, I heard the muezzin's call to prayer. Even in the forest, we could not avoid religion or a lottery ticket. Vinayagam announced that we had just entered Kerala—all the signs were now in Malayalam. We stopped outside Maveli, a small grocery store.

'Chechi, how much for that pepper?' Vinayagam asked, switching to the Malayalam term for 'sister'. We were one inch from Tamil Nadu and already my father's late valet had gone over to the other side.

Vinayagam used language to ingratiate himself into other people's lives. Out on the roads, India flourished on the strength of those casual relationships established within nanoseconds. People called each other 'anna' on the roads in Tamil Nadu; in Kerala, the word was 'chetta'. I heard 'bhai' and 'bhaiyya' up in the north. These terms of respect and consideration transcended religion, age, community, gender, belief, ethos, money, state and accomplishments. Surely, education had a greater responsibility—now more than ever before? To convey the particular spirit of a place and to mould human beings who would be as global as they were local?

It was this callous disregard of local life that bothered R. K. Narayan in his elementary years. When he learned the Roman alphabet, he was taught that 'A was an apple pie' and his English teacher would tell the students to memorize the line, without questioning exactly what a pie was: 'It must be some stuff similar to our *idli*, but prepared with apple.' Narayan observed how English was a stilted add-on for India: 'Among fruits, we were familiar with the mango, banana, guava, pomegranate and grape, but not the apple (in our part of the country) much less an apple pie.' When Narayan was five years old, he was initiated into education with religious rituals. 'I was taught to shape the first two letters of the alphabet with corn spread out on a tray, both in Sanskrit and Tamil.' But in the classroom in his school, Sanskrit and Tamil received short shrift. They were relegated to 'second language'; after all, the first being English was taught by the best teacher in the school, 'the ruling star of the institution, the headmaster himself'.[34] Like me, Narayan too was puzzled by the physical appearance of the English texts compared to the local books they used in the classroom. The English primer looked glossy and impressive with strong binding and colour illustrations.

Narayan's prescient words on relevance in education amounted to the simple truth that all learning had to be tailored to our individual selves and to our particular lives in order to be meaningful. One size could never fit all. This was the basic principle on which a tribal school in an elephant corridor had been founded. It was a value for any school to live by.

◆

As I left the classroom on my last day at Dalhousie, a tall thin boy followed me all the way to the office. 'Ma'am, can I have your email?' he asked. I had met him a couple days before on the courtyard of the school. A Kashmiri Muslim, he had just joined the school as a boarder a few months prior. 'Ma'am, after high school, I want to go to a foreign country,' he had said to me when I hung around talking to a few of them. 'Why a foreign country?' I had asked. 'Why not stay in India?' The boy replied that in Srinagar, schools were closed for months on end because of the border fighting between India and Pakistan. Some children stayed on in Srinagar waiting for their schools to reopen while some others received private coaching to keep up their education. Children who could afford boarding schools were sent away by parents whose livelihoods kept them working near India's borders. The day I was leaving, the boy wrote down my email. 'I really want to come to America,' he said once again, clutching my business card in his hand.

Later that evening Poonam asked me the most important question, one that we must all be concerned about: If the next generation is only going to migrate abroad, who is going to stay back here to build the future in India? Poonam was concerned that her students had no sense of community and did not seek technology other than Facebook and email; they did not use technology to learn about the world. It had not broadened their world any (contrary to what we might assume) because of their circumstances. Their parents were farmers and other agriculturists who had come into money because of rising land values. Sending their kids to this school was their idea of pursuing the 'American dream'. But it wasn't clear that their education would ultimately address the real reason a child must aspire for literacy at an English-medium school. It wasn't clear that the answer for everyone was an English-medium education. While reading Nawazuddin Siddiqui's words in an in-flight magazine, I was moved by his frustration over his inadequate English. He lamented that Bollywood was divided along the lines of English and non-English when the only criterion should be the presence or absence of acting talent.

In the new India, unfortunately, the perception of success was everything. The annual day celebration at a local school was one of Dalhousie's grandest spectacles. On the day, the traffic up to the mountains halted. Local hotshots, students from all the fancy boarding schools in the surrounding hills and even famous perfumed, high-heeled Delhiites arrived in the early afternoon at the high security entrance point of the school. From anywhere on the campus, it was impossible to miss the four words of the school motto that were plastered across the building: In Pursuit of Excellence. At the end of the annual day performances, one thing was clearly excellent in my opinion. Judging by the props, the costumes and the dances, it was obvious that the pursuit of money in the school was excellent, which in turn allowed for the tea, cakes and samosas to be exceptionally excellent and, accordingly, also allowed for the pursuit of a top-notch Bollywood choreographer to be excellent.

In contrast, for their annual day celebrations, Poonam's children would perform on the grassy knoll of her backyard and she would throw a dinner party for the children and their families in her home. 'I don't believe in the rat race. I want them to do it from their heart.' To prepare for the big day, Poonam would use her training as a semi-professional kathak dancer, coordinate with the teachers, listen to songs, go through steps, and tweak their performances.

But more than sweating annual day celebrations, Poonam spent an inordinate amount of time fretting over the format of exams and the quality of education. She worried that education was so mired in process, formalities, numbers and targets that it had lost its focus on reading, critical thinking, comprehension and analysis. Her words echoed those of Jerry Pinto, who teaches journalism at several Mumbai colleges, when he told me how, in general, humanities teaching in India had deteriorated and that the lack of critical thinking reflected on the poor quality of critical writing. In the meantime as president of Dalhousie Hilltop School, she was expected to meet the requirements of the CBSE board and those of all the parents who, while they knew little about the education system, were often consumed by the significance of test results.

A week after my conversations with the students at Dalhousie, my Toyota screeched down Chamba Valley towards Pathankot past speed warnings on perilous hairpin bends.

Billboards for schools littered the mountainside, all of them promising English-medium education and superior facilities for the next generation of overachievers. Speed warnings flashed past. One of them gave me pause: 'Don't Fast!'

I found myself wondering about the right way to sculpt the mind of a child. Having seen Vidya Vanam's simple precepts to education, it seemed Mahatma Gandhi may have been trying to tell us something—that the conduit for education was not as important as the content and that it was more important to learn one's lessons in the tongue that one understood best. It was entirely antithetical to what Poonam and other educators of English-medium schools espoused.

As my car reached the crossroads of Dalhousie—Jammu—Pathankot, a song from the past played on the car's radio and spilled out through the open window. The driver stopped the car and moseyed over to a tea stall for a break. I leaned back and crooned along with Mohammed Rafi and Lata Mangeshkar, thinking that this evergreen melody was at least as old as I was and discovering, much later, on Google, that the song was recorded in the year of my birth, 1961. 'Sau saal pehle mujhe tumse pyaar tha...'

I could understand all the words of the song even though I could not speak Hindi. I felt the confluence of many waters within me. Of the Tamil river that flowed within me, of the ocean of English that had hemmed me in during my adulthood and held me in its thrall. There was another layer of meaning that trickled out of the lines.

> A hundred years ago, I was in love with you
> I loved you then. I still do, now.
> And I will do so tomorrow.

This could have been India's song, in Hindi, about its undying love for the language of its colonial masters.

TWO

THE PRINCESS IN HER BUNGALOW

Three thousand kilometres southwest of Dalhousie Hilltop School, at the opposite end of the country, I discovered that in some families in India, the English language had been taught for over 200 years, for political reasons, almost as a matter of necessity. Inside the old royal family of Travancore, Her Highness Princess Pooyam Thirunal Gouri Parvathi Bayi had grown up hearing English spoken around her all the time. Consequently, when she began to learn it formally, it was almost effortless, as natural as paying obeisance to Lord Padmanabha, a representation of the supreme deity Vishnu. Every member of the royal family of the erstwhile Travancore kingdom was a dasa, a slave, to the god with the rare 'right-turning' conch. Even when Princess Gouri Parvathi Bayi travelled to other parts of the world, reminders of home popped up, in the most unexpected places.

On a visit to the Isle of Wight, she had just entered the Durbar Room in the Osborne House where Queen Victoria had breathed her last when the princess felt that something in that place was calling out to her. Sure enough, among the displays was a gift to the queen from her family—an ivory carving of Lord Padmanabha. Likewise, on another visit to the Windsor Castle, she noticed a throne among the exhibits, and told her friend that there was something about it that spoke to her. They walked around to the back of the chair and, there, engraved on it was the emblem of the Travancore royal family, Lord Padmanabha's conch. When she went back to her palace in the old city of Thiruvananthapuram, the princess discovered that in 1851 the throne had in fact been gifted by her ancestor, the Travancore maharaja, to his pen pal Queen Victoria, for the Great Exhibition at the Crystal Palace in London's Hyde Park. The conch seemed to be an extension of the princess herself. It was a feeling both inexplicable and unalterable, beckoning her, at the most unexpected times in her life.

Deep inside the ancient Sri Padmanabhaswamy Temple in Thiruvananthapuram, reclining under the hood of the serpent Adisesha lies Lord Padmanabha, Vishnu, whom Hindus worship as the Preserver of the Universe. According to legend, when a hermit blew into his conch during meditation, a snake crept out of it, and directed that he should be worshipped as Naga devata. Built on that sacred ground that was once a forest, the temple has stood sentinel to the fortunes of the Travancore kingdom—one of the oldest dynasties in India whose recorded history dates from 870 BCE. Stories about the temple also flourished. In 1870, a British missionary Reverend Samuel Mateer wrote about a deep well inside the temple 'into which immense riches are thrown year by year; and in another place, in a hollow covered by a stone, a great golden lamp, which was lit over 120 years ago and still continues burning.'[35]

Even before I landed in this city, I'd heard about the temple's magnificent seven-storey gopuram (tower) and the fabled Arattu procession that takes place in April and October every year. What is unique about this procession is that it shuts down the city's international airport for five hours so the deity, the king and the people of the city can walk down the 3-kilometre runway to the waters at Shankumugham Beach. There they immerse themselves, deity and dasa, in a ritual bathing in the Indian Ocean. Meteer's writings about life in Travancore denounced many of its ancient practices. Yet underscoring his writings was a sense of awe for the enigma of the place that he (and perhaps no one) would ever comprehend.

I'd landed at the Thiruvananthapuram airport early in the evening during a terrible downpour. In the pelting rain, it wasn't clear where the sky began and the ocean ended. Rain lashed the ground in inch-thick ropes and the umbrellas in Kerala were built to handle them, resembling little black tents with curved industrial strength handles. As my taxi crawled out of the airport, I realized how close the runway was to the waters of the Indian Ocean. Fishermen's boats lined the sands, reminding me of the events that unfolded in a novella, *Chemmeen*, that was centred around this southwestern coast.

'When the first fisherman fought with the waves and currents of the sea, single-handed, on a piece of wood on the other side of the horizon, his wife sat looking westward to the sea and prayed with all her soul for his safety.'[36] When the woman on the shore was chaste, the goddess of the sea, Katalamma, never failed to deliver her husband back to land, despite the treacherous whirlpools, sharks and storms.

Driving in that devastating rain, I understood why Princess Gouri looked for portents during her travels. Royals and commoners weren't exempt from tragedy and faith was the only thing that gave people hope. Princess Gouri lost her father in an air crash in Kullu when she was twenty-nine. In 1944, the princess was just three when she lost her six-year-old brother to a rheumatic heart condition. In a strange way, her life crossed mine, too, at the time. My parents were married the year of her brother's death and my father always told me that the sound of drums was missing at his wedding because the state of Travancore was in mourning.

I went to meet the princess at her residence on the grounds of Kowdiar Palace to glean a little more about her education, especially about her English lessons in the early part of the twentieth century. A conch frieze decorated the front door of her home. The doorbell by the front door was fused onto a base limned as a conch. It adorned light switches. I counted sixteen conches in each window grille at the bungalow. The royal vehicle had the conch emblazoned on the fender. Like all those of her lineage, the princess too believed that the 'valampuri shankha' assured fame, longevity and prosperity and as she spoke to me about her feelings in the presence of the sinistral conch, I listened, finding it hard to maintain my scepticism.

The princess spoke perfect English, as did her mother and her grandmother before her, and as did most educated Indians who had grown up in homes where English was also a familiar tongue. But Parvathi Bayi spoke with a certain flourish and colour, too, and with a wryness that came from an eye for irony, and with the sort of precision that I'd only heard from those who were educated in the early to mid-twentieth century, many of whom had been taught by Englishmen or by Anglo-Indians or by Indians who wielded the language as well as their imperial masters. There's a caveat, however. The second the princess uttered some words which ended in specific sounds—'hall', or 'soon', or 'people'—the pixie dust sloughed off her cotton kasavu sari. In a blink of an eye, the princess morphed into a commoner like me whose father could not afford to give his child a convent school education. All I heard was her strident affirmations and her weighty and hardened 'l' and 'n', which she enunciated, like most Malayalis—and all my maternal cousins who, like me, had also been born in Travancore—with the curl of her tongue against the posterior roof of her mouth.

Sitting in the bungalow adjacent to Kowdiar Palace, I discovered that, at seventy-five, Princess Parvathi couldn't be bothered about the trivialities of accent and style. Unlike the kingdoms in the north of India, the Travancore royalty had never valued opulence or artifice, eating out of banana leaves while seated on the floor just like the common folk did.

In any case, she said, how on earth did it matter that she spoke with an Indian accent or that the English that Indians spoke often showed the petticoats of its origins? 'Don't the French have an accent when they speak English?' she asked. 'And the Germans?'

The princess was right. She had put my common mind in its place and admonished me, in a sense, just as my husband often did. After four decades in America, he did not care a fig for the veneer of a westernized English accent or that his English showed the scaffoldings of his Tamil upbringing or that he had attended Krishnaswamy Mudaliar High School (not a convent school). Whenever I told him to fix how he pronounced the word 'embarrassment' (the stress was not on the third syllable) or 'equipment' (there was a 'u' before 'i') or 'distinguished' (the stress was on the second syllable), he was nettled by it. 'Who cares?' he asked, 'As long as I'm understood around the world?' His attitude was similar to that of Princess Gouri, except, of course, in one regard.

A few days before I showed up at her home, the princess had heard a speech given by a principal of a local school during which the woman used an object pronoun, as in 'Me and the students'. The formalities had barely begun but this had been an assault on Her Highness's ears. Princess Gouri was a classical dancer, an educator, a writer, a translator, an ambassador, a philanthropist, a wife, a mother, a grandmother, and a patron of the arts. In addition to all that, she was also a grammar fiend.

◆

It's the wettest state—whether measured by the rain or by the alcohol that flows through it. Kerala has an unhurried sameness. In my home town of Aluva (earlier called Alwaye), I saw it in the crawl of moss on brick walls, in the gabled windows with wooden lattices, the curves and curls of a brass manichithrathazhu (an ornamental lock) on a teak door, and the panoply of woods that lined the roads on drives from Paravur. Their names rang like a chant—plavu (jackfruit), thengu (coconut), eeti (rosewood), maanga (mango), irumullu (pyinkado), thambakam (Malabar ironwood), chandanam (sandalwood).

To mention Kerala, however, is also to celebrate progress, especially its forays into literacy with a focus on education and on health. In 1977, the World Health Organization drove a plan of 'Health for all by 2000 AD' and they fixed targets and indices for achievements—such as immunization, mortality during childbirth of mother or child, the control of communicable diseases, and life expectancy. Kerala achieved all these indices within five years. Its model of development was adopted as a standard by many developing nations. The state had always been progressive with a history of passionate educators.

When the Indian subcontinent was a British colony, it was divided into provinces and a collection of princely states of which Travancore was a high-ranking member with a '19-gun salute'. A pecking order had been established among royalty depending on how they performed, their income, their ability to keep in the good books of their rulers. The salute denoted a privilege with perquisites that were on display during the grand events hosted by the Raj. About 565 kingdoms were officially recognized and ruled by hereditary princes. Travancore, which had strengthened itself under the heft of Dutch militarist Eustachius De Lannoy by acquiring more land through warfare, was a trailblazer in education and social reforms. Outside of these princely states, the provinces were administered by the British and each province was ruled by a governor who was expected to keep the peace.

Even though Travancore formed a sliver of what finally grew into the state called Kerala after India's independence, the decisions of these Travancore kings and queens were pivotal to education and women's rights. Early on, the iconoclasts in this state were often women. By the time Princess Gouri's ancestor, Queen Lakshmi Bayi, died in 1814, she had eliminated the practice of 'gosha' with respect to association with Europeans at a time when the proximity of a foreigner was considered polluting.

A hundred years later, writer Aubrey Menen, whose Malayali father married an Englishwoman, experienced, first-hand, the repugnance central to gosha. Menen's grandmother, a proud woman of the Nair caste, could not bear to have her white daughter-in-law in the same house. 'My mother being foreign was ritually unclean, and therefore, whenever she entered the family house, she would defile it. The house would have to be purified each time, and so would every caste Hindu in it. It followed logically that if my mother stayed in the house, it would be continually in a state of being ritually cleaned.'[37] To get around this, Menen's grandmother put up her daughter-in-law in a separate building. She also delayed meeting her as long as she possibly could and when she ultimately acceded to a meeting weeks after her arrival, the meeting lasted all of three minutes and took place 'on a conveniently outlying veranda of the family house'.[38]

In the Travancore royal houses, in contrast, by the early nineteenth century, Europeans mingled freely with the royals. English governesses taught the royal children, and hence while they could read and write in Malayalam and Sanskrit, their English was also exemplary. The resources for learning were plenty and they sought Western ideas of scientific progress. A palace physician, an English gentleman called Dr Brown, instructed Uthram Thirunal Marthanda Varma, who reigned from 1847 to 1860, in chemistry and allopathy. In 1853 since social customs barred him from touching corpses and bone, the king got a replica of a human skeleton carved from ivory so that he could study anatomy and osteology.

The relationship between the court and the empire was friendly and large tracts of land were donated for both educational and religious purposes. In 1813 Queen Lakshmi Bayi granted sixteen acres of land, 500 rupees in cash, and timber from public forests for the construction of college buildings on the banks of the Meenachil River. The principal of the college laid the foundations of a modern secular education by implementing a curriculum with a strong concentration of subjects such as history, mathematics and geography, languages such as Syriac, Sanskrit, Latin, English and Greek. The academic programme at the college was expected to be 'no less rigorous than that at the University of Cambridge'.[39] Virgil's *Aeneid*, Cicero's *Orations*, Horace's *Epistles*, the works of Euclid and plane and spherical trigonometry were part of the syllabus.

In 1817, another ancestor who was also the princess's namesake, Queen Gouri Parvathi Bayi, was the regent during the minority of her nephew, Maharaja Swathi Thirunal. She declared education a state subject and made it the responsibility of the government to ensure the education of every Travancore citizen. However, while missionaries established schools where English was taught without discriminating gender, in many instances, orthodox families preferred to not send their children to school. Instead, if they were educated at all, their tutors would come to their homes. The English language had its beginnings in a confined manner among the general population through the Christian missionaries. Besides royalty, those associated with the church and missionary activities began to learn it first.

In the meanwhile, inside the royal household, a man called English Subba Rao (who had been taught by an English gentleman called Elias Schwarz) was the tutor of Maharaja Swathi Thirunal who ruled from 1813 to 1846. The kings of princely states were often polyglots because it was politically expedient. In Travancore, for instance, royals were trained in Persian, English, Portuguese and Dutch because treaties were often written in foreign languages and they were keen to understand the accords they signed. Swathi Thirunal's genius flowed into many disciplines. He was fluent in Malayalam, Kannada, Tamil, Telugu, Marathi, Hindustani, Sanskrit, English and Persian and he composed songs in several languages, all of which were now a celebrated part of the Carnatic classical repertoire. Into each of his lyrical gems, Swathi Thirunal embedded his signature mudra, the word 'Padmanabha', offering benedictions to the god whose gopuram he could see from the music room where he created many of his famous musical compositions.

A little after Swathi Thirunal ascended the throne on attaining majority, in 1829, Persian sloughed off as a court language. Now English education propelled the empire. Colleges in the three presidencies offered degrees in arts, law, medicine and engineering. While the royals interacted with the British Raj, English became a language of communication between the king, his dewan, the resident of the princely state and Great Britain. In another decade, English became the preferred language for entry into government jobs, creating a new class of people who would aspire for those positions upon learning the new language of the masters.

The maharaja died young, by the age of thirty-three,

but during his reign, he established the first free English school. He also established a school in every village of his dominions—something that had not been done in England, Scotland or Ireland—and insisted on educating every child, male and female. There was not a child who had reached eight years of age in his kingdom who was not capable of reading and writing.

Kerala's first printing press was set up in 1820 in Nagercoil (then in the state of Travancore) and Swathi Thirunal was so impressed by Reverend Bailey's invention that he invited him to Thiruvananthapuram to set up a printing press in his capital city. Keen on participating in scientific advancement, Swathi Thirunal sanctioned the construction of an observatory and named John Caldecott its director. He sought to furnish it with the best instruments to be obtained in Europe. Krishna Rao, a Telugu Brahmin minister, was a great favourite of General Cullen, the resident of Travancore state, and he now began to have designs on joining the Travancore service. He began to poison General Cullen's mind against Dewan Subba Rao who had been Swathi Thirunal's English teacher; he also leaked stories about how the king was unhappy about the expenses pertaining to the observatory to be built by Caldecott. When the maharaja got wind of the machinations of the wily Krishna Rao, he wrote a letter to Caldecott. Almost two hundred years later, the letter's language comes across as verbose and archaic, but it demonstrates how articulate the king was and how well English had permeated into India in the time of the Raj. Many of India's illustrious lawyers and administrators were known for the arsenic-edged wit that they had inherited from their English role models. In this letter, the king, his pen mightier even than his sword, hacks to pieces Krishna Rao's reputation.

Here I must not omit to say, in diametrical opposition

to what the Resident has been pleased to intimate to you as my sentiments that neither such mean idea has ever entered into my head, nor have I, either directly or indirectly communicated anything upon this point to the above purport, but on the contrary, whenever Krishna Rao, who, you know, is a vulgar minded man and a total stranger to any learning at all, endeavored to persuade me that there is no utility by the continuance of the observatory establishment, I sued to check him and at the same time express to him my sense of the high advantage derived from this establishment in a scientific point of view, as I am fully sensible that by reason of my patronizing it, my name, however undeserving of any celebrity is favorably noticed even in distant regions, among the scientific personages of the day.[40]

◆

When she was about five years old, right around the time India gained independence, Princess Gouri played hostess to eighteen-year-old Pamela Mountbatten, the daughter of Lord Louis Mountbatten, the last viceroy of British India and the first governor general of independent India. Lord Mountbatten and his family were headed for the Periyar Game Sanctuary (now part of the Periyar Wildlife Sanctuary) in the Western Ghats and they had stopped to greet the Travancore royals 3,000 feet up in the hills at Peermade. As per etiquette, Lord Mountbatten sat at her uncle's table and Lady Edwina at her mother's table while the little princess had been assigned to take charge of Pamela. She had been coached to ask Pamela what she wanted to drink.

'Would you like coffee or tea?' she asked.

Since Pamela responded with 'tea'—and that being a

foregone conclusion—the princess had been primed to ask the subsequent question.

'Would you like milk or lemon with that?'

At the end of the tea and the mingling, Lord Mountbatten was so taken with how well-spoken the five-year-old princess was that she was whisked away for a photograph with him, a picture that the princess could not locate as I sat with her at her guest house at Kowdiar Palace. But in her descriptions was a revelation of how children of the Travancore royal family were groomed early for formal, diplomatic functions.

As was customary in the state of her birth, the princess began learning to write the Malayalam script by scrawling with her finger on sand so that she never lost touch with the earth. The priest held her finger and made her write out the words 'Hari Sree Ganapathaye Namaha Avignamasthu...' invoking Lord Ganesha to remove all obstacles in her progress to education and the Goddess of Learning, Saraswati, to pave the way. One year after she began learning Malayalam, at about four years of age, the princess was initiated into the English alphabet, although she was already speaking the language fluently by then.

Early on, the princess was perplexed by the unpredictability of English. 'Cut. Put. But. They're written the same way but pronounced differently,' she would say to her English tutor, Mrs Myrtle Pereira, who turned up at the palace for her lessons every day.

'That's the way it is, child,' Mrs Pereira said, suggesting that the best way to master the language was to accept its inconsistencies, memorize them and move on. The princess had asked a thoughtful question to which the response was labyrinthine. The English language had evolved over a thousand years of the clash of civilizations. Every time the English language met a people and a culture—first the Romans, then the Anglo-Saxons, the Vikings, the French and then the colonies—it received another overhaul. New words washed out the old. New sounds hissed in. In Middle English (approximately between the twelfth and sixteenth centuries), the words 'cut', 'put', and 'but' along with many others with that vowel sound in them would have had 'oo' sound (like the French 'ou' as in the word 'vous'). They would have rhymed, although they may not have sounded as they do to our ears today because vowel sounds changed, too, through regions as well as through time. In the early Modern English period, the 'oo' sound was thought to have morphed to an short 'u' sound as in the word 'foot' but this change in the vowel supposedly happened to only some words and not to others. While Mrs Pereira may or may not have known all this, she was wise in telling that 'child'—a very Anglo-Indian usage, indeed—not to question the quirks of the language that provided her sustenance.

An Anglo-Indian, Mrs Pereira belonged to the legion of India's Eurasians who were masterful teachers as well as sportsmen, yet they were looked upon with mild derision, as second-class citizens, in India and certainly in Great Britain. During the rule of the British East India Company in the late eighteenth and early nineteenth centuries, British officers and soldiers often married local women and had Eurasian children, owing to a lack of Englishwomen in India.

Like Princess Gouri, almost every Indian educated in the India of the twentieth century had a story about his or her Anglo-Indian teacher. In her early years, Mrs Pereira taught the princess to form her letters on four lines on a black slate. Then the princess learned to write them on double lines, connecting her letters in a cursive hand. When she wrote a composition, she was told to not repeat words as much as possible. Everything she wrote had to have a rough and fair copy. When she wrote 'thank you' cards to her teachers, her mother and grandmother supervised the writing for grammar, content and handwriting and insisted that she write words of gratitude acknowledging her teachers. The royal children were homeschooled until it was time to enrol in a university. But times had changed, observed the princess, her lips curved downward in disapproval. Now it was a big deal if the gifts she gave received an acknowledgement by way of an emoji.

Princess Gouri recalled how Mrs Pereira came to the palace school clad in a skirt and blouse and always talked about going 'back home'. Home, Britain, was just an entity in the imagination of most Anglo-Indians who had been born and raised on Indian soil. Across the country, Anglo-Indians were often employed in the subordinate departments of the government—with the police, railways, telegraph, customs and the port. They were fixtures of India's many non-Catholic English-medium schools, coveted for their English language skills, their commitment to discipline and their athletic prowess. Growing up, I remember hearing them being mocked with terms like 'Chutney Mary' whose origins I did not understand. It was commonly used in Kolkata, which had the biggest population of Anglo-Indians, to describe a low-class woman with cheap taste trying to pass off as upper class. Anglo-Indians were disparaged for many reasons because while they ate Indian food, they adopted Western wear, aspired to go 'back home' while being categorically barred from 'whites only' clubs. After Independence, in the sixties and seventies, most Anglo-Indians left India for the United Kingdom, Australia or Canada. Although they were the only community given reserved seats in the assemblies and the parliament, they stood out like pomegranates among gooseberries.

Now as an immigrant to another nation who had given birth to two children in the United States, I felt I understood their predicament; the deracinated angst of the Anglo-Indian was not different from that of my children whose brown skin belied their allegiance to the American soil into which they had been born. The hypocrisy of the Englishman also stuck out in sharp relief. The English had the gall to call Indians caste-conscious when it was well known they were inherently class-conscious.

Among the things I owed the Anglo-Indian community were expressions—now buried and hidden between the pages of my father's *Encyclopaedia Britannica* and my love for my favourite *Bournvita Quiz Contest* on All India Radio—that marked my adolescence in India. When I asked a friend if my 'Sunday' were longer than 'Monday' "I was, in fact, wondering if my petticoat were showing from under my dress or skirt". I never understood how we assigned the name 'Hawaii chappals' to beachwear for the feet. Apparently, it was a term made popular by Anglo-Indians. I learned to call them bathroom slippers or flip-flops after I landed in America.

When I was in school in Chennai, an Anglo-Indian music teacher taught us to sing a hymn that, in my memory, predates every Hindu bhajan I'd ever learned. Long before I was taught to love this or hate that, I remember singing at school assemblies a song about the beauty of Creation while the teacher accompanied us on the piano.

> All things bright and beautiful,
> All creatures great and small,
> All things wise and wonderful:
> The Lord God Made Them All.
>
> Each little flow'r that opens,
> Each little bird that sings,
> He made their glowing colours,
> He made their tiny wings…

Myrtle Pereira finally did go 'back home' to the United Kingdom. Princess Gouri stayed in touch with her long after she moved, exchanging letters until the teacher died.

◆

Although most Englishmen and women were barred from making friends with the natives, some, like Kaye, rebelled against that notion. Like Kipling's Kim she 'consorted on terms of perfect equality' with the children of servants who worked at her parents' home and the small boys and girls of the bazaar.[41] Out of the interactions between the Indian and the Englishman rose a treasure chest of language containing Indian words in the English dictionary. In linguist David Crystal's view, this was possible only because of the inherent flexibility of the English language to absorb the colour of every language and culture it encountered.

Among the words in the English lexicon are words we use today without realizing their colonial origins: 'pyjama', 'juggernaut', 'pundit', 'teak', 'congee', 'coolie', 'bangle', 'jungle', 'bakshish', 'curry', 'korma', 'tamasha', 'yoga', and 'pariah', among hundreds of others.

Had I been born in the avatar of a pukka English memsahib in colonial times, I'd have lived a life grander than those of the maharajas and maharanis of the time. While I lounged in the drawing room on a warm morning, a servant would have kept me cool by swinging the punkah, a large fan on an oblong frame, suspended from the ceiling with a rope attached to it. I might have wandered off into the garden to smell the cabbage roses and the frangipani, even as the mali walked about tending to the plants and the gorawala sat by the horse carriage swatting flies off his face. Between the laborious sitting and the ambling about into the veranda of my bungalow and the garden, if I so desired, my khansama, the head of the kitchen, would have ensured that a cup of tea was brought to me, while I sat down right in view of the peepul tree. But if my preferred seating looked especially dusty on that fine morning, I'd have pointed it out to my ayah, my personal maid, who would have then scrambled inside to put in a quick word with the sirdar, the chief of home affairs, whose duty it was to keep everything polished and shining and whose other task included wafting away those horrid flies during my meals. It would have been a life in paradise but for the heat and humidity that may have made my calico drawers weigh down—not that they were made of jute—but I thank the Lord for there was a durzee attached to my household to make me new underclothes and repair our clothing and curtains and a dhobi to wash them all. It would have been the perfect life indeed but for the night watchman, the chowkidar, who gave me the shivers because it was rumoured that he was a member of a criminal gang and that employing him was merely insurance against being looted and killed by yet another thug. This should have been a life of nirvana, if only I did not live in mortal fear of being ground to chutney by a dreadful tropical disease or did not have to live at such a great distance from my children, as journalist and playwright J. H. Stocqueler wrote in *India Under the British Empire*, because the continual companionship of native servants is unfavourable 'to the formation of that peculiarly "British" character which every Englishman holds to be desirable in his child'.

Despite the innate desire to avoid contact with the locals, the household staff in English homes was vast. At the viceroy's home in New Delhi, no less than fifty boys were employed to scare away birds from the lovely Mughal gardens and a total of about 5,000 servants were deemed necessary to run the governor general's mansion. There was an abundance of servants, each with a specific duty.

Consequently, many other words slipped into English language over the decades: sahib, zamindar, mahout, doli, jawan, durbar, howdah, bibi, halwa, jalebi, izzat, maidan and shikari. I recognized how my mother tongue, too, had foisted its words onto English: cheroot was from churuttu, cot was from kattil, mango from mangai, cash from kasu, although in the case of kasu, Tamil may have acquired it from Portuguese.

'Ayah' was a word that recurred through the pages of Kaye's memoir with a lot of affection. The word described a category of native maids employed by Europeans living in India during the time of empire. The word had its origins in the Portuguese 'aia' which described a nurse or governess. While Kaye was cared for by native ayahs, most of her English friends were supervised by governesses or nannies. Kaye felt truly sorry for the nanny-children. 'The nanny-children envied our greater freedom and our ability to chatter to any Indian we met in the Bazaar or the Mall, in our own or other people's houses,' she wrote, describing how ayahs let their charges run wild in a way that no British nanny would have permitted in a post-Victorian era.[42]

In the short stories and poems of Rudyard Kipling were a slew of other words that transported me into an altogether different world and time. Some words died out because the object they described had become antiquated and distanced from the present day. One such word was 'palanquin'—also spelt as palankeen—which emerged from the Hindi word palki. Mentioned in Indian literature as early as the Hindu epic Ramayana, the palanquin is a covered sedan chair or litter carried on four poles. It derives from the Sanskrit word for a bed or couch, palyanka. Menen described being transported to his grandmother's home thus: 'I went by palanquin—a hammock of red cloth, with rather worn embroidery of gold thread, swung on a black pole that had silver ornaments on either end. Four virtually naked men, two in front and two behind, carried the palanquin at a swift trot.' Menen wrote also about the art of the trot. 'If the four men trotted just as they pleased, the hammock would swing in a growing arc until it tipped the passenger out.' The men trotted according to a complicated system, which Menen never really figured out. 'Watching them and trying to follow it was as difficult as trying to determine the order in which a horse puts its hoofs down. The men kept their rhythm by chanting.'[43]

Like the word palanquin, the Persian word maidan entered the English lexicon during the Raj. I had heard endless stories from my father about the maidan inside the Palakkad Fort where he and his siblings played cricket as adolescents. I heard a reference to it, again, the day I chatted with Princess Gouri, and this time the metaphorical use of the term was hilarious. At a community dance, she had been appalled by the sari blouses worn by some of the dancers. 'Some of their backs... showing all that skin on their back!' she said, brows raised, 'it looked like a maidan.' While I laughed heartily at her description, the princess remained serious. She said she found a solution to the problem the following year; she distributed blouse pieces with embroidery already done on it so that the dancers would be forced to stitch modest blouses with the pre-fabricated design on their backs. The princess had drawn her bounds on immodesty in an original, yet diplomatic, move.

I detected in her confession a certain hypocrisy, too, because I recalled that she too had once rebelled against the prevailing forces in the sixties when some members of her royal family had balked at her dancing in public. At seventy-five, Princess Gouri continued to perform on stage in order to send a message to women that they must not fear the wrath of others to express themselves.

In the princess's gait, I detected the self-confidence of

Menen's Malayali grandmother. The contradictions in her I saw in the princess too. Our bounds of modesty were prescribed, after all, by the truths of our own traditions. When Menen went to meet his grandmother at long last, he was shocked to see her naked from the waist up, like many of the women of the time. She also didn't hesitate to convey her contempt of the white man in no uncertain manner, saying she couldn't believe that a white man would bathe in a tub of dirty water—like a buffalo. 'Always bathe in running water,' she said to Menen, laughing at the backwardness of the white man's bathroom.[44]

Long after the English dominions shrank and Travancore was no more, the royals were loved and admired for their simple lives in the city of Trivandrum (as it was then called). On meeting the princess's grandmother, Sethu Lakshmi Bayi, in 1925, Gandhi wrote that he found himself in the presence of a modest young woman. 'Her room was as plainly furnished as she was plainly dressed. Her severe simplicity became an object of my envy. She seemed to me an object lesson for many a prince and many a millionaire whose loud ornamentation, ugly looking diamonds, rings and studs and still more loud and almost vulgar furniture offend the taste and present a terrible and sad contrast between them and the masses from whom they derive their wealth.'[45]

The Travancore royals, like other families in India, lost their ruling rights when Travancore merged with the Indian union and their privileges were abolished by a constitutional amendment. But they continued to serve the temple, however, and their reverence to the deity continued unhindered. Princess Gouri's daughter, a journalist, wrote about their ties to Lord Padmanabha: 'Whenever any member of my family leaves or returns to Thiruvananthapuram, they go to the temple to mark their attendance. When flying in, we prefer sitting on the right side of the aeroplane as it offers an aerial view of the temple as we touch down.'[46]

In recent years, the royal family had been in the news because of a lawsuit against the temple authorities. The ensuing battle and investigation inside several vaults of the temple of Lord Padmanabha confirmed that it was the richest Hindu temple in the world. One of the men behind the lawsuit died from an unexplained two-day fever kindling superstitions that anyone who questioned the wealth would die an untimely death.

I never broached the topic of the treasures with the princess as I sat in her bungalow, surrounded by the many manifestations of the conch. No one knows exactly how the temple of Lord Padmanabha came into existence in the forest of Anantha infested with snakes. Tales abounded about the unopened last vault with the conch and snake insignia on its door. Some stories told of trenches that linked the land, sea and the sun. Others claimed that the only reason that the tsunami of 2004 spared this coast from devastation was the divine energy that buttressed the soil. A four-day prayer ceremony, devaprasnam, was held to ascertain the will of the deity. The result was not encouraging. The vault remained sealed. It was much better for Lord Padmanabha, the princess and me, indeed all of us, that some things in life remain a mystery.

THREE

GO NATIVE IN DELHI

For seventy-eight weeks between January 1987 and July 1988, a majority of Indians, my parents included, were glued to their television sets. Every Sunday at 9.30 a.m., life ground to a halt all over the country while everyone watched the epic *Ramayan*.

A frisson of television-induced communal harmony crested through the country from Kashmir to Kanyakumari during the half hour that this mythological tale played on screen; Christians, Sikhs and Muslims were as much in its grip as Hindus. They all watched the peregrinations of God on earth even though the deity, Lord Rama, was a creation of Ramanand Sagar's Vrindavan Studios that churned out what today seems like some of the tackiest visuals and special effects that anyone had seen.

During that long viewing season, Tully, too, was under its spell. 'I became a fan—to the disgust of almost all my friends, because of course it's fashionable to rubbish the Sagars' *Ramayan*,' he wrote a few years later reflecting on the production that defined the collective spirit of a nation, while dwelling on the irony of how belief in the deity had divided Muslims and Hindus in India.[47] It struck me that, by the standards established by the old imperial order, Tully had gone native.

During the Raj, as we've seen, Englishmen were leery of socializing with Indians and identifying with the local culture, philosophy, food and customs lest they be accused of having 'gone native'. English children born in India were raised with an awareness of 'them' and 'us'. The English language and the accent were sacred, too.

'We were English, not Indian,' Tully wrote in an essay about the Raj during his father's time.[48] Born in Calcutta, in 1935, he had never been allowed to forget, from his youngest days, that he was different. He was not allowed to play with children who only had Indian or Anglo-Indian nannies because their parents couldn't afford a 'proper nanny'. Once when his English nanny found him learning to count from 1 to 10 in Hindustani from their driver, she cuffed Tully on the head, saying, 'That's the servants' language, not yours.'[49] When he was packed off to school up in the hills of Darjeeling, there was no one to watch over matters of social comportment. He wrote that he 'learned enough Hindustani and Nepali to amuse the rickshaw pullers and porters who carried people and freight up the steep streets and lanes. My father would not have approved if he'd known.'[50]

European society in the Calcutta of the Raj was striated by race and perceived class. This was not all that different from the caste system. Tully's father worked at a management agency as a 'boxwallah', and was not in the same class, for instance, as those with plum jobs in the Indian Civil Services who had attended elite schools in Britain. The undercurrent of his father's class consciousness shaped Tully's mind.

Years later, in 1965, Tully returned to India as a correspondent for the BBC and upon retirement in 1992, he stayed on in India, in an ultimate act of defiance against his father and, in my view, against the whole colonial establishment.

India held memories for four generations of his family on his mother's side. Many months after my meeting with him in New Delhi, I heard Sir Tully wax eloquent on the power of smell in evoking suppressed memories on BBC's *Something Understood*. The nostalgia evoked by his words brought back a line from *A Passage to India* that I had underlined for myself when I read it some years ago: '...every life ought to contain both a turn and a return.'[51]

Tully's Indian roots were in New Delhi, a natural choice for retirement for a man whose work and friendships had tethered him to the place and even more so for someone whose natural passions for Indian politics would make the city an obvious choice. I suspected, however, that the city's connections with the English language and the world of publishing were an added attraction. The English language had been written and spoken in New Delhi by some of the most skilled craftsmen of the English language in the world. India's first prime minister was the face of English prose during and after the Raj.

At Nehru Memorial Library one afternoon, I read a study of Jawaharlal Nehru's writing compared with the brilliant prose of Winston Churchill by a British military historian called Tom Wintringham who was a talented wielder of the pen himself. 'Compare pages from two books on great events. One has the pomp of a Moghal durbar; sentences move with the gross dignity of elephants; paragraphs are marshalled armies, armies of old Emperors, with banners, with drums, with the pride and stir and tumult of the East. On the other page, words move like a bar of music; emphasis is in the placing, the rhythm, the straightness of things seen or said, not in the piling of colour over these things; sentences and paragraphs are complete in themselves yet connected as precisely to the flow of the language as in a scientist's account of his discoveries.'[52] Wintringham wrote that Indian children would 'learn better history and better English' from Nehru than from Englishmen like Macaulay.[53] He invited people to analyse scientifically several of Nehru's letters. 'They will find in Nehru, far more than in the men of our House of Commons, use of the familiar word rather than the far-fetched; concrete words rather than abstract; single words instead of circumlocutions; short words instead of long.'[54]

Growing up, I'd always associated Delhi with erudition and articulation. There were those news readers and anchors at Doordarshan and All India Radio whose diction was unparalleled, in both English and Hindi. There was also Indira Gandhi whom few could better in oratory. I remembered reading pieces by Sham Lal, the famous man with a red pen whose famed library evoked awe while his red pen evoked terror. When he passed away, his subordinates wrote about having trembled under the wrath of his uncompromising standards for good English. The essays he wrote for the *Times of India* are still relevant today, his language immensely readable. Then there was Delhi's resident and now late writer, Khushwant Singh, who had been much maligned for his politics. But Singh was a maverick, and spun a revolution in journalism as the editor of the *Illustrated Weekly of India*, a magazine that I'd devoured in the seventies and eighties. By the late nineties, Arundhati Roy, yet another famous Delhiite, wowed the national and international community with her masterful fiction. Delhi presided over the pristineness of the language. In this old city, I met many who spoke the Etonian English of Shashi Tharoor although more and more I'd begun hearing the earthy, cosmopolitan accent of journalist Barkha Dutt (both alums of St Stephen's College) whose greatest oratorical prowess was her ability to deliver pitch-perfect openers on television programmes, panel discussions and conference kick-offs. It seemed natural that Delhi should be India's English publishing mecca since it had once been a salon for Urdu poets. The Urdu language had been leached out of

Delhi by India's partition, yet the blood of many Mughal kings and courtiers had soaked into its soil. The city's artistic legacies lived on in its imposing edifices and its dankest alleyways.

The day I was driven to meet Tully, my autorickshaw swung into Mathura Road and passed by the sixteenth-century tomb of Abdur Rahim whose story had moved me. When Emperor Akbar's father died in 1556, Akbar was barely fourteen years old. His uncle took charge of him until adulthood, keeping predators at bay; in return, when Akbar reached adulthood he showed his gratitude by taking under his wing his uncle's widow and their child, Abdur Rahim, who, later, would emerge as a gifted poet in Akbar's court. Stories like that skittered off the sudden domes of Delhi whenever I turned a corner in this city. An entire city had been rebuilt over seven times. Through their many births, older architectural structures had survived. Tongues had endured. Poetry, literature and music had triumphed over decadence, decay and death and had been distilled into a performance art in the form of the qawwali three minutes away from Tully's home, outside the tomb of the Sufi saint Nizamuddin Auliya. Who was to say that the English language too would not shine in a city that celebrated all literature. It seemed that if you were a peddler of words in Delhi, you were marked for success—or infamy—and that you lived on the edge in some way, torched by the scorn of others, and simultaneously scorched by the upheavals of both the nation and the city, as was one poet whose vision shaped the Urdu language in the twentieth century.

Ahmed Ali, a poet, scholar, diplomat and critic, was forced to leave India at Partition; years later, after he had made a life for himself in Karachi, he was still seething about it. Ali couldn't bear to return to Delhi but he was forced to do so when his flight to Australia made an emergency landing in Delhi because of a mechanical failure. Ali refused to get out.

When they asked him why he was being belligerent, he sat in his seat and quoted the words of the acclaimed Urdu poet of the eighteenth century, Mir Taqi Mir.

> What matters it, O breeze,
> If now has come the spring
> When I have lost them both
> The garden and my nest?

Perhaps Ali had forgotten his own evocative words in his rumination on the city in his novel *Twilight in Delhi* (1940) in which he asserted that Delhi was a city of renewal, of ancestors who had risen like the phoenix to build another life. He had forgotten the city's relationship to the rest of the world visualized by Urdu poet Mirza Ghalib from the previous century.

> Ik roz apni rooh se poocha, ki dilli kya hai.
>   To yun jawab me keh gayi,
> Yeh duniya mano jism hai aur dilli uski jaan
>
> (I asked my soul, 'What is Delhi?'
> It replied:
> 'The world is the body, Delhi its soul.')[55]

During my trips to Delhi, I struggled, sometimes, to see Ghalib's portrayal of the city. One evening I found something doors away from where Tully lived, right by a tutor's advertisement about French lessons. The warning, in couplet form, veered far away from Mughal lyricism and busted the myth about the artistic gifts of Delhi.

> No Parking In Front Of Gate
> Tyre Will Be Deflated.

◆

An octogenarian now, Tully used a cane in public spaces like Jaipur Literature Festival where I first ran into him. But he moved about without any aid inside his home, his large frame bundled into a thick cardigan, a muffler wound around his neck, hobbling a little in the chill of January, as if there were a constant ache in his knees.

His voice had lost the edge of youth since the time he had been a correspondent for the BBC. But even now his commentaries regularly aired on the radio, each half hour session a rumination on a way of being: Simplicity; Preparation; Popularity; and Saintliness, most of them focused on building character. Perhaps it was his background in theology that gave him a philosophical bent of mind but in his writings on India, he seemed to be a field worker unafraid to probe and become the insider even when he, paradoxically, seemed like an outsider. Tully often wrote narratives about specific people, using their circumstances to get at a larger truth about India. I liked the intimacy he established with his subjects. It was an India I didn't really know, having spent over half my life away. The very first time I read his essays in *No Full Stops in India* (1991)—I hoped I'd be able to meet him at least once in my life. More than two decades later, on a wintry afternoon, I stood outside the tall gate of his modest house in Nizamuddin West.

I let myself into a sliver of a garden. A young woman ushered me up the steps to the inside of a home where the scent of dog hovered like the Delhi smog. A Labrador barked fiercely at the far end of the room. My dread over my impending meeting with the knighted award-winning journalist morphed into terror in the presence of canine hostility. Holding the dog back, the owner hobbled over to where I stood. 'Sony!' Tully shouted, barking orders at the dog. 'Sit down! What's the matter with you?' I wondered aloud if she had been named after the Japanese brand. 'No-ooo,' he intoned while Sony continued to emit a low, menacing growl, 'she's an *Indian* Dog.'

Sony was an icebreaker and soon we began chatting. His affection for India came through in that meeting. He preferred to use the word affection when he talked about India because 'love blinds you', he'd said often and it gave him 'the distance and the objectivity to offer constructive criticism'. In an introduction to one of his books published in 1995, Sir Tully gushed over India's natural bounty, describing, among many moments, the scent of pine in the Himalayas and the wonder of a sunset in the Arabian Sea in Kerala where 'the sun slid like a great red dome below the horizon'.[56] Sir Tully had never sought to go back to where he came from because he felt he belonged in India and observed how unusual it was that he, a foreigner, was now accepted as a part of India. He was swept away by feeling. 'It would need a poet to describe what India means to me, and I am no poet.' I wished to tell him that there were many such moments in his work that deeply moved me because they made me introspect on my own relationship with India long after I'd sought American citizenship. Like him, I was also an Overseas Citizen of India (OCI). His writing revealed his vulnerability in his interactions with people across many strata of society. Sometimes when I read these pieces aloud to my husband, we were both in tears.

I began to talk to him about his arrival in India. In the dimly lit living room with yellow cushions and sofas and a bookshelf, we began talking about his decision to stay on in India. The woman who had let me into the house brought a pot of tea with milk and sugar which she set on a low table on which were plates and knick-knacks from many trips. Gondh and Bhil paintings adorned the walls. Ganeshas graced the shelves. On a far wall I saw etchings of the old Calcutta's

Chowringhee Road. I remembered reading that his first home in Calcutta was set in the middle of a huge expanse of land which could have easily accommodated a tennis court in the front and the back.

I had also read about his father's expectations from Tully, his oldest child. 'His life was filled with correctness—the right way to hold a knife and fork, the right way to sit (and stand and ride a bicycle), the right way to talk to servants—and I managed to get most things wrong.'[57] Tully now told me how his father sent back his son's letters with edits marked in red pen, with a view to perfecting his language. He had been horrified by the slightest tendencies towards the 'chi-chi' accent in his children. And now as I listened to Tully's English and detected the occasional singsong cadences of Indian English, the inevitable result of more than half a century spent living in India as an active participant and an observer, a fleeting thought crossed my mind. When your body was dusted in turmeric, how could your nails not turn yellow at the edges? I wondered what his father's reaction might have been over Tully's decision to stay back in the country of his birth after retiring from the BBC.

'I didn't see any point in going,' he said, when I asked him the clichéd question without once thinking about my decision to stay on in America after over thirty years of living there.

'You feel rooted here now?'

Tully paused for a second. 'You might say I'm stuck,' he shot back, laughing, as he set his teacup in its saucer. 'All I say is I live here.'

◆

At the exclusive Delhi Gymkhana Club on Safdarjung Road, the word 'imperial' was dropped from its name when India gained independence. In recent times, the club issued a circular specifying a dress code that was somewhat outmoded in today's India, in language that would have received a complete overhaul had the circular been submitted for proofreading at any of Delhi's elite English-medium schools. It stipulated several dos and don'ts.

Kindly note that:
i.   Only tucked in T-Shirt with collar and without slogans Permitted
ii.   Full Sleeves Shirt must always be tucked in
iii. All permitted shoes must be worn with socks
iv.   Kurtas with Jeans/Pants is not permitted
v.   Torn/distressed/faded jeans strictly Not Permitted
      'ONLY BUSH SHIRTS CAN BE WORN WITHOUT TUCKING IN'
      Members are requested to cooperate

The five enumerated rules for dress raised new questions in my mind. It seemed as if no other shirt was permitted, judging by (i). However, rule (ii) invalidated (i) by stating that a full-sleeved shirt always had to be 'tucked in' and it made me wonder about half-sleeved shirts. How must *they* be worn? What about rule (iii)? Could 'unpermitted' shoes be worn without socks, and if so, could someone enumerate the 'unpermitted' kind? And did (iv) imply that a kurta with nothing at all underneath was allowed on the premises? The last one, (v), made me wonder about what the difference was between 'strictly Not 'Permitted' and 'not permitted' and I certainly didn't understand the point of the last two dangling, unnumbered rules.

Delhi Gymkhana Club isn't the only club in India with such antiquated sartorial rules. Across India, there are any number of clubs that were once within the purview of the British. These clubs were still chugging along but they were now relics, outmoded and stuffy. Most, however, were still prized for their promise of exclusivity for those in positions of power, prestige and a particular income bracket.

One morning inside the Bengal Club in Kolkata—where I had been rudely refused entry the previous evening—a member, Sanjay Sarkar, was gracious enough to show me around the place that had once been Lord Macaulay's residence from 1834 to 1838. He called me out on my hypocritical stance, pointing out that everyone in the world wanted exclusivity.

'And what's wrong with that?' Sarkar asked, blowing smoke rings into the air as we sat in a room with rosewood panelling where a sullen uniformed bearer hovered about, tray in hand. 'We all want a little of that, don't we?'

He looked at me keenly from behind his glasses. 'You wanted your children to go to an exclusive college, didn't you?' Sarkar went on to state that there were many golf courses in the United States where entry was only by membership. He waved his cigarette about the room. 'And look at us sitting here. It's nice and quiet,' he went on. 'If everybody up from the street could come up here then what exclusivity do you have?' I couldn't argue with that. It was human nature to covet being in a place that was off limits to someone else. Still, it's one thing to restrict club activities to members, but quite another to refuse the public entry to places of historical value.

The exclusivity of the Bengal Club reminded me of the time of the Raj when Indians were not even allowed into these clubs set up by the British. At every one of these clubs, I entered a world that was, even over a century later, at a complete disconnect from the world outside. The language inside the clubs, too, was often a throwback to another period.

While reading about these clubs I discovered that the word gymkhana was born in the Indian subcontinent. An amalgam of Greek and Hindustani, the word 'gym' is derived from the ancient Greek 'gymnasium' which refers to a sports club; 'khana' describes an enclosure. In India and Pakistan, gymkhana applies to a smart sporting club, whereas in Britain and other parts of the world, it refers to an equestrian club or automobile competition. Like the word 'gymkhana', India retained words long after they were outdated in the rest of the world. The word 'issue' is still used in India in reference to one's children. A distant uncle in India wondered how many issues my husband and I had. I wished for him to know that while we had two children, we had a million issues between us. There were other words that still lingered in the shadow of the Raj.

When British cars were in use in India, the 'dicky' became popular as a place to store luggage and then, in all future avatars of the car, the word was adopted for any storage space in the back of the car. While trying to understand the notion of the dicky and its antediluvian character, I pored over books on classic vintage passenger cars from 1905 to 1942. Inside each of the books was a little card holder—a remnant of the antiquated library system—which was an attachment to the page (also called a 'dicky', it turns out). The dicky, in general, referred to a false front even though it was often in the rear. As one who had spent a large part her life in America, I saw how the word 'dicky' would be unusable there, however.

'Amma, your father told me that "dicky" was a very bad word in America,' Vinayagam said one day. In the nineties, my father had instructed Vinayagam to not use the word around people with American sensibilities such as his daughter and her family. He was taught to use the term 'trunk' instead but Vinayagam found it hard to change his ways. I explained the difference between a dicky and a trunk to Vinayagam. Early in the twentieth century, automobile manufacturers built racks on the back of cars for adding trunks. The 'trunk' of the car was, literally, a removable piece of luggage, unlike the integral part of the car that it is today. The notion of the dicky was very different from the trunk, I had discovered. The dicky was nothing but an addition to the car. It was referred to as 'dicky seat' in British English, also called a 'mother-in-law seat', and was often an upholstered exterior seat that folded into the rear deck. When unoccupied, the space under the seat's lid would be used for storing luggage. The dicky was also an optional space where a servant might sit. I theorized that, given the many members of a retinue who accompanied the Indian maharajas (and now, politicians) on their excursions, the word 'dicky' stayed on in India for many decades afterward.

Some English words acquired new meanings as they rolled into new societies. The history of the word 'stepney' intrigued me. It's possible that the spare tyre went by the name 'stepney' because the wheels were manufactured on Stepney Street in Llanelli, Wales. In 1904 shop owners probably owed hugely to the Stepney family who had been aristocrats in the town for generations. The early motorcars were made without spare wheels; a spoke-less wheel rim fitted with an inflated tyre gave a driver a solution for a puncture. The Stepney Spare Wheel manufactured spare wheels that were fitted in all new cars. The inventor became wealthy as the company set up agencies across the world. In time the word became used in the colonies for the spare wheel. Long after the Britons forgot about it, the word continued to be used in India and Pakistan. It acquired new meanings, too. In Delhi an easy-going member of staff, who is not of much help, could also be called a 'stepney', someone who is called upon when the real thing isn't working. The word assumed other connotations in my part of India. When I was growing up in Chennai, a stepney was a reference to a mistress, a concubine, of a man whose marriage had lost its sheen.

Thus English words sometimes lost their original lustre in India and in a different breeding ground, new expressions were birthed, too. While I was walking down ancient Chandni Chowk with a heritage lover one morning, he told me that the expression 'bite the bullet' may have stemmed from the days of the Raj. The Revolt of 1857 had arisen from insensitive treatment of Indian soldiers in the British Army. The grease on cartridges containing gunpowder was believed to have been made of pork or beef fat. The soldiers would have to tear open the cartridge with their teeth. Pork is abhorrent to Muslims while cows are deified by Hindus—and the reaction to being made to bite into these defiled cartridges was believed to have stirred the rebellion by the soldiers. The more familiar idiom 'bite the bullet' is thought to have originated from 'bite the cartridge'.

References, turns of phrase and the expression of a sentiment are often endemic to a place and a time and certainly in Delhi, the English language had blustered through its alleys like the loo before the monsoon, upending values in a city that had been dyed in court culture and etiquette, 'blowing so hard that sand rained down all night and came between one's teeth and covered the bed', as Ahmed Ali observed in *Twilight in Delhi*.[58] I was reminded of his lament about how Western fashions and thought had infiltrated traditional families and their ways of life, occupying the spaces between Urdu and Hindi. 'The leaves of the henna tree became seared and wan, and the branches of the date palm became coated with sand. The dust blew through the unending noon.'[59] Like its author, the protagonist, Mir Nihal, believed that every visitor had wrought so much havoc in Delhi and shaped its core. 'It has seen the fall of many a glorious kingdom, and listened to the groans of birth. It's a symbol of life and death and revenge is its nature.'[60]

In Delhi I certainly sensed a cantankerous manner, a constant mien of raised hackles, of people always having to look behind their shoulder.

The history of a place diffused into the minds of its people. A friend who moved to New Orleans a few years ago said that the people in her city embraced her and made her feel very welcome when she landed there and tried to begin a new life. 'It must be having to deal with hurricanes, high winds and flooding,' she said, reflecting on the generosity of spirit in the town. I learned that New Orleans was the first town in America where, on Sunday afternoons in Congo Square, slaves could raise the money to buy their way to freedom.

Even though New Delhi had only been a capital city under the empire from 1911 to 1947, a period of thirty-six years, some of India's most difficult as it wrenched itself away from its colonial master, here I felt the weight of class, money and title. In Delhi more than anywhere, people wanted to show off their material acquisitions. And why not? Here, every resident had lost it all time and again and risen from the ashes of past accomplishment. 'Although all men may be equal in God's eyes, they can never be equal in the eyes of other men,' summed up Tully in one of his works, wrapping up most succinctly the spirit of Delhi.[61]

Entitlement was the byword of this city, I realized, the day I walked down a road in Delhi's famed Defence Colony. A feminine voice assaulted my senses from behind the canopy of dust-covered trees.

'Excuse me!' a woman cried from up above. 'Why are you taking a picture of my home?' She had emerged at one of the balconies on the second floor of a building on my left. There was another of India's convent-educated women whose English was a dead giveaway of privilege and power. In her gait, I saw the confidence of many women in Delhi who knew someone who knew someone who might try to twist the arm of a prominent politician or bureaucrat. Svelte, dressed in a kameez and churidar, the woman decided to tell me, obviously an outsider in her community of homes once built for India's armed forces, that I was out of place in her city and locality.

'India's a free country,' I yelled back. 'And this is a beautiful road. I have the right to take photographs.'

She seemed unconvinced. 'But why my home?' she asked.

'But what gave you the impression that I was interested in your home?' I asked. It was an apartment building of offices and residences. 'I take a lot of pictures of a multitude of things.' I waved my cell phone at her. 'With this.' The woman shook her head in annoyance, turned around and vanished into her home, banging the balcony door shut behind her.

For my part, I rolled my eyes, shook my head in irritation, and proceeded to walk on towards the metro station.

◆

'The golden rule in radio was to be simple,' Tully told me, while chatting about writing for an audience like that of the BBC. Writing script for the radio was a challenge because a listener couldn't go back to 'read' the script or experience it like he could a book or a newspaper, at least in those days when listeners did not have the advantage of the memory of the Internet. Writing for the radio had made him factor in quick comprehension and I realized then how that experience on the job had imbued his writing, too, with candour and simplicity. 'It has to be simple but not simplistic,' he said, and I realized the critical importance of suppressing oneself and one's ego and voice while letting a story unravel itself.

An essay he had written about the sway of English in India had made an indelible impression on me. English had become a 'killer' language, he had proclaimed and one of Tully's contacts in Chennai, a gentleman by the name of Ramakrishnan, who was passionate about Tamil, told Tully that 'English did not just kill. It maimed.'

Around the world, English had indeed uprooted cultures. A young Filipino friend told me how English had supplanted her mother tongue, Tagalog, so much so that in Manila, her countrymen spoke mostly English, peppered, of course, with expressions typical to the Philippines. In parts of Africa, too, the English language had erased memories and retold the history of the place. Akwaeke Emezi expressed this feeling perfectly in an NYPL podcast ('Debut novelist Akwaeke Emezi Recenters Reality') on the release of her novel *Freshwater* (2018). In her fiction, she was interested in exploring the realities that her countrymen had been separated from and the ways in which they had been invalidated. In the podcast, Emezi likens colonizing to cleansing, 'to a group of people coming and saying, "Hey, everything that you believed for centuries and that your family has believed for generations is fake and we're going to tell you what's real and you're going to believe that and everyone after us is going to basically say these are the things that are real and these are the things that are not real."'

Tully, too, had written about this decimation of stories and histories at some length: 'It has often been said that if you want to destroy a people, first destroy its language. The British were too subtle to try that: they degraded Indian languages by installing a new language of the elite—English. Just as the British were quite happy to keep the caste system intact provided they were acknowledged as a superior caste, so were they happy to promote the study of Indian languages provided English was acknowledged as the link language of the elite.'[62] .

Sometimes Tully's writings were didactic in nature, as in *No Full Stops in India*. It was a plea to Indians to reckon with and reclaim what was great about their past. He hoped India would promote economic growth that protected ancient culture and not just ape the 'sterile' west.[63]

I recalled the exhortations of the guide in R. K. Narayan's eponymous work. Railway Raju addressed his gathering of followers one day: 'I want you all to think independently, of your own accord, and not allow yourselves to be led about by the nose, as if you were cattle.'[64] Tully's writings underscored those of Narayan on how India needed to find its own solutions based on its ethos '...because the old colonial mentality still survives—the servile mentality that believes that anything Indian must be inferior. Nothing has done more to keep that feeing alive than the English language. As English reinforced their superior status, the elite, not surprisingly, made no serious attempt to provide an Indian link language when the British left.'[65] The aspirational quality of English left people with a reduced sense of who they were.

In his years with the BBC in India, Tully had heard about Indian contributors being rejected because of their 'thick accent'. 'It's too Peter Sellers', was the feedback Tully received.[66] He couldn't believe the double standards of his organization. A thick European accent was viewed differently from a heavy Indian accent. BBC producers would never dare tell a Frenchman that his accent was not up to snuff because 'they are only too happy to find Frenchmen willing to speak our language'. In telling this tale, Tully was pointing at how some of this stemmed from the lack of pride in India for its regional languages. India had not ever sought to develop its own 'ideology' or 'attitudes' or 'institutions' and had adopted those of the West instead. In the sixties, writer Ved Mehta posed the same questions. 'We produced carbon copies of their literature and newspapers, administration, officers. Can we make our own standards? How long will it take?'[67] The answers to India's problems had to emerge from past traditions; any and all knowledge driving those solutions had to be targeted to India's present circumstances. I recalled what parenting experts often said about how to mould one's children; in the same family, every child was as unique as the five fingers of a palm and it behoved a parent to not enforce the same expectations on each.

Tully's incitement also reminded me of something that my friend, Shanthi, said when she found me frustrated with the way my work for American consumer magazines was being edited. It left my work seeming colourless. It left me feeling voiceless. 'So when are you going to write for yourself?' Shanthi asked. 'When are you going to write what you want to write?' Her words set me off on a journey over the next decade. I began to work on telling the stories that I wanted to tell. Just as my friend goaded me to ponder what it was that I really wanted to do, Tully was prodding us too. He had understood something about India at a level that many Indians had yet to do.

In contrast to the Indian attitude towards their languages, Tully had noticed a different disposition in Bangladesh. A few Bengali writers confirmed this as well. 'When I go to Bangladesh...lots and lots of people speak perfect English—but among themselves they speak only in Bengali,' Tully said to me. He further observed that Hindi was a particularly unfortunate language. 'It's looked down on. There is not the same pride in Hindi as in Tamil or Bengal or Malayalam.'

I saw in Tully's words a twisted re-enactment of the white man's burden, refashioned, for the explicit purposes of showing the Indian what was superlative and original about his own homeland.

At this point in our conversation Tully went into his office and printed out one of the columns he had published in the *Hindustan Times*. In the article he had questioned the inadequate use of government resources in government schools and bemoaned the massive waste of public money.[68] The lack of quality public education in India was one of his pet peeves. He lamented the ill effects of it on the poor who often sacrificed money in the belief that private education would provide a better future for their children. 'These parents are, unfortunately, depriving themselves to send their children to these so-called English-medium schools,' he said, pointing out the dual damage when they emerged from school 'neither speaking English nor their own language' confidently. Very often, he said, the private schools too were disappointing. Before I left his home Tully told me to pay a visit to Sardar Patel School, known to teach in Hindi until Class VI while retaining English as a subject. After Class VI the school adopted English as the medium of education. A handful of such schools exist all around India where the focus is to impart Indian values while making their students global citizens.

It struck me, as I left Tully's home, that in many ways he had become the pluralist Indian. He was a practising Christian but his living room was adorned with Ganesha and Hanuman figurines. He had imbibed Indian philosophical thought, embraced eclectic cultural wisdom and lived on in India, offering constructive criticism. I walked away sensing his angst over the aftermath of colonization, feeling that my country was a broken home in which a step-parent had wreaked havoc, upending values, breaking relationships and severing communication. But hope sprang eternal in the human breast and I realized that change—some great, some good, some unsavoury—was the only constant.

◆

By the time I left Delhi that winter I had met two fabled men who made their living in the world of words. While Tully was among the Who's Who in the literary stratosphere of Delhi life teeming with power mongers, the other man, Mithilesh Singh, a bookseller at Khan Market's Bahrisons, was famous in his own way, too.

About fifteen minutes away from where the Sufi saint Nizamuddin Auliya and his famous disciple, Amir Khusro, were buried, a few old English bookstores still chugged on even as others had folded in the face of mounting competition from online behemoths, rising costs and diminishing profits. The story of Bahrisons is interlaced with the history of Delhi and India.

Between 1941 and 1951, New Delhi's population had more than doubled to almost two million people as a fallout of India's partition. New neighbourhoods were built to house the influx of people. Almost all the refugees started from scratch, having left their jobs and belongings in Pakistan with, literally, just the clothes on their backs. One such man, Balraj Bahri Malhotra, had heard that shops in Khan Market were being allocated to refugees and in 1953, buffered by a loan, Malhotra opened a bookshop in a narrow corner of Khan Market. Over the decades its shelves multiplied and today it is the famous Bahrisons with more outlets across the city. In the late nineties, it would offer an opportunity for Mithilesh, a poor young man from Bihar. I had the chance to observe him in action.

On the first day, as I hovered about browsing the shelves, a distinguished elderly gentleman whom I instantly recognized— Kapil Sibal—strode in. Heads turned in recognition of Sibal, a poet and lawyer turned politician who was a fixture on Indian television. He made a beeline for Mithilesh, who greeted him warmly. On the second day, a Caucasian gentleman stood in front of Mithilesh wondering if a certain book were available.

'Would you have *Far From the Tree*?' the man asked.

'Oh, by Andrew Solomon?' Mithilesh said, looking up from the desk where he sat writing on a sheet of paper. The man answered in the affirmative.

'I think we have a copy, sir,' Mithilesh said, and then yelled out an order in the direction of a staffer who scooted up the stairs. He brought the book to Mithilesh within minutes. Solomon had just published this account of families who struggled with issues of identity, hope, transcendence, illness, struggle and belief. While Solomon's work was well known in the United States, I was surprised at Mithilesh's instant recall of his name. His ready association of every book title to its writer took me by surprise for the next few hours as I, unbeknownst to Mithilesh, observed him. When another customer asked him for something else, he told the clerks to hunt it down, directing them to the appropriate shelves lining the stairs en route to the attic. When they couldn't find it, Mithilesh verified the details on the computer. 'Oh, that's why!' he said to the customer. The book hadn't yet been released, he said. If a book was not spotted on the shelves, on the other hand, that is, if the bookstore had exhausted its stock of a book, as he told me on the day I asked him for *Words* ('By Farrukh Dhondy?' he'd confirmed), he would have it mailed to my address within one or two days, thus saving me a return trip to Bahrisons as well as the trouble of finding space in my luggage.

Mithilesh had been born into a landowning middle-class family in Bihar. He had attended a village school and applied himself to books at Bhagalpur University before he came to work in New Delhi. When he arrived in the city at the age of twenty-one, he knew a smattering of English words, but was clueless about how to string them together. But Mithilesh was affable of manner and willing to work hard. A newspaper story titled 'Dial M For Mithilesh' pasted on the store's bulletin board showered encomiums on him from the world's A-list writers. They extolled Mithilesh as a deliverer, a man who could put just about any book into people's hands within a matter of seconds.[69]

'I wanted to become something in my life, ma'am,' he said to me that afternoon upstairs where we talked in some quiet. He told me that mathematics came to him effortlessly. For instance, he didn't need a calculator for additions of huge sums. His memory was uncanny, too, he said, and his brothers had felt he would be an asset in a 'book shed' in Delhi. 'It was December 1996,' he said, enunciating 'was' as 'waj' the way many people hardened the 'z' sound to 'j' in the north of India. But Mithilesh spoke confidently, using English idioms seamlessly, too. On the first afternoon I watched him at work, I heard him telling a customer that the title of a particular book 'rang a bell'.

He began many of his responses with 'well,' using it in a casual, expansive way. Thirty years later, he was a confident English speaker, one whose grammar was not perfect, but who was an asset and a role model in an exclusive world of an English bookstore. By the year 2000, he was speaking pidgin English.

I recalled Tully's point in the article for *Hindustan Times* that it was not important for a school to be English medium. That all that was needed was for the subject—English or any other—to be taught well at a good school, a pertinent detail about a value system that the teachers at Vidya Vanam had put into practise. It came back to Mahatma Gandhi's belief that the language of instruction was hardly as important as the concepts that were being dinned into a child. When Mithilesh entered the rarefied atmosphere of English speakers in Delhi, he knew only 'library English'. I felt that he epitomized what

Tully had prescribed all along. He had picked up English while working hard at his chosen profession. His work ethic, along with his uncanny abilities, took care of the rest.

I gleaned more about Mithilesh as we talked. Every day he rode into and back from work from Lajwanti Garden in a motorcycle gifted to him by his boss. He didn't have time to read English books because his life was too busy. His wife did not speak English but his children were being educated in an English-medium school and their English was 'not bad'. He worked a twelve-hour day six days a week and took every Sunday off. Before I left the store that afternoon, Mithilesh told me that he had mastered his job through sheer hard work. He decided to do well what he did from the day he was twenty-one. He had known nothing else. 'Work is worship,' he said. 'I always say that whatever good that has happened is because of Shiv,' he said putting his hands together and turning his eyes towards the skies. 'I believe that Shiv is taking care of me.'

In the hours I spent at Bahrisons, it became apparent that there was no one Mithilesh did not know but it was even clearer that everyone knew Mithilesh Singh. I forgot to ask Tully whether he knew Mithilesh. But when I mentioned his name to Mithilesh, he smiled. 'Oh, I know Tully sir,' he said. 'He comes here sometimes.' I never corroborated that with Sir Tully who mentioned in his writings that Faqir Chand & Sons, one of the first stores in Khan Market, established in 1951 was one of his favourite haunts.

The trajectory of Tully's career had been impressive, yet I found myself awed by Mithilesh's record. There was a power in becoming indispensable to an organization. I spoke to Mithilesh's bosses and they acknowledged his memory and his contributions in a reverential tone. Yet, during our interview, Mithilesh teared up when I told him that his English was very good. His whole demeanour was one of reverence, of astonishment that someone like me would appreciate him for his skills in the English language. I recalled writer Pavan K. Varma's lament to me about how impressed those Indians who could not speak the English language always were of those who could. Fluency in English was never on par with agility in another bhasha.

On my exit from Bahrisons I ambled through the market that was now one of Delhi's cool hang-outs, wondering about the similarity between the two men I'd just met—one, a middle-aged god-fearing Indian who was fluent in Hindi and English and the other, a devout octogenarian Englishman who spoke both English and Hindi—both of whom were feted for doing their jobs superlatively well. The Indian felt that his English was not good enough. The Englishman also, owing to his love and commitment to India, spoke decent enough Hindi, although he too confessed to me that it was no good at all.

FOUR

DRIVING MISS UNIVERSAL

It was not often that Vinayagam and my late father's maid, Ganga, were on friendly terms. On those peachy days he sometimes called her 'my darling', whereas on most days he addressed her as 'kezhavi' which meant 'old woman', in Tamil, maintaining that she was, after all, old enough to be his grandmother. That morning, the day we were setting out to see Ganga's village that was four hours away, the young man had been rather kindly disposed towards the seventy-year-old harridan and he'd offered her some Marie biscuits along with her morning cup of coffee.

'I don't want it, kanna,' she said, using a Tamil term of endearment often used for one's children. 'Only because I cannot afford it,' she said, waving it away. 'I'll put on weight.'

Ganga used the English word 'weight' in the Tamil sentence, rather like the way high-society women bantered about their extra pounds. Brow raised, Vinayagam glared at the skinny old termagant.

'Weight-aa? You're going to compete in Miss Universal or something?' he asked. 'Ayyo, loose-u kezhavi!' he snarled, telling her she was coming off the hinges. Then he marched towards the prayer alcove which he had been decorating with fresh chrysanthemums and roses and began barking orders to her from there. Ganga disappeared into the kitchen, and busied herself washing the coffee cups. After that she mopped our little porch and drew a fresh kolam on the stone floor right outside our front door.

The previous afternoon Vinayagam had warned her that we would be setting out early to beat the traffic. Ganga had arrived promptly at 5.45 a.m. so she wouldn't incur his wrath. When I opened the door to her, I'd been shocked at her new avatar. There she was in a starched cotton sari and a crisp white blouse and she walked in with a regal air about her.

'Ayyo! Look at you!' I'd exclaimed, stunned that she'd dressed up thus for the drive to her village. I told her she looked like a movie star. Around her neck sparkled a gold chain. Gold bangles glinted against her dark brown wrists. 'My family in the village has to see I'm doing very well, Amma,' she had said, smugly, a smile staining her rust-brown teeth. She set her red-and-black wire bag on the floor. 'Especially today when I get down from that fancy shining car with my owner-Amma.'

◆

In a little while, we set out, snaking through smaller roads in T. Nagar towards Anna Salai. There were four of us in the car with Vinayagam at the wheel. Saravanan sat to his left. He had been my father's office boy and yet another devoted caregiver in the last year leading to his death. Ganga and I sat belted at the back.

Chennai was prettiest at dawn. At that hour, before the cacophony of Chennai traffic decimated all peace, I could hear the sonorous peal of a temple bell. Idols of gods and goddesses peered out of alcoves in trees. People walked on tracks at local parks. It was also the hour of the scent of jasmine, holy ash, curry leaf and cow dung just before the press of exhaust fumes assaulted the air.

Past Poonamallee, one of Chennai's bottlenecks where

buses and roads met before they branched off to different parts of the state, we made for NH 32 in a southwesterly direction, heading for the village of Seppetai near Gingee, where once Ganga and her late husband had tilled their land, right by the foothills of one of India's oldest stone fortifications.

To get to her village of Seppetai, Ganga usually hopped into a municipal bus from Chennai. She made the trip often. There was always something calling her back—a wedding, a death, a girl attaining puberty. Of late, it had been tussles over property for which she had to go to court. Ganga never travelled by a luxury air-conditioned bus even when she could afford it. 'I don't care if it blows all my hair away,' she said, laughing. 'I will only go by regular bus.' Often, she had to stand the whole way. I understood why this luxurious ride in the Toyota made her feel special and I also wasn't oblivious to how Vinayagam didn't let her forget that such a car ride was way above her pay grade. I heard it in his snarky retorts as he drove us.

I also knew that women like Ganga were a threat to men like Vinayagam because they knew to put him in his place. I remember how, one morning, Ganga had stepped into the house and greeted me with a 'Hullo, Amma!'

Vinayagam had been incredulous. 'Kezhavi, you look like you were born into the English language,' he said, 'the way you're addressing my boss—in English and all?'

'Sweetheart, you may not know this,' Ganga said, placing her red-and-black wire bag on the kitchen floor. 'But I was born very well.'

'Really?' Vinayagam asked, scorn lacing his voice.

Ganga moseyed up to where I sat cutting up a winter melon. 'My cousin used to be a writer in a bank.'

Vinayagam shut the door of the fridge and turned to her. 'You mean he was a peon, kezhavi.' In the times of the

British Raj, a scribe for bureaucratic work was also referred to as a writer.

'And, you know, my uncle was an attorney,' she said, ignoring this provocation. 'A rather big one in the village.'

The young man laughed. 'That's why you're in and out of courts all the time?' His references to her litigious streak fazed her not a bit. 'What say, kezhavi?' She ignored that too but she made her position clear by speaking her mind.

'You know, even though I was born well, I've ended up having to wash dishes,' she said, heaving a sigh. 'But I'm proud about what I do. I do it well.' She paused. In her eyes, I saw the glint of a tear. Then Ganga referred to herself in the third person, a sign that she was out to establish her worth, thus building a moat between herself and the undesirable element in the house. 'No one dares to walk up to Ganga and complain about her poor work ethic.' Depending on the situation, Ganga knew to disregard Vinayagam's taunts, as on the morning he was doing her a favour by driving her to her village where her relatives awaited our arrival.

We passed hamlets and miles of lush banana plantations and coconut groves punctuated by the occasional engineering college or polytechnic that had bloomed all over South India since information technology started fuelling the nation's dreams. South India's highways were fast becoming the thoroughfare for cheap labour for the multinational companies that had mushroomed along them. This highway that we were travelling on sliced through villages. For over a thousand years, weaving had been a local industry but now Foxconn buses plucked people from their homes and ferried them to soulless jobs at multinationals, fed them at their workplace and brought them back to their homes, holding them hostage by the carrot stick of steady money, offering three times what they would make as weavers or labourers in a good month. Over a hundred years, these companies would most certainly wipe out the memories and the debris of a culture once buttressed by cottage industries. In Kanchipuram, the traditional korvai style of silk weaving had already fallen victim to this slow but sure decimation of craft and art. Agriculture too had succumbed to this alteration of landscape.

Farming families of those like Ganga and Saravanan had been compelled to forage for survival in cities. The mass exodus from India's villages had complicated the lives of cities whose resources and infrastructure were limited. But for people like Ganga, who had once lived off their land, the city of Madras—renamed Chennai in 1996—offered the only hope, even though it reinforced and often exacerbated their poverty.

◆

Madras was not the first of British East India Company's trading posts in India—Surat in northwestern India had already been established in 1615. By 1639, the Company was looking to set up a post in the south. Its rivals, the Dutch and the French, had already established theirs. Sir Francis Day chased an ideal parcel of land on the eastern seaboard and he found a friend in Naik Damarla Venkatadri of Wandiwash. In a few months, he secured land that was once a plantain plantation—in present-day Fort St George by the waters of the Bay of Bengal—owned by a fisherman called Madrasen, a Christian fisherman whose village took its name from its parish, Madre de Deus in Mylapore.[70]

On 22 July 1639, a decree worded by Sir Francis Day— written well before the standardization of English in the middle of the eighteenth century—established the British East India Company's claim to the port of Madraspatam which would become the city of Madras.

> Whereas Mr. Francis Day, Captain of the English at Armagon, upon great hopes by reason of our promises offten made unto him, hath repaired to our port of Madraspatam and had personall Conference with us in behalfe of the Company of that Nation, Concerning their trading in our territories and freindly Comerce with our subjects; wee, out of our spetiall Love and favour to the English, doe grant unto the said Captain, or whomsoever shall bee deputed to Idgitate the affaires of that Company, by vertue of this firman, Power to direct and order the building of a fort...[71]

Almost four hundred years after the firman was issued, that plot of land had burgeoned into a city of 4.6 million. Under British rule, this seaside settlement became India's first municipal corporation under the empire and, as the Madras Presidency, it incorporated almost the entirety of South India as well as several regions in the east. Included in its purvey was the land 160 kilometres away where Ganga had spent most of her years raising her family and harvesting her produce. Far away up in the hills, if Ganga squinted into the sun, she would have seen the fortress at Gingee built in the thirteenth century during the time of the Vijayanagara kings. At its steepest point, at some 900 feet, the fort was accessible only by climbing through thick forests while its walls sprawled over 12 kilometres and enclosed three massive hills. Built over gargantuan formations of rock that had challenged every ruler, Gingee's fortifications had been nearly impregnable, stumping even the Maratha kings who later occupied it for twenty years.

Soon after Madraspatam came into being, a Capuchin priest, Father Ephraim, started a free school out of his house in the 'White Town' (where the Europeans lived) around the newly built Fort St George. In 1688, after the city corporation of Madras started operations, a school was established in Black Town (the area where the Indians lived) for the purpose of teaching 'native children to speak, read, and write the English tongue and to understand Arithmetic and merchant Accompts'.[72] It would, of course, be many decades before education became available to Indians in a steady, disciplined fashion. St George's Anglo-Indian Higher Secondary School on Poonamallee Road—the first Western-style school in India—opened, and a gentleman called Andrew Bell joined as its superintendent in 1787. He modelled the teaching after the system of education in the pyol schools that he had observed in the villages where a student monitor attached to a teacher helped coach the students. A pyol is a raised platform on which to sit and it stands at about knee-height, flanking the main door of a house.

Bell applied the monitoring method to teach a large number of students and went on to become an evangelist of the idea, inspiring Queen Charlotte of Great Britain and many other schools in the country. Astute with his finances, Bell also made money in many different capacities in Madras and when he went back to England a decade later, he continued to receive a pension for another thirty-five years. His contribution was memorialized upon his death in 1832, with a tablet in the south choir aisle of London's Westminster Abbey. The tablet shows a relief of a seated man with a group of schoolboys and the inscription above it reads: 'Sacred to the memory of Andrew Bell D.D. L.L.D. Prebendary of this Collegiate Church: the eminent founder of the Madras System of education, who discovered and reduced to successful practice the plan of mutual instruction; founded upon the multiplication of power, and the division of labour, in the moral and intellectual world, which has been adopted within the British Empire as the national system of education of the children of the poor.'[73] His fame later evoked scepticism, because, after all, there was nothing revolutionary about the concept of a master standing in the deck of his house, teaching a line of poor students, some of whom simply picked up the material faster and related it to the other students.

And Ganga would have agreed. If Reverend Bell had dared explain his 'Madras System' to Ganga then or now, she would have pooh-poohed him, saying that it was not a new idea, for that was how girls acquired new kolam designs back in her village. An experienced woman conceived and drew the kolam, rice flour pinched between her fingers, on a clean mud bed or a concrete slab, and someone older and more experienced interpreted it to a bunch of girls and they discussed its intricacies. The next morning, the upgraded kolam artwork, magnified and embellished beyond anything they had discussed, decorated another person's doorstep.

On our drive to her village, Ganga told me about how so much learning was contained in the art of kolam. She also described her early years. Ganga believes she was born in the Hindu year 'tarana' which approximates to the year 1944. Her father, a religious Naidu man, had prayed every morning for twelve years until a son was born to him when Ganga was about two years old. But the child fell ill a few years after. Villagers believed that their deity, Mariatha, gave but also took away for reasons no one understood. The day that the goddess wrested her brother from them, Ganga's father lay down in sorrow. He began running a fever. 'My mother told me how our family cow lay her front feet at our doorstep, mooed twice mournfully and ambled out of our home, never to return,' Ganga said. Her father died a few hours later.

Despite this tragedy early in her life, Ganga recalled a

life filled with frolic and laughter. She capered around rice fields, peanut farms and haystacks. As she entered her teens, she ran around their mud huts with a coterie of her friends, observing other people's kolam designs in their front yards. She used these designs as inspirations for her own work, practising in mud for drawing the kolam outside her home. She loved deciphering how someone had drawn a design. She analysed the dots in the pattern and tried to visualize how to enlarge it or how she might make it more intricate.

Ganga never received any formal education but these artistic experiments allowed her to learn arithmetic, geometry and spatial relationships. Her story mirrored that of many of India's poor whose only means of livelihood was agriculture. For those yoked to the plough, education often took a back seat since government initiatives didn't always reach the farthest corners of India. The absenteeism of teachers, not just students, dogged establishments.

But in the late 1950s, after Ganga attained puberty, her mother and her uncle sought a suitor. Ganga was betrothed to a man thirty years her senior who had several acres of land and cows and was related, albeit in a distant way, to her family. He was desperately looking for a wife, his fourth, it turned out, who would bear him sons. A year into the marriage, however, Ganga was riddled with questions and advice. When was she going to have children? Why hadn't she borne her husband a son? Soon Ganga prayed to every god and swallowed bitter drinks. One of the herbal fertility mixes was crushed vembu, the juice of neem leaves. She lay back while her husband held her head and two other women pinned down her hands and legs while yet another funnelled the concoction into her throat. In quick succession over the next decade, Ganga would have two sons, a daughter and a third son. But even before she turned forty, her husband died.

Looking for a way to make a living, Ganga, her daughter and two of her sons boarded a bus to Madras.

◆

By the time Ganga reached Madras in the eighties, it was one of the most celebrated cities in India for education. Not only was Madras known for its educational institutions along the length of 'Marina Beach by the turn of the twentieth century, the city had some of the best-stocked libraries in India. By the end of the seventeenth century, the British East India Company sent a bale of calico cloth by ship to London where it was sold. The money realized was used to purchase the first shelf of books that would occupy a place at Fort St George. When the library formally opened in 1671, the first books were on theology. In the 1800s many more libraries opened in Madras out of which one of the most well-known institutions was the Madras Literary Society in Egmore. Today, it is a crumbling ruin held together by passionate volunteers who fret over the restoration of old manuscripts. The country's tropical heat and humidity hurts the preservation of rare books and manuscripts and hence several of its old public libraries—treasure houses of the nation's rich history and literature—are in a similarly dilapidated state. The spectacular architecture of these libraries harks back to an era when education was prized in its provinces and kingdoms.

In 1921, the editor of the *Madras Times*, Glyn Barlow, wrote about how a tourist to Madras would have been overwhelmed by the numerous signs of educational activity. 'Apart from the multitude of juvenile schools in every part of the crowded city, the number of academic institutions is large, and educational buildings are among the most prominent of its edifices.'[74] And despite the state of some of these buildings, driving alongside what's believed to be the world's second longest urban beach,

I felt, once again, the lofty vision for education in the Madras Presidency. Over the last few decades, English-medium schools and colleges had sprung up everywhere, and education was still one of the biggest preoccupations in the city. Almost a century later, however, it seemed that the English language in its written form—in all the libraries, clubs, banks and certainly inside the courts that Ganga frequented in Gingee—was used more to obfuscate than to illuminate.

When I griped about the sorry state of the English language in India to Vinayagam, he had a standard answer to my peevish protests. 'When the people don't have enough to eat, how will they care about monuments or English spelling, Amma?' I realized the import of his question the day we stopped at the foothills of the fortress at Gingee. Standing at the grassy walkway leading to the rocky path, I turned to Ganga and asked her if she had ever climbed up all the way to the fort. She told me that grand as it seemed from her village, she had never once thought to climb it. It just hadn't crossed her mind. Vinayagam was not completely off the mark about how poverty, education and awareness were all connected. The Englishmen who sought to make Madras a grand centre for education couldn't even make a dent as large as a mustard seed on the Gangas of the hinterlands.

◆

Ganga did not let on that she could not read. On her antiquated phone, my number had the photo of an apple against it. She distinguished each person by a picture. But she knew to squeeze the most out of the basic cell phone, using it to collect debts, make her appointments and put her family members in place using foul Tamil slang that I didn't understand. Sometimes, English sneaked in as on the morning she received a call from a relative from the village.

'Now, you listen to me, you, I'm going to be dontcare!' Ganga shouted into the tiny black gadget, her left arm on her hip, spit sailing in ten directions from her betel-stained lips. 'And you can go and tell that turd-brain that Ganga said that to him.' She had just made noun out of a phrase. American English had leaked into the hinterlands of South India, where once women like Ganga used to work, thrusting rice saplings into the wetness of paddy fields. Ganga continued to hiss into her cell phone, rattling off another bucketful of curses at the caller. At the close of her tirade, she told the good-for-nothing at the other end that so-and-so was nothing but a head louse under her broom.

When I expressed my shock to Vinayagam at having heard her say 'dontcare' in the way she had used it, he laughed. He said my ears would burn in embarrassment if I understood Tamil slang well enough. Presently he said 'dontcare' was a Tamil word—just like 'cool' and 'night' and 'tension' and 'stress'.

Ganga's comfort with the English language was significant to me in several ways. I was struck by the number of English words that now weighed down our sentences in the vernacular—even when we didn't need to use them. I was taken aback most by the way in which English nouns had been subsumed, subverted and transformed into verbs or adverbs to suit the vernacular. Expressions had been transmogrified in strange ways into a language that, at any given time and place, was understood right away by a certain coterie of people. A friend told me how the day he was trying to book a flight in India at a travel agent's office, the two clerks, both of whom weren't very comfortable in English, spoke to each other in a pidgin English and managed to understand each other perfectly well even though my friend had some trouble with it. I saw it in the interactions of Ganga, Vinayagam and

Saravanan who used English words in a particular way and knew what it meant. Vinayagam explained to me that the term 'touch-up' alluded to making out with a lover. A whole other English, one I wouldn't recognize because it was shorn of all grammar and rules, was being used and referenced on the streets of Chennai by those who hadn't had the privilege of an English-medium education.

It was a world I didn't understand, just as I would never be able to empathize with why someone like Ganga was preoccupied with the notion of caste. During our drive to Gingee, Ganga pointed out that the four of us in the fancy Toyota Crysta were each of a different caste. 'He's a Mudaliar,' she said pointing to Saravanan sitting in front of me. 'And Vinayagam here is a Nayakar. I'm a Naidu and you, Amma, are a Brahmin.' It seemed puerile and out of context for her to have even brought this up; yet, it was something that those with less privilege thought about and navigated all the time.

Vinayagam often told me that Ganga was more shrewd than she let on, that she was one of the most hidebound people he knew and that at our home she would not carry out some tasks that were beneath her perceived station in life. He claimed that the only reason he got any respect at all from her was because he matched her 'level', as he said, using the English word, owing to his own birth into the Nayakar caste.

Our car crawled over twenty feet of unpaved road leading to Ganga's hovel in Seppettai. Sugar cane swayed in the light breeze. As she descended from the car, Ganga hollered to a young man on a moped who spluttered to a stop by our car. 'Now go and tell everyone that Ganga is here! With her owner-Amma!' There was excitement in her eyes and her demeanour. This was the closest I'd ever feel to a zamindar.

As we entered the muddy walkway to her old home, I saw

Ganga totter. Her eyes welled up. She turned away. I sensed that she couldn't walk into her late son's home without being pierced by sorrow every time. I was unaware that this was the first time she was visiting his home since Amavasai drank himself to death two years before. She pointed to a room on the right side of the hovel. 'That's where he died,' she said leading the way in.

Her daughter-in-law greeted me warmly and hovered about asking me if I wanted something to eat or drink. Ganga collected herself in time and harassed her daughter-in-law as to what else she had to offer me. 'How about some sugar cane? What about groundnuts?' And then she walked up to a room and filled up a large bag of unshelled groundnuts which she promised to shell for me when we went back to Chennai. The four of us then walked down the path leading towards the coconut trees. A stream gurgled to our left and Ganga told me how it spilled over its banks in the rainy season. To the right, the land stretched in brown patches as far as my eye could see, bordered occasionally by a row of coconut and moringa trees. Ganga drew an imaginary line in the air to show the edge of her sons' lands—once hers and those of her late husband—and how she had now given it all away to her children. On it her daughter-in-law and extended family continued to grow black gram, groundnut, green chilli pepper, and cowpea.

◆

While Ganga had no appreciation whatsoever for the English language in the spoken or the written form, Vinayagam lamented that he was unable to understand what was being said when a group of people spoke English fluently and at speed. He understood some of it in context but he felt lost when more complicated vocabulary and idiomatic expressions were used. I understood Vinayagam's frustrations because chauffeurs like him, more than people with other skill sets, could earn a higher salary when they were fluent in English.

On the last day of June, two weeks after my father passed away, we stopped our daily subscription to *The Hindu*, ending a seventy-year association with the newspaper with whose English my father would never found fault. After I made a life in the United States, however, I began to find its language a tad wordy and obscure.

The first issue of *The Hindu* appeared in 1878 as it joined India's fight for Independence. Its editors and reporters had been schooled in the King's English by Englishmen in institutions like Presidency College of Madras whose alumni roster read like the who's who of India. The temerity of the fledgling version of *The Hindu* seemed to be in stark contrast to the opaqueness and caution of the present-day avatar of the newspaper. The man who started the newspaper, G. Subramania Aiyer, along with five others, did not mince his words while criticizing the callous ways of his British ruler or the orthodoxy of a section of Hindu society. During the Salem riots of 1884, *The Hindu* railed against the then Governor of Madras Presidency, M. E. Grant Duff, for his stance. 'Oh! Lucifer! How art thou fallen? Oh! Mr Grant Duff, how you stand like an extinct volcano in the midst of the ruins of your abortive reputation as an administrator! Erudite you may be, but a statesman you are not.'[75]

G. Subramania Aiyer was a crusader for social reform and women's empowerment and spoke truth to power with an audacity that would ultimately hurt and impoverish him. Against the custom of the day, he sought to have his daughter Priyammal—she had been widowed at the age of thirteen—married to a boy in 1889. Aiyer also wrote in support of Dalits, opining that 'no amount of admiration for our religion will bring social salvation to these poor people'.[76] Besides that, Aiyer wanted to raise the age of marriage and sought to abolish caste, child marriages and nautch parties. The conservative Tamil Brahmin readers took umbrage at his writings and *The Hindu* received defamation suits and suffered heavy losses culminating in the ouster of Aiyer.[77]

The newspaper regained its glory over the next century and in 1965, *The Times* of London listed *The Hindu* as one of the world's ten best newspapers. Discussing each of its choices in separate articles, *The Times* wrote that *The Hindu* was 'the only newspaper which in spite of being published only in a provincial capital is regularly and attentively read in Delhi'.[78] The newspaper's main attraction, for me, in recent times was its array of supplements focused on literature and the performing arts. Nonetheless, my affection for the paper ran deep. It was one of my last links with my departed father. Furthermore, it would always be the newspaper that had taught me the English language.

In the Madras in which I grew up, the love for English was an obsession, especially among those who sought an English-medium education. In some families, the language had replaced the mother tongue, the craze for English being such that families spoke English inside the home. No wonder people like Ganga, Saravanan and Vinayagam often felt they were excluded from conversations and groups.

English had always had a lot of social and political clout in South India, especially in Madras, where the disapproval of Hindi as a national language manifested itself as an unseemly love for English. In 1965, when the time came to transition to Hindi for all government communication, the people of the state of Tamil Nadu told the central government in New Delhi that they wanted English to continue. The state began pressing to secede from the Indian union for the cause of

English. The political unrest led to several suicides.[79]

As we've seen earlier, C. Rajagopalachari made a case for why English was critical for India's future. In a letter to the central government, he explained that if the centre and the people must speak the same language, Hindi was a poor choice since several states did not speak Hindi. Furthermore, all progress in science and industry was available only in English. Hindi would have to catch up; it would take not only time but a lot of work. This lack of access to knowledge would halt the progress of the nation, he argued. He stated that he had doubts about India's ability to rule itself but on the question of the English language, he had no doubts whatsoever, despite the general feeling that English would continue India's oppression by caste.

'Let English continue,' he wrote. 'This stone which the builders refused is become the headstone of the corner. So the Psalmist sang. The builders had rejected it as being of curious shape, not a rectangle and none of its sides square or oblong. But it became the keystone of the arch and its strange shape was its merit. Not one of our own languages but this strange one will keep the arch firm and all the languages together. It is the Lord's doing and marvelous in our eyes. So be it.'[80] Prime Minister Jawaharlal Nehru heeded the advice of the South Indian statesman.

Almost a half-century after Rajagopalachari wrote his famous argument, India would have reason to thank his foresight because the language would become the country's ticket to the information superhighway. No matter the economic advantages, in a city where English grammar was once revered by the educated elite, the language had twisted into a comical version of itself. While my father's life hung in the balance at MedIndia Hospital in Nungambakkam a few years ago, I was often distracted from my sorrow by the many signs around me. I recall that one of them went thus: 'Visitors not allowed other than visiting time.'

A week after the emergency surgery gave my father a lease on life, he was released from the hospital. My sister, Vinayagam and I were thankful for the extra time that had been granted my father after a harrowing week at the intensive digestive care unit. By the middle of November, he was back at his house where, after a few weeks of care, he was also back at his dining table, pen in hand and paper on table, writing letters again—always in several rough and fair drafts—one to the bank, another to the mutual fund manager, yet another to the accountant general's office of the Government of India and a last one to the temple committee at his village in Kerala.

Decades of life in the Indian government had chiselled my father's English with the precision granite carvers displayed miles away at the rock temples of Mahabalipuram. It had also weighted it down with words of reverence and servility typical of the sahibs of the British Raj, not to mention wonderful Indianisms.

My father wrote to the government asking for his pension matter to be sorted out. 'I request you to please confirm the position stated above,' he wrote, 'and kindly note in your records your payment to me during 2009–2010. Please do the needful and revert at the earliest.'

The letter to the temple committee read thus:

I received the Samooham circular of 20-6-2012. A series of health problems kept me confined to a hospital in Nungambakkam here and the house for almost five months. I'm somewhat normal now. The weight loss, however, is six kilograms. I could not therefore write to you earlier. Presently I am sending herewith a crossed demand draft for a modest Rs. 3000. The long treatment drained quite some funds of mine. Please accept this sum. I wish you and the Ratha Samithi all success in their efforts. With best wishes and a happy new year to all.

Despite the leaden prose my father wrote after years of being steeped in bureaucrat jargon, I'd almost never seen him employ bad grammar or poor spelling until a few months prior to his demise. The city of my youth, on the other hand, had gone in quite another direction and I was angry at my father for becoming inured to it.

English stared out from many yellow posters on electric junction boxes around Chennai. Sometimes it issued warnings about fistula or piles with English and Tamil sections on the same sheet. In some versions of the posters, the first word was 'sex' and it was followed by a question with the word 'impotercy?' When I read the small print below the headline, I got more clarity: 'Shortly sperms comeout'; 'sperms water type'; 'sleeping time sperms release'. The clause that followed wrapped it all up in bold type with '100% guaranty': 'Penis small size'. Now I knew I could recommend this Dr Sajal in Chennai's Periamet (Canara Bank Opp.) not just for anyone with sexual dysfunction but also for anyone who wished to apply for a position to edit the poster.

At a park with many walkers who were educated in English, I saw signs about how 'cleanliness was next to godliness', a fact I too learned in school in kindergarten in Chennai. But adjacent to that sign was one that exasperated me: 'Please donot pluck the leaves of this devine tree.' Chennai also had many varieties of the 'No Parking' sign. Sometimes it was a warning with one word: NoParking. Just like the many 'Tolet' signs which I often read as 'Toilet'. Vinayagam told me to stop analysing all the spelling mistakes. He told me, once again, that my perspective was coloured by privilege. I tried to convince him that what frustrated me was the lack of attention to detail even in places where mistakes were inadmissible.

At Chennai's Music Academy, a venue frequented by wealthy, educated patrons, many of whom are connected to India's biggest industrial houses or the newspaper business, the sign on the electric box said 'Music Acadamy'. Neither they nor the musicians—many of whom are the elites of India and speak and write excellent English—had cared about the existence of such a sign. The word 'available',—not an overly complicated word—was the most misspelt in the entire city. At Grand Sweets & Snacks, a board mentioned that assorted sweets were 'availble'; but at Easwari Lending Library, a busy private lending library, the books were only 'avilble'.

In complete juxtaposition to these bloopers, I saw another problem when I opened *The Hindu* on some mornings. Its music reviews could be so bloated that I just didn't understand them at all. 'In the concert of T. M. Krishna, his style bristled with conjured-up creativity served in different moulds.' The writer also mentioned that the musician's new bani—a Tamil word encompassing the musician's tutelage and imbibed style—'seems to suggest that he is in the process of discovering fresh dimensions to expository patterns. It had familiar traits but was wayward in execution.' [81]

◆

On our drive back from Ganga's village, we stopped at the foothills of the Gingee Fort and walked up to where the hike up the rock began. Ganga had never been that close to the fort and she marvelled at its magnificence. As we took in the panorama of the fields around us, Ganga told me about how she had learned to count by drawing kolams. She was happy she had learned to read numbers because that helped her recognize bus routes and travel around the city. She could do math in multiples of five. For a few years, Ganga floated a 'chit fund' scheme charging high rates of interest while making money off of those who desperately needed cash. She could do the math to know what she was owed to the last rupee when her debtor didn't pay up.

Even though she couldn't read and write any language, there were, however, three English words that she knew to write. They were the same three she wrote on 1 January every year because her first big boss, Periyaiyya—'the big boss' who was her 'owner' when she first moved to Chennai in 1982— expected the three words, along with the year, written below a big kolam outside his doorstep.

'On the morning of every new year, after I'd drawn the kolam and written the words, Periyaiyya would tell me to come around to the front of the house,' Ganga said. 'He looked resplendent in a white shirt and white veshti and an angavastram over his torso, this plank of holy ash across his forehead, and a sandalwood and vermilion dot below it.' He would look at the kolam and her writing and say, 'Ganga, onakku vaasikka teriyattalum, nee azhaga yezhudariye. (Even though you don't know to read, you write beautifully.)' Ganga paused, her eyes misty. 'And now he's looking at me from up above.' She smiled, looking up at the heavens. Ganga told me how he had always made her feel that she was not an unlettered woman. She had felt very special every new year when he pressed a hundred rupee note into her palm with his very best wishes to her for a happy new year.

Besides the three words that she knew to write, Ganga strung many English words into her Tamil sentences as she spoke. I recalled how one morning when she walked into my father's home, she told me she felt a 'weakness' in her body. Other words slipped out of her mouth used in the right context, their meaning always intact: side, salt, tea, cup, finish, soap, road, ground, school, station, airport, mileage, night, mood, court, police, train, government, bus, appeal, problem, connection, road, hotel, stay, order, allow, adjust, interest, military, last, land, property, bank, ground, movement, register, record, copy, door, lawyer, bank, cheque, photo, sink, teacher, machine, tailor, housing board, soap, collector, office, telephone, ready, ordinary, weakness, dull, and deposit, among others.

After we returned home from Gingee that evening, Vinayagam pointed out that Ganga knew all sorts of English words especially when they were related to the court system. 'Women who go to court are not considered nice women—at least in my community,' he said to me after Ganga had left for the day. I retorted that Ganga was the most empowered woman I knew and that she was gutsier than many who had many degrees to their name but weren't intrepid enough to challenge someone in court. Ganga was always at the lawyer's office filing one appeal or another about this property or that and always demanding her rights as the fourth legal wife of her late husband. I couldn't digest Vinayagam's cynicism. I was awed that Ganga knew her way around the court system even when she had not seen the inside of a school or a library. By her own admission it was street smarts that lifted her out of her bad circumstances. One morning I discovered exactly how proud a woman Ganga was.

Vinayagam was talking animatedly with me in the kitchen as I hovered by the stove cooking. He raised his right arm to point something out to me when Ganga walked up right behind him with her mop. 'Ayyo, kezhavi!' Vinayagam cried. 'Next time, warn me when you're creeping up behind me! I could have killed you, see? And then, if you go, I'd have to call your son to take care of your cremation and we'd have to arrange for this and that.'

Unfazed by the taunt, Ganga grinned, baring the jagged edges of her teeth. 'Kanna, don't fret. Just call my son and take him to the bank where I've stashed away money for my cremation expenses.' Cackling, Ganga said she never ever wanted to be indebted to any of her children when she left the world. She waved five fingers in the air. 'I've left 50,000 rupees for when I go.'

Vinayagam didn't appreciate her moxie and retorted, 'Old woman, money alone is pointless. You have to tell the bank that your son must have access to it.'

Then, the two of them—the young man who was savvy about banks and paperwork, and an old woman who could not read or write but knew what 'debosit' meant—began hashing out the nitty-gritties of notaries, deposits and banks and stamp papers, in a most civil fashion. There I stood, in the meanwhile, watching, listening to their debate, reflecting on how the subject of Ganga's final journey out of this world seemed to give my late father's man Friday an unusually high degree of satisfaction.

FIVE

JAB ENGLISH MET HINDI

'Indians are the only ones who say "can", no?' he asked, chuckling, as he washed his hands in the kitchen sink. Kranti Kanade, whose Airbnb I was staying at, had swooped down on my slip as I asked for a towel using 'Can I' instead of 'May I'. At thirty-seven, this illustrious alumnus of Pune's Film and Television Institute of India (FTII) resembled all those smooth-cheeked Bollywood heroes of the seventies in whom sadness lingered even after they had won over their lady-love.

Kranti listened intently as I talked and when it was time for him to answer, he paused for a while. When he spoke at last, he articulated his thoughts in nuanced ways, charting out the complexities of India's predicament. He reached often for the word 'complex'. India was complex. The people were complex. Its history was complex. India's romance with English was complex. He held forth in an English that revealed so much about his upbringing and his love for the vernaculars of his life—Marathi and Hindi—about which his thespian parents and his freedom fighter grandfather were passionate.

When he said 'village' with the rounded 'w' as in 'willage' I realized why Mumbai's famous street food could never be 'pav bhaji' but 'pao bhaji' because in both Marathi and Gujarati, every 'v' was always to be rounded out with the lips. And that, I understood, was precisely how a mother tongue bled into one's English. Days after hearing that, I figured out why Deolali, a town a hundred miles from Pune, had entered the vocal cords of the British Raj as 'Doolally', a word that the Raj used for those who were messed up in the head, something today's world calls PTSD. In Kranti, his Marathi had seasoned his English, just as lemongrass peppered masala chai in these parts.

In the mid-eighties, Kranti attended a boarding school in Nashik called Boys' Town School run by educators from the dwindling Parsi community, Zoroastrians who had fled to western India from Persia between the eighth and tenth centuries. Kranti's fascination for new words and his attention to grammar rules began then, in elementary school. He obsessed for over a month over question tags. During that zany time he'd flit around practising his lessons, annoying those around him with contrived sentences using appropriate question tags such as 'She has gone there, *hasn't she?*' and 'You're coming here, *aren't you?*'

Like my father and grandfather who both swore by it, Kranti too had grown up on Wren and Martin, the high school English grammar and composition or collectively, a series of English textbooks written jointly by P. C. Wren and H. Martin culled out of the *Manual of English Grammar and Composition* by J. C. Nesfield. Although the grammar book had been written primarily for the children of British officers residing in India, Indian and Pakistani schools in the postcolonial era adopted them, too. Through my years in India, all those who loved English held it in as much reverence as they did the Bhagavad Gita. Still, I wasn't sure I'd be too ruffled if someone were to say: 'We're going there, isn't it?'

Indians were known for their non-adherence to the correct question tag. The subject and verb of a sentence must agree and any second reference in the sentence must refer to the same subject. If I accused my husband of polishing off all the pani puri, I might ask 'You ate all the pani puri, didn't you?'

But most Indians used 'isn't it' as a general purpose tag. This was a defilement of English and a dead giveaway that one's grammar wasn't up to snuff. I understood why Kranti fussed so much about grammar.

Still, when he brought up the point about 'can' I was struck. Years of living in the most informal state in America had snipped the old graces that we had been taught back in school in India and I knew that if I'd wanted to ask Kranti for a towel with which to wipe my hands, I should, rightly, have asked: '*May* I have a towel, Kranti?'

The grammar Nazi now picked up a towel, laughing as he stalked across to where I stood looking a trifle embarrassed, while his mother, Shakuntala, a well-known actress of the Marathi stage, hovered about the kitchen in a silk sari, listening as Kranti talked about the house he had built on land they owned. After his father passed away, Shakuntala had told him she wanted to get away from the city to live in her own farmhouse. Kranti had assured her that he would redesign their home instead. He would make the farm take root in their home in Pune, the greenest town I'd seen on my recent travels through my native country. It had been one of the foundries for India's freedom fight against the British. Now home to defence companies, high-tech firms, top-flight educational institutions and a film institute that honed the skills of the most celebrated mavens of India's hyperactive film industry, Pune was an intellectual and artistic centre that was a three-hour drive from Mumbai where I had landed ten days ago.

◆

At the Mumbai airport, my Uber driver, Babasaheb, had responded confidently in English. 'Where are you standing, madam?' he'd asked. Within minutes I realized, however, that Babasaheb too was a master merely of the gerund. He wielded a larger gaggle of English nouns and a few basic verbs—'come', 'go', 'coming' and 'going' being the most employed in his line of work—but mostly he reminded me of my chauffeur in Chennai, Vinayagam.

At my home, whenever I called out to Vinayagam, he yelled back in English for effect: 'I coming, madam, please wait!' When I corrected Vinayagam, telling him to insert the 'am' and say 'I am coming', I found myself unable to explain why the English language was conjugated thus, with the 'to be' verb, when Indian languages were not. One day my long–winded explanations and justifications led to yet another complication. Vinayagam prepared my father's lunch and brought it to our dining table. With the confidence of Grammar Girl, Vinayagam summoned my father thus: 'Saar, you are lunch is ready.' That day I realized that just as I would never master the French reflexive verb, English conjugations would likely elude chauffeurs whose medium of education had been a regional bhasha. In contrast to Vinayagam, Mumbai's Babasaheb shot from an arsenal of English words.

Before the week was out, I'd discover that in this city of celluloid dreams, cultures and classes collided in unpredictable ways. Here the English language too had assumed an unscripted trajectory. As one of the city's prolific writers and translators, Jerry Pinto, said to me, English had become a transactional language in India, not just in Mumbai. In my view, nowhere was the element of transaction manifest as in the creation of the city of Mumbai.

In 1661 the seven swampy islands which together formed Bombay were part of the dowry that Catherine of Braganza brought when she married Charles II of Britain. In a transaction that would define the ethos of the place Charles II rented the islands to the East India Company in 1668 for £10 a year. During the colonial period that followed, out of the two major cities, Bombay and Calcutta, the former was more progressive, innovative and nimble because of the many communities that had fired up businesses there. Relations between Hindu and Muslim businessmen were better in Bombay than in Calcutta. Indians reported to Englishmen in Calcutta. In Bombay, however, Indians collaborated with Europeans. As a child, I'd seen Bombay's sense of equality in the sixties and seventies even on buses and trains. In the south of India women and men sat on different sides of the bus. In Bombay, in the early days, men and women sat together homogenously in a prescient sign that they were equal collaborators in the world.

On my latest visit I saw Mumbai's natural adeptness and progressive nature also in the pidgin English of the drivers who whisked me up and down its roads. The city's intrinsic work ethic had rubbed off on its people even though their English was sanded down to a skeletal form, scaffolded by Marathi, Hindi and Gujarati. I had heard that in Mumbai, Uber drivers were often locals and a match for the sharp local cabbies. This was not true of Uber drivers in many other cities in India and hence Babasaheb's felicity in English did not surprise me one bit.

Babasaheb had assumed the sobriquet of the late Mumbai icon, Dr B. R. Ambedkar, a Columbia-educated lawyer who had fought for the rights of the Dalits. Like most Mumbai cabbies Babasaheb was quick on the uptake. He recognized, in a flash, the name of the building where my cousin lived in Chembur's Diamond Garden. We torpedoed on in his Maruti Suzuki Wagon R passing high-rises where laundry flapped about on all the balconies of the town's dreary buildings. Thanks to both negligence and the intense monsoons that ravaged the city every year, their facades often wore discolorations resembling mascara streaks marring the cheeks of a tearful woman.

As we sped down western expressway, Babasaheb traded

the details of his life with me. He worked from 10 a.m. to 10 p.m.—'Drop-Pickup-Drop-Pickup' was the rhythm of his existence—except for a break to eat the tiffin packed by his wife at around 2 p.m.—but, thank goodness that at least Mumbai's traffic was 'systematic' he said, in English. A proud Maharashtrian, he was making a good living—he owned his vehicle—despite his stunted seventh-grade education in the village. When I appreciated his city over all other cities, Babasaheb took that as a compliment, placing his hand on his chest and bowing his head ever so slightly as he navigated city traffic, as if he himself had put wrench to nut and built the old city of Bombay—from Alexandra Dock, right by one of India's natural harbours, all the way up to Vashi, where newcomers bought up properties.

Soon it was Babasaheb's turn to pry into my life. 'Are you a Bollywood writer, madam?' he asked. I laughed and shook my head.

'Main non-fiction writer hoon. Journalist, haina? Bollywood writer nahin,' I said at a dreadful attempt at Hindi.

Babasaheb chuckled. 'Mumbai mein "writer" means writing for Bollywood, ma'am,' he said with a wide grin. Even as early as 1927, when India had started cranking out silent films, Bombay had seventy-seven permanent cinema houses.

Babasaheb wondered if I worked for a paper. 'Like *Saamana*?' he asked. *Saamana* was Maharashtra's Marathi newspaper, a mouthpiece for one of the state's political party, Shiv Sena. I was left chafing at the inadvertent insult.

But I too did Babasaheb a bad turn before I emerged from his car. I complimented him on his good English and told him to read the *Times of India* daily to improve his English. That was a gaffe on my part. While the *Times of India* had been birthed in Mumbai and was now India's biggest English-language daily, its profits were directly proportional to its advertorials and it had never regained its old glory as a purveyor of the King's English.[82]

Mumbai's hodgepodge of cultures embraced a salmagundi of the English language, while truncating or decimating every language that arrived to become a part of it and, naturally, archaic English was now a relic in contemporary Mumbai. Closer to Alexandra Dock, at one of the famous old Irani cafés of Mumbai, Kyani & Co., vegetable patties were sold as vegetable 'pattice' and mixed vegetable as 'mix' vegetable. A sign called 'washbasin' pointed me to the sink. I wasn't sure, however, that I could be cavalier towards one warning in one of those cafés: 'Outside Eatables not allowed.' While 'eatable' was both an adjective and a noun, prefixing it with the word 'outside' as Indians often managed to do for convenience with every noun, was handy and efficient. But it was prone to misinterpretation by search engines lacking natural human intelligence to parse intuitively. On one run through Google, for instance, my search of the term 'outside eatable' returned this: 'Eldorado Candy G-String 7970. *To be sweet and sexy, slip into this edible candy g-String! Elastic holds the candy in place and one size fits most.*' Indianisms received unexpected reactions from foreign minds and, apparently, Google was no exception.

For Indians, efficiency always trumped the rule of law, just as on the country's roads. Every Indian had foisted his own preferences on the English language. Since Indian languages were position independent, we code-switched effortlessly. We often felt a word in our hands, added a little salt, sprinkled some mirch, some jeera and some ajwain, and squeezed, kneaded, pulled and twisted it like roti dough, rolling out a whole new kind of masala bread.

In Mumbai this parlayed into each community brandishing its version of English. At Chembur's Kottakkal Arya Vaidyasala, a clinic dedicated to herbal oil treatments popular in Kerala, a sign offered 'cunsaltation', instead of 'consultation', a word with Latin origins. This attitude to language was not unlike that of Jerry Pinto's grandmother who, in Pinto's description in *Em and The Big Hoom* 'omitted almost all the important words in every sentence'.[83] Pinto observed that it was probably because 'she had had far too many languages drummed into her ears—first Konkani in Goa, then Burmese in Rangoon, then Bengali in wartime Calcutta, and now English, in which her child spoke and dreamed.' Pinto's droll description of his grandmother's manner of speech—'she spoke in code'—could very well be a reference to Mumbai's own patois.

The English language had bumped along Mumbai's streets—as a white cricket ball rolls through town picking up fuzz and dirt—gathering the grime of street talk and the argot of different quarters as it drifted through town over the decades. English also grew inflated with 'kindly' and 'needful' and the passive voice between the carriage returns of native typewriters that Naval Godrej had dreamed up and built at the Godrej plant at Mumbai's Vikhroli suburb. The active English of the living, spoken by 'Mumbaikars', as they called themselves, was not unlike Creole, a fusion of several tongues.

'Hinglish' advertisements targeting the youth of the country soon became the norm in a city touted to be India's commercial capital. English embodied the need to be heard, seen and read by a higher class of people, and to advertise in English became 'an Indian weakness' in the words of journalist Binoo John'.[84] In time the language of the street permeated the billboards of advertising reflecting how daily Hindi incorporated many English words as when a taxi driver took a particular route owing to a traffic jam: 'Yeh route mein jam hoga.'

When I came of age in the seventies, the irreverent yet topical advertising campaigns of Amul butter represented what would become touchstones in my writing career many decades later. Which writer wouldn't kill to write a line that captured the imagination of millions of people? There were other timeless advertising slogans too that touched a chord. In 1998, Pepsi's Hinglish slogan became a national rallying cry of a martyred soldier in the Kargil War—'Yeh Dil Maange More', meaning 'the heart desires more'—proving that an amalgam of English and other regional languages spoken with a pan-Indian sensibility was often more urgent, more strident and more effective in seizing the attention of India's young consumers.

I suspect that this was what Kranti Kanade referred to as the 'cool English' that everyone in Bollywood and in many of India's metros preferred to speak in the twenty-first century. It was only a matter of time before Indian English turned English on its head. And thus in yet another grand irony, by the year 2015, 'Arre yaar', a term that Bollywood had used for decades—which, literally, means 'hey, buddy'—had burrowed its way into the Oxford dictionary. In that year, 'churidaar', 'bhelpuri' and 'dhaba' were the other three entries, adding to the warren of more than 2,000 contributions from the various Indian languages into the English language.

◆

In Pune's Fergusson College, Kranti was told he could not write a script for an inter-collegiate theatre competition. Instead of challenging its own student community to write the script, his college simply hired a professional scriptwriter. Kranti was riled. He felt cheated, voiceless. Here was yet another proof of how institutions cared more about trophies than about nurturing talent. Kranti simmered with the unfairness of this for decades before he corralled it into his work in a film he titled *CRD* (2016). In this as well as his other films, the theme he examines is how the outside world constantly tries to stamp out individuality and uniqueness.

Kranti considered the English language part of this inexorable force and disliked how English tainted content was received and consumed. 'If Prannoy Roy is interviewing you in English on NDTV, it is considered a national interview as opposed to a local journalist interviewing you in Marathi or Hindi.' He thought it was preposterous. Wasn't language meant to communicate, to reach either super consciousness or levels of creativity? English had compromised perceptions about art, too, he said. 'So how does it matter to a beautiful potter—whether he knows English or Japanese, or not?' As Kranti vented, it dawned on me that English had become that filter through which we assessed the value of something or someone. Had English shifted, ever so slightly perhaps, our moral centre? Kranti questioned this placid acceptance of the shift. To him, as for Tully, English was that juggernaut that had crushed India's individuality.

This persistent questioning was Kranti's signature style. In his films, too, his protagonists were idealistic to a fault, safeguarding their originality against the machinations of an invading world, often at the cost of their reputations—and sometimes their lives—to live the most original life they could. I noticed a physical manifestation of this ideology in his home.

Kranti's terrace was flush with organic fruiting trees and plants: tomatoes, methi, coriander, lime, papaya, guava, and other species poked out of pots packed together under the full sun. He grew enough produce for home consumption.

'Every house has to have a mango tree in front and back, you know,' he said, the incessant chirping of birds drowning out his voice as we stared over the sterile rooftops of other buildings below us. We towered over the city. Below us television antennae sprouted, like weeds, from barren rooftops. Kranti accused people of wasting their spaces, when they could easily do their part for the environment. 'Couldn't every neighbour put some money into a terrace garden?' he wondered aloud. The ficus tree he had planted two years before had grown so madly that its canopy now weltered over the road. Ashoka, banana, coconut and mango trees rustled at the front and the back of his home.

Kranti's house divulged little about himself or his background. His grandparents had been doctors and leaders during the Indian independence movement and had been active in developmental politics in the post-Independence period. But there was hardly anything in Kranti's spartan home that allowed me to label him. The filmmaker hadn't assigned a name to his home, a typical feature of most Indian bungalows. I saw no idols. Sparse wooden furniture adorned the living quarters. The living room, the dining area and the kitchen opened out to the koi pond in the middle of the house. The openness of the interior and the way in which a light breeze flowed through its living spaces struck me as different from the layout of most contemporary Indian homes. He had fashioned his home to be a meeting place where people from the community would gather for discussions and concerts. Kranti's sensibilities had been sculpted by his parents who raised him to be an artist. Shakuntala and Satish Kanade had managed a school for rural children and had run a theatre organization, Kalavaibhav, for more than thirty-five years. Sartre, Camus and Kafka had cast long shadows in his home; by the age of ten, Kranti was acting in school plays. The result was a global consciousness and an activist mindset that Kranti then ploughed into his own art decades later. 'We were totally atheist—no god—it was much easier to focus on rationality and creativity.' Kranti paused again, staring into space. 'Rational answers are always better than the traditional answers,' Kranti said, at last, with a hint of a smile. (Or as my husband might put it: 'Logic always trumps bullshit'.) It was probably that rational streak that made his parents enrol him into English-medium schools—as did many parents who could afford such education for their children—even though they were steeped in the regional bhasha and literature.

Kranti loved the English language as a painter loved his brush. He admitted to loving it despite its peculiarities. He loved it even more, he said, because it enabled him to speak to his wife whose mother tongue is Gujarati. Moreover, English had expanded his world view bringing European and American films into his living room when he was a teenager. English had been a boon to him but he knew its place in his life. It was merely a perk, a vehicle for him to get to another place. However, he was painfully aware that this was not true for most of his countrymen whose penurious circumstances had put English out of reach to them. For them English was a destination in itself, a holy grail, an unattainable goal, because it was a skill they would have to work to master that would then lead them towards other trappings of the good life. For them, English would loom large as an intimidating force that by its very inaccessibility lowered their self-esteem by several notches.

At Pune's film institute Kranti had been privy to the struggles of some of his classmates for whom English had not been their medium of education. They never fully grasped Western literary cinematic concepts owing to their inability to process English at a higher level. The language divide at the institute was thus stark, an invisible wall separating students whose only cerebration, really, should have been over the medium of their art. English had colonized people's minds when, in the grand scheme of things, the nuances of English mattered not a whit to the common man. English was irrelevant to 90 per cent of India and, consequently, the

English language had to be put its rightful place in society, especially if so much of India had to catch up.

◆

All men are brothers, no?
In India also
Gujaratis, Maharashtrians, Hindiwallahs
All brothers—
Though some are having funny habits.
Still, you tolerate me,
I tolerate you,
One day Ram Rajya is surely coming.

From 'The Patriot' by Nissim Ezekiel[85]

In Mumbai (and indeed, all over India), wallah—the word occurred in different forms, as 'wala' or 'vala' or 'walla'—was an ubiquitous organism ticking in different corners of a city that chugged day and night. The suffix of wallah to a name or a role meant agent, doer, keeper, man, inhabitant, master, lord, possessor, owner and it often became synonymous with what he manufactured or the service he provided. One of those mornings in Mumbai, I was interested in visiting a historic old place by Ballard Estate where men specialized in the puri.

I'd planned on lunch at Pancham Puriwala, a hole in the wall eatery that is right across from the gothic marvel of Mumbai's landmark Chhatrapati Shivaji Terminus train station. I'd been told that if I were lucky a spot at a table of strangers was all that I would get. Fearing for my life, I stepped in.

The man at the counter turned towards the centre of the space after he spotted me. 'Singal lady!' he hollered in English over his shoulder. Meanwhile, dozens of pairs of eyes

in the space turned to me, the only woman in a
beehive of moustachioed men. In less than fogenic
however, I was seated at a narrow ledge of a taute,
I was elbow-to-elbow with two unknown vallahs her
topis, and another unknown wallah in form. Western hite
In the 1860s, before the demolition of the Fort ramparts there
was a pond known as Fansi Talao or Gallow's Tank, across
the road from this eatery where murderers were hanged in
public ignominy. Criminals were pilloried, had rotten egs, old
shoes, mud and brickbats thrown at them. After watching a
public hanging, people filed to Pancham Puriwala for a quick
bite of puri-aloo.[86] When my plate with its four puffed puris
and piping hot aloo palak was served, I tucked in as fast as
I could, thankful that the puris I ate were dissociated from
public hangings.

After my meal, I made for the station where I stood
shoulder to shoulder with a group of Mumbai's dabbawallahs
who balanced long wooden crates of lunch dabbas on their
head. Watching them, I recalled the words of Rohinton Mistry
in a story he had titled 'Lend Me Your Light'. 'The tiffin
carriers would stagger into the school compound with their
long, narrow rickety crates balanced on their heads, each with
fifty tiffin boxes, delivering lunches from homes in all corners
of the city.' When the boxes were unpacked, the smell would
be 'thick as swill'.[87]

I recognized the characteristics of the city in the resilience
and fortitude of these dabbawallahs who ferried the food with
such uncanny precision from point to point come rain or
shine, and in Mumbai's horrific monsoons, too, their work
epitomizing the character and resilience of the city to which
they owed their sustenance. Their efficiency became a case
study at Harvard Business School. A 2012 Harvard paper
described how the 5,000 or so dabbawallahs transported more

000 lunchboxes throughout Mumbai, conducting
th of 260,000 transactions every day with scarcely an
u

me and ain I spotted this can-do energy and optimism
n ores of th less fortunate in India that I found impossible
to xplain. In umbai, I found this drive in the other prominent
'wallh' in e city—the Parsi. Sometimes Parsi names were
mrely Elish translations of the owner's vocation: Lawyer,
Doctor, Paymaster, Engineer, Confectioner, Readymoney,
Motiwla, Screwvala, Engineer, Contractor, Rotiwallah, and
Keswallah, among many others. Parsi writer Farrukh Dhondy
wrote in his book Words about a family name of Saklatwalla on
his mother's side that was really 'Sack-cloth-wala'. He reckons
that his ancestors must have made gunny sacks, importing
raw jute from Bengal into western India to make jute sacks
that are used for storing everything from grain to potatoes
to sand all over the world. Today this small community of
Parsis has shrunk to about 60,000,[88] yet their enterprise and
philanthropy has infused Mumbai with their work ethic and
value system.

In the late eighteenth and nineteenth centuries, Mumbai's
trading communities of Parsis, Gujarati Hindus, Baghdadi
Jews and Khoja Ismailis were often equal partners in building
what was often the first enterprise in a city of ample first
ventures: the first cotton spinning mill, stock exchange, cement
production company, railway. The first successful modern
factory originated in Bombay: Cowasji Davar's Oriental
Spinning, 1854. India's first stock exchange opened in Bombay
in 1875. Steel production began in 1913 by the company started
by the Tata family that also powered the hydroelectric industry.
Industriousness defined the people of Bombay and the city
knew much less racial and communal strife.

By the early part of the nineteenth century, the Parsi

community owned half of Bombay, renting out their magnificent houses to the British. In accordance with Zoroastrian doctrine, Parsis bequeathed their money to charities that benefited both the community and the city. As Rohinton Mistry says in the voice of Jacqueline, the Goan Catholic ayah, the Parsi bosses 'thought they were like British only, ruling India side by side'.[89]

Everywhere in old Mumbai I saw evidence of Parsi largesse. Near Flora Fountain, I came upon a plaque laid in 1871 by the governor of Bombay for the Sir Jamsetjee Jeejeebhoy Parsee Benevolent Institution whose mission was to educate children unmindful of religion, caste or creed. The words explained the Parsi heart. 'Happy is he that hath mercy on the poor; and he that giveth to the poor shall not lack.' A foot away from it, a caboodle of children in uniform giggled as girls tugged at each other's pigtails outside the massive white iron grille gates of the school, not different, perhaps from the Parsi-run school in Nashik where Kranti Kanade had once learned to appreciate English grammar and a whole lot more.

◆

December was chilly in Pune but the afternoon sun warmed my ears and neck. We were seated at Kranti's long balcony, with the sun playing hide-and-seek. Kranti told me that the building of his house in Pune was also a sort of dissent on his part. 'I constantly try to revolt against everything,' he said, pointing out that instead of adding more rooms, he found other ways to keep a large part of the house accessible and bring the outside in so that people could 'sit with this beautiful light falling on [their] faces'. 'In my own personal life or my art or my work I constantly strive to revolt against everything,' he repeated.

Kranti's movies left me with a melancholy I could not

shake off. They riled up dormant feelings in me because he asked me questions about what I held dear, often subverting my world view. Was revolt and dissent the only way to achieving one's potential? Was I somehow less relevant and valuable in the world when I submitted to the authority of another?

In his movie, *Gandhi of the Month*, Kranti addressed issues of ferment and chaos in the nation. Even *Mahek*, a more upbeat movie with many hilarious moments, hit me hard. It posited that the educational system had been created to stifle a child's imagination. Every film of his was an exploration of lost innocence. But I also wondered about Kranti's chosen path. Would being a Bollywood director have been a surer way of reaching a wider audience in order to get his messages across? I remembered having heard a valuable piece of advice from singer Harry Belafonte in one of his speeches. He urged people to first have a platform to reach the masses and then use that to try and change the minds of people.

Popular art was often that fastest way to grab people's attention. Kranti didn't care for it, however. He was not impressed by Chetan Bhagat, for instance. 'At best I would say is he's a simple narrator. That is not literature,' he said. 'Literature has to ignite a revolution in each individual.' He looked into the distance. I understood Kranti's gripe because I too didn't care for Bhagat's work. Still, as a maven of the publishing industry observed to me, Bhagat had paved the way for Indian writers to be heard and to market themselves effectively. By shunning elitism in the approach to his art, Bhagat had endeared himself to a large number of Indian youth. His stories were accessible for those whose first language was not English. Bhagat was telling India's tales, that, too, in Indian English. Did it mean, conversely, that by shunning the popular in art, Kranti had embraced the very elitism he shunned? I wasn't sure about the answer.

I could see why Kranti was frustrated. The priorities of Indian cinema had changed—the early films had often been a commentary on the state of affairs. Thoughtful films were not getting made even by those who were graduates of a stellar institution like the FTII. Years before, Kranti had started work on a Hindi feature film in Bollywood titled *Poona Masala* for which he had signed on the top stars, lyricists and musicians of the day. But Kranti could not go through with it and he abandoned the project midway.

◆

Far removed from the Hinglish of Bhagat's books, and the language one heard in colleges and on the streets, the seventeenth-century baroque style lived on at the 300-year-old St Thomas Cathedral Church at Horniman Circle. Here a plaque installed by the East India Company in 1784 extolled the courage of one gentleman, Lieutenant Colonel John Campbell, who 'Defended Mangalore During a Siege of Eight Months, Against the United Arms of Mysore and France, And After extorting from the Inexorable Sultaun An involuntary Eulogy, With Honourable Terms for his Small but Brave Garrison, Sunk at the age of Thirty Three, Under the Hardships Experienced, In the Discharge of his Duty to His King and Country'.

While English from the era of Samuel Johnson and Lord Byron still survived, unseen and unread, in the quiet corners of Mumbai, the language had morphed along with the changing metropolis. This evolving language has been significant to Indian cinema from its inception.

In the early years, every movie had a working title in English. The first films, even the silent movies—such as *Light of Asia* (1925) and *A Throw of Dice* (1929) starring Himanshu Rai—had subtitles in English. In the earliest film posters, too,

I noticed how the name of every movie title was painted in Roman letters. In 1936, *Miya Bibi* was released and its English title was *Always Tell Your Wife*. *Amar Bhoopali* (1952), set in the waning days of Maratha Confederacy in the early nineteenth century, was a true story about a simple cowherd who had an innate gift of poetry; its English title was *The Immortal Song*. Hand-painted posters unique to Indian cinema often displayed the titles in three languages—English, Hindi and Urdu.

After World War II, the 'masala' cinema—a mixed-genre film that combined song, dance, and romance—was spawned by Bombay's cosmopolitan character and its hodgepodge of language and culture in a city flush with the promise of capital. Its genesis was a debate at an Indian Cinematograph Enquiry Committee formed by the British government in 1927. They were in a quandary. More and more women left the confines of their homes to throng cinema halls. The increase in crimes and moral depravities of men and women in India were ascribed to the 'so-called educative value of these cinema shows'[90] and the abominable love scenes that led young people astray. Worried that American movies would render their women promiscuous,[91] the committee of three Britons and three Indians opted for Indian cinema with an Indian ethos crafted for an Indian audience. In time the Bombay film industry became a leader and a brand. But what really began to have cachet in this city, India's Tinseltown, was a duality of the regional bhasha and English. It became an asset that commanded respect—from both moviemakers and from the audience.

As the aspirational classes sought to move into the cities and acquire the English language, perspectives shifted. If there were no English in cinema, it was not a realistic portrayal of Indian life and hence unattractive to the aspirational class. For stories to be authentic, English had to find its way into a movie title, a song and the dialogue. On the other hand, offering pure English fare excluded the aspirational class for whom a regional bhasha suffused with English helped to improve one's English. Too much of English tossed a film into the bucket of elitist art cinema: *In Which Annie Gives It Those Ones* (1989), *English, August* (1994), *Hyderabad Blues* (1998), *The Last Lear* (2007), and *Finding Fanny* (2014) remain India's famous underground productions in English. They would remain examples of how while English was the language of the head, Hindi, or, better yet, Hinglish, would remain the language of the heart.

'The English bit has always impressed Kapoor,' wrote one of India's first gossip columnists, Devyani Chaubal, recalling the legendary filmmaker Raj Kapoor's fascination with women like actress Zeenat Aman who had attended convent schools. The columnist discussed Kapoor's preferences, quoting him. 'The other day while watching an old RK film, he told Zeenat: "Don't think you are the only convent-educated girl. Thirty years ago, I had a leading lady who wore jeans, spoke English and used French perfume." In fact, all his leading ladies— Nargis, Padmini, Vyjayanthi, Simi, Dimple and Zeenat—speak English and have impeccable manners.'[92]

This correlation of English to social status is the filter through which people were still assessed in India's film industry even though, more and more now, especially as presented in Chetan Bhagat's many novels, a country bumpkin could end up dating a city girl who spoke English. They could fall in love, too, as we got to see in the movie *Sultan* (2016), where a villager is smitten with a city girl. To woo her he admits to her that he's an 'anpadh' (uneducated). While her eyes speak English, his eyes are illiterate, he says. No matter her feelings, she has stolen his heart and he knows that in the larger scheme of things his English matters little. After all, while he likes her face, she certainly likes his 'bass'—and here he pats his own behind as he sings lyrics in Hinglish that celebrate his infatuation with her.

This mishmash of English and colloquial Hindi remains the currency of Bollywood movies. A movie's first screenplay is often written in English and then translated into Hindi by a dialogue writer. The entire language of communication on most sets continues to be English. Today, many actors cannot read Devanagari and are hence given their Hindi dialogue in the Roman script. Aspiring and established Bollywood actors are well aware that fluency in English has a bearing on their marketability. Success often eludes those who cannot speak English fluently or happen to speak the language with a mother tongue accent. For Kangana Ranaut, a talented female actor, English was the marker by which she was judged, not by her acting prowess, and she maintained that the world of English was meant to create an inferiority complex for those who had not walked through its portals.

A certain double standard was germane to Bollywood. Mumbai's Hinglish movie titles were often hard to stomach yet apparently easy to digest for the movie-loving public: *Love Aaj Kal* (2009), *Jab We Met* (2007), *Go Goa Gone* (2013) and *Delhi Belly* (2011). Movie titles sometimes showed up with intentional gaffes in grammar and spelling. *Horn 'Ok' Pleassss* (2009) would never have been okay, yet the title passed muster. In a flagrant misspelling of the word 'stories', the title of *I Hate Luv Storys* (2010), a romantic comedy produced by Karan Johar and Ronnie Screwvala, hinted at the hypocrisy of Bollywood's movers and shakers. The dapper Karan Johar, Bollywood's favourite filmmaker and television personality, was known to have poked fun at some actors for their halting English, yet he couldn't see anything wrong with introducing an error in the English title of his production because he belonged to that exclusive English-speaking club in which English slip-ups were permissible just because they emerged from the club. It reminded me of an observation at a writer's workshop that 'it was perfectly acceptable to break the rules of good writing—*after* one had mastered writing'.

In Bollywood, too, then, English had become a hydra, hard to embrace and hard to vanquish. It was all complicated, as Kranti Kanade had said to me one too many times. English held its sway even with incorrect spelling and incorrect grammar. India's hypocrisy over English and its equivocations on how it viewed the haves and the have-nots, were contained, represented and showcased in Bollywood every day.

◆

Kranti was frustrated with his countrymen over their embrace of Western ways without introspection over the ideals that were markers of Indian civilization. He was bothered by the notion of exclusivity too. He couldn't understand why his neighbours did not want to open up the park next door to the public. It was a beautiful park, he said, something that would be of value for ordinary citizens to exercise in; but his neighbours in the gated community wanted to keep it off limits. Every night after midnight, a gate cordoned off the homes in his society from the rest of the world.

'So how do we create, at a very deep level, a divide-less society where we treat each other equally with love and respect? How? That is the real question. Eshwar bhi unke nahi, baori bhi nahi unki.' Kranti wondered why the poorest of the poor in some parts of India didn't have access to God or to the water in the well. Decades after India's independence, there were villages in India today where Dalits did not have the freedom of access to all parts of their village. Fortunately, cities had largely broken that divide. Kranti praised the man who once upbraided Mahatma Gandhi. 'That's what Ambedkar had said that time to his untouchable class that "you leave the villages and go to cities where your identities will be merged".' Listening to Kranti wax eloquent that day, I understood why he could never have painted with Bollywood's brush.

In his movies, I found a poignant extension to his inner turmoil and a depth of feeling and experience that I had rarely seen. In *Gandhi of the Month*, one of his characters, surgeon-activist Sailesh, comments on the reverence towards English in India: 'We still revel in those cheap copies of condensed Shakespeare,' Sailesh says, wondering why the schoolboys at Wellington School must recite an English prayer instead of an Indian one. Pat comes the American headmaster's response: 'Because English is also their mother tongue!'

I felt that Sailesh's anguish was, in fact, Kranti's soliloquy over India's predicament: 'We're the porters of the world, the customer care donkeys. Today our boys know Bruce Springsteen but they don't know Kishori Amonkar. We queue up in front of British and US embassies chasing false dreams. We judge ourselves through their eyes. This must be stopped. We must stop it now or we'll perish.'

It was clear to me. Kranti's art had to merge with his heart. To live in harmony with his environment was consequently an important personal goal for him. As soon as I moved into the tidy but spare room and bathroom in his Airbnb, I noticed how loose wires poked out of the wall way above my head where once the air conditioner had been fitted. When he found out that 16,000 people in a nearby village didn't have access to electricity, Kranti decided he could live without air conditioning in his home even though the temperatures soared in the summer. He ripped out all the units in his home.

Now, all day, a light breeze billowed about through the long open doors and windows of his home, the water in the koi pond rippling every few seconds as a tanpura at a concert. At the edge of the pond, a pensive Buddha lay his head on his thigh, pondering the stillness of the water through which he—and the rest of us—could see the night blooming white water lilies and the pebbles beneath.

SIX

BANGALORED!

Shouting into the phone, Nograj accused one Mr Panduranga of being a half-baked fifth-grade English teacher. He said he had been receiving 'complaintuu after complaintuu' that Panduranga was 'beating the childrens and not giving a proper knowledge'.

Incensed at this charge against his work ethic, the teacher responded that there was absolutely 'no need to kindly test my English'. Nograj continued to heckle the teacher. That made Panduranga even angrier. Now it was his turn to yell into the phone. 'You are saying my English wrong? What is your own English?'

My sympathies lay with the teacher. Nograj (which is how the name Nagraj is often pronounced in a Kannada accent) spoke English using grammar rules that fit his mother tongue, Kannada, a language native to his home town of Bangalore.

I noticed how on any such calls that Nograj initiated, he, as well the person he called, lashed out with a stream of invective until the call ended with the recipient disconnecting the call or with Nograj shedding his accent and ending the prank. Nograj then emerged as the suave radio jockey Danish Sait, whose talents included fluency in five or more Indian languages and the ability to wield a rainbow of Englishes besides American, British, Australian and Caribbean.

When Danish was not the crude Nograj, he might be Chacko, Manjunath, Asghar or Salim, each representing a stereotype with its own baggage of biases based on education, religion and upbringing. In his six characters I sensed an empathy that I recognized in the characters created by the late R. K. Narayan. Danish's short-lived sketches of India's Everyman were as incisive as they were funny.

Whenever he was in character as Nograj, however, this thirty-year-old born into a progressive Muslim family was the insufferable, self-righteous politician who, on any given call, liked to enumerate a rash of accusations with the use of adverbs such as 'firstly'. Deriving his own rules of grammar for the English he spoke, Nograj used the word 'twosly' while making his second proclamation in a list. Emphatic about his many theories Nograj always finished his tirade with the following question: 'Can you able to understand?'

The morning I met Danish Sait in his home, he welcomed me into his sunny yellow living room where an Usha sewing machine sat on display by the television. He had just co-written a film script with Saad Khan titled *Humble Politician Nograj*, where the word 'humble' was rather contradictory in relation to the word 'politician'. In it, Danish would play Nograj, his most popular radio character. (The film released in 2018.) He had no qualms about playing the stereotypical corrupt politician even though his maternal grandfather, Azeez Sait, had been a renowned politician in the Congress Party. Danish created and polished his characters by watching how regular people interacted during the phone pranks that he aired on Fever 104 FM where he was a radio jockey.

Out of a dozen radio stations in Bangalore, Fever 104 FM is primarily an English station with radio jockeys like Danish juggling a potpourri of languages on the air. Despite the mesmeric effect of television, broadcast radio has a 99 per cent reach and rural India still relies on it.[93] There are about 180 community radio stations across India that broadcast in languages that would never find any airtime on television because of the minuscule population that speaks those languages.[94] Besides, a radio is also much more affordable—at less than ₹50 apiece—and during my travel on India's roads, I realized how effective this hundred-year-old gadget still is in reinforcing not just the mother tongue but also the English language.

Until the eighties, the Queen's English had been the standard for both English radio and television, with stalwarts like Melville de Mellow setting the highest standards in both reportage and the use of the English language. For his work from war zones to his coverage of political upheavals, De Mellow was an institution unto himself. During the Indo–Pakistan war of 1971, de Mellow visited several battlefronts with his microphone, recording the memories of military officers who were in combat—'on the ground, in the air, and on the high seas'.[95]

> They stood fast, fighting and bleeding, and then inch by inch, foot by foot and yard by yard they began to fall back, but it was never a rout. Yard by bloody yard, they fought it out. This was the Chhamb inferno with its lobbing grenades—heroic abandon—mud—blood and the spray of automatic fire.[96]

I know that my father and my grandfather found his impromptu reports as moving as reading printed prose.

In the early seventies, I became an avid follower of another radio maven, Ameen Sayani—best known for *Binaca Geetmala* and the *Bournvita Quiz Contest*—and I recall the impression his voice and his diction made on me from our Marconi radio. Radio still has a big place in my life; public radio has a coveted place in journalism in the United States and I listen to the radio every day. Radio has an immediacy and a real, ear-to-the-ground feel and has a way of weaving its way around my life and my schedule. Some of my favourite anchors on the radio are like old friends. The constancy of their voices is reassuring and calming. I know that Bangalore's radio stations had those too and among those recognized voices were those of Darius Sunawala and Danish Sait whose English had none of the Etonian polish of de Mellow; instead it was a pleasant Indian by-product of English-medium education—often a colourless, odourless pan-Indian accent nurtured inside convent schools run by Malayali nuns whose English had many cadences of Malayalam.

This is common in most parts of India; the English spoken in and around Mumbai is stained by Marathi; the English in Tamil Nadu resembles Tamil. But the accent that most people aspired to was often to be found only at elite boarding schools such as St Xavier's Collegiate School of Kolkata, the Doon School and Welham Girls' School of Dehradun and the Lawrence School at Lovedale. As the teaching staff at these schools—once made up of Englishmen and Eurasians—died, retired or moved to other parts of the world, the language of the colonial master slowly died out. These days, we rarely hear this 'proper', rather antiquated accent. Some of the only men and women still to be found in India speaking that language are renowned journalists, industrialists and statesmen—Tavleen Singh, Tarun Tahiliani, Swapan Dasgupta, Suhel Seth and Shashi Tharoor, to name a few—whose names were often fixtures on the rosters of literature festivals.

In contrast, the Indianized upper-crust English that Danish spoke dropped no clues about his place of nativity or background. Yet what fascinated me was how Danish drew his strength precisely from those giveaways of speech and demeanour. He told me how he people-watched during his off-school hours in his mother's department store, Value Mart, when he was a child. He walked through the aisles of the store where all his stage avatars were born—between stacks of Pringles, Whisper sanitary napkins, Eveready batteries, Nilgiris bread and Cadbury's bars. There he discovered his passion for strange accents and mannerisms—the shrug of the Frenchman, the swagger of the Punjabi, the scepticism of the Tamilian and the nasal twang of the Malayali. As soon as a customer left the store, Danish would begin riffing, recorder in hand, appropriating the voices from the pageant of people that had floated past him.

During our meeting he entertained me with the typical local dialect. 'Table has become tableuuu. Book is not pustaka but bookuuu,' he said, laughing, pointing out how Kannada had influenced the English heard across the city. He told me what an autorickshaw driver might say when asked for directions: 'Where you want to go, saar?' Danish then conveyed how the driver's directions might begin in English: 'Go straightuuu, take rightuuuu...' and so on and so forth in an English suffixed by the inflexions of Kannada. The same autorickshaw driver might demand 'won and off' ('one and a half') or 'dubbul' fare if he had to go far out of his comfort zone. Danish said it took a certain chutzpah on the part of the non-English speaker to attempt to speak in English. But that's how we were as a people. 'Our country is about finding solutions. Our roads are so terrible. But the people deal with it,' Danish said, referring to India's make-do attitude. 'There was always a way around every problem. I'm not going to fix it but I'll go around it and move ahead.' Danish had honed in on what I too had observed about the country of my birth especially now that it had leapfrogged into the world of high-tech. The globalization of English simply did not mean that everyone would speak or use English in daily life. Some of the Uber drivers did not speak English. Yet they could use the app to ferry customers around and actually eke out a living. Speech recognition software had made rapid strides and it wasn't hard to imagine a day when a command in one language would result in a response and an action in another. Graddol's belief was not altogether far-fetched, that in the years ahead, speech recognition systems may altogether eliminate the need for English.[97]

I saw how Danish's ear for accents and his empathy had infused his work with gentle humour. Danish imbued all his work—radio shows, emceeing, product sponsorship and acting—with the richness of his interactions with people. With practice, his avatars became virtual people whose voices would be played on SoundCloud over 32 million times. He told me how his mother, Yasmin, a gifted mimic herself, gave him pointers about accents and speech patterns. His gift for improv was a perfect blend of both his parents' talents: 'I had my mother's tenacity and my father's adventurous spirit.'

◆

In a story on technology, *India Today* magazine once called Professor N. Balakrishnan (better known as Balki) one of the top fifty people in India driving the country's technological destiny.[98] Balki had built the supercomputer centre at Bangalore's Indian Institute of Science (IISC), one of India's ace research institutions established in 1909. He had retired from IISC but was busier than ever since he was on the board of many companies.

Balki spoke English the way my husband did—like all those whose education was not at a convent school but at a school where concepts were taught in the mother tongue. Mostly, their grammar was excellent because the English language had been taught as a subject at school; their pronunciation of words and their usage of prepositions could vary, however, depending on their teachers, their environment at home and their circle of friends. Balki had a professorial manner of interjecting into my observations. 'Correct!' he exclaimed often, holding his pointer finger aloft in the air, especially when I grasped the point he was making. When I listened keenly enough, his Tamil leaked from the edge of his sentences in the subtlest of ways. I heard it when he uttered words like 'almost' and 'already'. He pronounced 'al' as in 'ul' in 'ultimate'. There was also the way he said the word 'digital', the second 'i' of the word always inaudible.

Years of teaching, travelling and interaction with people from different parts of the world had given his English a different patina. After over four decades in Bangalore, the last twenty of which were spent at the helm of India's technological overhaul, Balki believed, especially now, that what gave people like him the edge was the exposure to the English language at the right time.

He was a product of the era that prized the scientific temperament. Jawaharlal Nehru had laid out a vision about scientific advancement for India. Science was a 'philosophical and literary pursuit' for him. In a speech in 1948 he declared that 'Nobody talks or ought to talk about English science, French science, American science, Chinese science. Science is something bigger than countries. There ought to be no such thing as Indian science.' He contested the Western monopoly on science and wished to 'ground modern science in India's cultural traditions and contribution to world civilization'.[99] He wished for science to address India's problems such as ill health and poverty. A little before Nehru yet another man moulded the scientific shape of the princely state of Mysore, of which Bangalore was a part. M. Visvesvaraya, an engineer with vision, had built dams and roads and he brought his experience to building a section of Bangalore. Thus the city of

Bangalore itself with its many engineering colleges, research labs and electronics industries, was a poster child for both Nehruvian aspiration and Visvesvaraya's drive. Well before Balki was born, the princely state of Mysore had established itself as a place with a progressive and of scientific spirit even in Nobel circles. In 1979, Balki went on to get his doctorate degree from IISC.

Balki and a legion of scientists would agree that India's edge in science and technology stemmed from the colonial experience. Several generations of middle- and upper-class Indians were educated by British systems and their aspirations helped subsequent generations pursue advanced studies. Their exposure to the English language helped them compete on the world stage. Thus, both Bangalore and, subsequently, all of India, too, were in the right place at the right time when the information technology industry around the world needed trained software engineers. India's labour force was perfectly positioned. Nehru could never have imagined that the scientific progress he envisioned would bear out in several different ways for India at an opportune moment.

Balki had witnessed four decades of radical change. The last two, in particular, had been frenetic. In 1991, with the economic liberalization of India, Bangalore grew at a feverish clip. The needs of the IT industry began to decimate the city's greenery. Tower cranes blotted the sky. Education may have eluded India's poor, yet, scientists like Balki believed that technology would bridge the gap between the poor and the elite. He insisted on using the term 'digital democracy'—not digital 'divide'—with respect to India.

I saw the truth of Balki's phrasing play out by the ancient Shiva temple of Srikalahasti in Andhra Pradesh, the day I visited a young painter skilled in the laborious art of kalamkari fabric painting. He painted designs in his humble home and carted his cloth to a water pump in the afternoon and dried the fabric on the mud. For much of the time that I spent watching him, he didn't take his eyes off his cell phone; he was busy responding to questions and taking orders on WhatsApp. Technology had provided this artist with a solution to be in touch with top-notch designers around India. The common man, who may never have imagined getting a phone line in his residence, could now buy a rudimentary cell phone and be connected to the world in an instant and run his business through his phone.

For the first time, in India, money, status and fancy English were not essential for access to a public utility. Technology had demolished old barriers and ushered in an era of fairness. Every year, over a hundred million Internet users added themselves to the global market and by 2020 there would be an estimated one billion unique mobile subscribers in India alone.[100] Like linguist Crystal, Professor Balki sensed the power of such a market and the relevance of high technology in helping people realize their ambition. Though technology could render the English language irrelevant in the future, there was no question in Balki's mind that India was launched onto the world stage owing to its familiarity with the English language. I gathered that Balki was not unlike the poet Mohan, the character in R. K. Narayan's *The Bachelor of Arts*. Both men could read and write in Tamil and English, yet they both believed that English was 'the language of the world'.

Curiously enough, in recent times, as he worked on projects on machine learning, Balki had begun confronting the complexity of the English language and the greater predictability of Indian languages and their phonetic nature which lent themselves nicely to analysis by software systems. Balki told me how Indian languages were not only phonetic, they were often pronounced exactly the way they were written, an attribute not often seen in English.

'Our Indian languages are word-order-free languages,' he said. We did not have worry about which part of the sentence went first. Balki showed me how that would never fly in English. Indians also brought their cultural sensibilities to their comprehension of Indian words, he said, and proceeded to give me an example. For instance, since the Tamil alphabet used the same letter for 'p' and 'b' and 'd' and 't', the pronunciation of certain Tamil and English words sometimes reflected this. Now Balki looked up at me, his eyes shining. 'But would any man from Chennai ever call Bank of Baroda Pank of Parota?' We burst out laughing.

◆

The morning I visited Danish in his apartment, I discovered that Fraser Town had been part of the Bangalore Cantonment and that the locality was still referred to as the cantonment area. Once a military garrison under the British Raj, the word cantonment originated in the French 'cantonnement', from the French verb 'cantonner', which means 'to confine'. The cantonment included a cluster of suburbs: Benson Town, Cleveland Town, Cox Town, Cooke Town, Austin Town, Murphy Town, Richards Town, Langford Town and Richmond Town, as well as the bazaar around the old Russell Market and the parade area by M. G. Road and Brigade Road. The first industrial enterprise in the cantonment began in 1889: Bangalore Breweries began producing beer so that British soldiers in the barracks would not saunter over to the native quarters of the old city seeking cheap liquor.

Long before the word 'bangalore' was allowed in a game of Scrabble—not as a proper noun but as a word alluding to the Bangalore torpedo, an explosive built in Bangalore and first used in World War I—the city had adopted English names such as St Marks Road, Lavelle Road, Cubbon Park, Infantry Road, Artillery Road, Brigade Road, Cavalry Road and Parade Grounds.

Bangalore's cool climate made it attractive for the British who suffered in the extreme heat of the plains of India. It became a hub for the British and Anglo-Indians working in the military. In time English became the lingua franca among the educated classes of the city. After Independence, the city's salubrious weather and its many parks and gardens attracted retirees from around the country. While I'd been growing up in Chennai I thought of Bangalore as an unhurried, yet cosmopolitan, city. One afternoon at the State Central Library in Cubbon Park, I sensed its obsession with books and literature. A roomful of people sat in pin-drop silence; the only sound was the rustle of newspapers. A head or two went up to follow me all the way as I crossed the room, the way people did when they perceived an interloper in their midst.

A customer at Blossom Book House on Church Street told me that the reason the city began to have some of the nicest independent bookstores was because the city boasted inveterate consumers of the printed word, both in English and in the languages. 'I don't know why. I suppose it's because Bangalore has always been a leafy, laid-back city,' she said, disappearing into the aisle for fiction, where I also found all the non-fiction by Atul Gawande.

On the ground floor at Blossom, I found used books from the 1700s that had probably been jettisoned in the estate sales of erstwhile bungalows of old Bangalore. This was the town that held a wake for Premier Bookshop, a book lover's haunt since 1973. Writers and students mourned its passing when it pulled down its shutters in 2009 selling some of its books for a hundred rupees each. The owner, T. S. Shanbhag, donated the remaining stock to libraries in the city and everything was sold or recycled, including the 'Premier Bookshop' sign.

This was not different from the death of many bookstores in the San Francisco Bay Area, thanks to the growth of online booksellers. Amazon, in particular, was the juggernaut that had annihilated many small independent stores under its wheels. In Bangalore, though, Amazon had even changed a city's contours and, some might argue, its mindset.

At Brigade Gateway in the old quarter of Malleswaram, two dozen apartment structures hugged an enclave called World Trade Centre where Amazon filled most of the floors. In the nineties, Bangalore sloughed off its leisurely stride and remodeled itself as India's Silicon Valley. High-tech employees rented or owned swanky apartments at Brigade Gateway with magnificent views of the city. A sky bridge connected to Orion Mall from where another sky bridge linked to Sheraton Hotel, where a room could cost anywhere between ₹10,000 and 70,000 a night. Thousands of cars were parked below Brigade Gateway—among them, from what I could tell, were Maseratis, BMWs, Porsches and at least one Rolls-Royce.

In stark contrast to the city's street-side metal jewellery vendors on Commercial Street were these bright, young engineers from Amazon peddling their sharpest edge, English. On any morning at the massive enclave of Brigade Gateway, the words that buzzed all around me were those that high technology had pumped into the English lexicon—'google', 'access', 'bug', 'debug', 'impact', 'tweet', 'ping', 'update', 'tag', 'bio break', 'ping', 'bandwidth', 'xerox', 'morph' and 'cache', among a slew of others—and these too now flowed alongside the rapid called Indian English.

A friend who lived in an apartment at Brigade Gateway coached engineers on placement to the United States. She fretted over English usage and cultural practices. In her two-day training program, she taught consultants to use deodorant, eat olives while drinking beer (it helped control belching!);

explained how coconut oil was a 'nono', even though it had recently become quite the favourite in skincare and haircare in the West; and warned them to avoid Lifebuoy soap as it smelt rather unpleasant.

She also advised them about slipshod communication. 'What is the thing that travels the fastest after light?' she asked her trainees. (The answer was 'Email'.) An email that used the word 'revert' was abhorrent, she warned. The word was a landmine for those from India. It meant 'to put something back into its old state' and had nothing to do with replying to someone, she explained. She also taught her young trainees to say 'v' with the teeth against the lip as in 'validate', not 'walidate'. Behind the engineers and IT consultants, a phalanx of etiquette coaches tidied up language and comportment and nowhere were these more in demand than in Bangalore, the back office of the world, a clubbing and pubbing paradise that never went to sleep. In the midst of these shiny glass buildings, who could ever imagine that aeons ago, Bangalore's humble beginnings had something to do with boiled beans?

According to legend, in the eleventh century, King Veera Ballala went out hunting and lost his way in the woods. When he arrived, exhausted, at a lonely hut at the end of his wanderings, an old woman saved his life by giving him a handful of boiled beans. Grateful, the king named the place 'Bendakalooru', the place of boiled beans.[101] This little settlement would ultimately grow into the place called Bangalore, where the British set up one of their bases.

In 2005, the city's fabled writer, the late U. R. Ananthamurthy, spearheaded a proposal to reinstate the city's original name. He made a case for why the official name of a city must reflect the language spoken there. Japan was 'Nippon' in Japanese. London was known by its English name and was not the French/Spanish/Portuguese 'Londres'. In his pitch,

the writer argued that the sound 'u' (or 'oo') was an enabling
sound in Kannada, and that the pronunciation of 'Bengaluru'
was merely an organic extension of the city's language.[102]

◆

I discovered the following record of the kingdom of
Mysore—in an old tome called *Mysore: A Gazetteer Compiled
for Government* by Benjamin Lewis Rice in 1897—under the
well-lit dome of State Central Library. Around me, Kannada
literature, Sanskrit literature, and reference books of the last
several hundred years graced the shelves that stretched along
the circular wall of the room. I pored over the gazetteer,
wonderstruck by the details about the land around Bangalore
and its rich agriculture.

> Not only does she abound in the picturesque features
> of lofty mountains and primeval forests, of noble rivers
> and mighty cataracts, but—to mention only a few of the
> products specially pertaining to her—she yields by far
> the most gold of any country in India, and her treasure
> in the past, carried off to the north by Musalman
> invaders, may have found its way to Central Asia among
> the spoils of Tartar hordes; she is the peculiar home
> of the sandal and also of teak, a special haunt of the
> elephant, rears a famous and superior breed of horned
> cattle, supplies as the staple food of her people the
> nutrient grain of rági, was the cradle in India and is still
> the chief garden for coffee cultivation.[103]

There were few signs of this lushness now amid the traffic-
infested cacophony of Bangalore life. But there was
that bedevilling swath of silk at Mysore Saree Udyog on
Commercial Street; the parade of handmade wood and cane
furniture in the stores along Kamaraj Avenue; the fragrance

of mounds of lime outside Russell Market in Shivaji Nagar, and a slew of other sights where the words of the Mysore gazetteer eulogizing the luxuriance of the old Mysore state rang true. I felt it in the girth of the old kapok tree at Lalbagh Botanical Garden which was an oasis of peace. It was impossible to not feel the legacy of this state in the confluence of roads right by the ninety-year-old Russell Market, where M. F. Norrona Street met Meenakshi Kovil Street, a thoroughfare named after the Hindu temple. As I walked up to the door of St Mary's Basilica, the noonday prayer from the mosque by the beef market floated in towards the church and the temple.

Built in 1927 in an Indo-Saracenic style with minarets and domes, Russell Market is one of the oldest markets of the city. After a fire gutted part of the market in 2012 the traders organized themselves to prevent the market from being razed to the ground to make way for a mall. The sign outside the market read: 'WEL COME. RUSSELL MARKET'. Below that it said: 'Perishables Around The World Avaliable Here.'

Inside the market, I was struck, however, by the signs that advertised 'Indian and English' vegetables. When the British introduced cauliflower, cabbage, carrot and radish into India, these were referred to as 'English' vegetables, These vegetables were never used by orthodox Hindus during religious festivals or ritual offerings for ancestors. On my visit of the Lawrence School at Lovedale, I was mesmerized by the hills and dales surrounding Ooty where carrot and cabbage grew in beds between low-lying terraces of tea. I discovered, however, that there was nothing 'English' about carrots because they had existed in Asia, in the purple form, for centuries even though the carotene version that was ubiquitous today in most parts of the world was likely introduced from Europe, which is probably why the carrot got classified as an 'English' vegetable in the mind of Indians.

My amble through Russell market that day was revelatory. The challenges of Indian English were not unlike the identity crises of the produce sold in the market. It was no longer clear what an English or an Indian vegetable was. The cauliflower may once have been an English vegetable. Yet the ubiquitous gobi manchurian, fried cauliflower sautéed and spiced in a Chinese style, was one of India's own culinary delights. While I couldn't fault a shopkeeper inside the market for his lack of clarity on Indian and English vegetables, I was, however, annoyed that the sign above his store said 'Russul Market'. It dawned on me, that a debate on the phonetic spelling of English names—and the suggestion for a new, overhauled spelling for all the English names in his city of Bengaluru— would have found a most animated proponent in the humble politician called Nograj. The irony of the metaphor was not lost on me. Just as vendors in Bangalore's Russell Market couldn't tell apart the Indian vegetables from the English ones, the speakers of Indian English couldn't often classify the words they uttered. The bhasha and English had traded so many words and expressions that most speakers did not notice when they were using an English word while speaking an Indian language or when they were reaching for an Indian word while cobbling together a sentence in English.

I recalled having read a paper in which an English professor had explained that the word 'rate' in the Indian context alluded to something that has a fixed price and is unnegotiable. A vegetable vendor might say, 'Nahin sahib, yehi rate hai.' (Sorry, sir, this is the rate!) I'd always known that in an Indian context, 'rate' equated to 'price' whereas, outside India, 'rate' referred to quantity or frequency.

So many English words had infiltrated Indian languages that some of us did not even have terms in our vernacular for these concepts. I stepped out of Russell Market that day thinking that India's proclivity to hybridize and bastardize—and harmonize—was certainly in evidence within its four walls. The coexistence of Indian and English produce right by the beef and chicken market, the lentil granaries, the fruit vendors, and the rose and jasmine garland merchants bore testimony to decades of India's pluralism and tolerance.

◆

In the plethora of Danish's acts, I began to see the morphing of the English language. I suppose the growing irrelevance of 'proper' English language instruction in India began at the exact moment that India's advantage with English thrust it onto the global stage.

As Gurcharan Das observed in *India Unbound*, a young man in Tamil Nadu whom he met told him he didn't see the need to learn English any more. In the new India shaped by technology, all he needed was the knowledge of 400 English words in order to pass the TOEFL exam. He had dreams of big riches and, as Das observed in *India Grows at Midnight*, wanted to be the next 'Bill Gay'. I saw evidence of that all around me in the way Vinayagam, Ganga, the Uber drivers, and the kalamkari artist navigated the world with a smattering of English.

While Danish poked fun at those who couldn't speak the English language, I saw his exaggerated farces as projections of the poor people's frustrations at the government. His empathy came through in the way he presented Nograj's plight after demonetization in December 2016. Nograj wept copiously that all of the 500- and 1,000-rupee notes he had stashed under the bed, in his safe and in his wife's bra—had become extinct overnight.[104] Danish's world view was not unlike that of Nograj, sometimes. A selfish, bigoted megalomaniac of a politician could teach us a thing or two about our own insecurities.

Danish told me that he made it a point to talk to everyone and find out more about them. 'Find out something about where the person interacting with was born. Find out the nativity. Try to find a way to reach out in some way,' he said. I tended to do that with all those who drove me up and down the city. Their stories told me so much about a changing India. The Uber driver who drove me to the outskirts of the city to watch Danish's live show was a mechanical engineer by day. He worked at a multinational from 9 a.m. to 5 p.m. and drove an Uber at night to make more money. We'd been on the road since 5.55 p.m. and a distance of 33 kilometres which should have taken us all of twenty minutes in any other country had already taken us one hour and forty minutes. The young man spoke perfect English.

On this long drive, the radio kept me riveted. While Arijit Singh kept me swaying to his melody 'Tu meri bahon mein duniya bhula de', the advertisements entertained me and piqued my curiosity about how English beat through India's physical arteries in choked cities. 'It is not fair,' said a male voice on the radio in English (and Hindi). 'This is not fair. This is just not fair. Right when I was booking my Coldplay passes, mera data khatam hogaya. Who'll give me the passes now?' A female voice chimed in reassuring him that he'll get them from Radio Mirchi 95 FM as long as he spread the hashtag '#mirchiwalikushi' on Twitter. She asked him to help spread the word about the Global Citizen Festival India which would feature entertainers such as Shah Rukh Khan, A. R. Rahman, Jay-Z, Aamir Khan, Arijit Singh. 'And more!' she said. 'Only on Radio Mirchi!'

English radio now encompassed other languages, too, and the day I was at his home, Danish demonstrated how a radio jockey in Chennai might approach his lines by slipping in and out of English, Tamil and Hindi. 'Radio 91.9 FM Fever—Idhu Bollywoodin Superstar! The time is now 7 o'clock. Aaj aap ke pas hain mauka to win a fantastic prize. Ippo onga mobile phonea yedunga, oru text message anuppunga. And aaj aapka savaal yeh hain...'

Balki had been right all along, that the word order in Indian languages made it almost effortless to segue between languages. And I saw also why, when I reached BMC layout to watch Danish and friends perform improv, Danish rocked the show because it was the easiest, most natural thing in the world for anyone who had been brought up and raised in a city like Bangalore.

Life here lent itself to unscripted comedy—with its many colourful personalities, unexpected accents, and random situations. Danish's brilliance and dexterity to enter and exit situations in his improv sketches mimicked the daily tamasha of life in India. It reminded me of the day a well-dressed, soft-spoken gentleman jumped into my autorickshaw in the middle of an intersection and began talking to me about this and that and asked the driver to drop him off at yet another busy junction, assuming all along that of course I would pay his share. Unbeknownst to all three of us, the gentleman had converted my vehicle into a share-auto in which I ended up footing the entire bill.

Experiences like these were a part and parcel of Indian life. They made life in India at once exciting and exasperating. They were of course the stuff of rib-tickling comedy. Naturally, I could see why the stand-up comedy scene in India was electric. In particular, I saw why this city of the youthful vibe, Bangalore, was where India launched most of its new products, and why it was also ground zero for a debate on more serious issues—feminism, micro aggressions towards women and the state of Indian marriages—aired by India's brightest female comedians. In this pulsating, 24/7 city of contradictions, Indian English—warts, accents, pretence and all—was growing hands, legs and tentacles. I could actually see David Crystal's prediction come true that India's English could gain currency as one of the most powerful Englishes in the world. After all, history had shown that the language that fired up people was always the language of commercial heft. It had happened to Latin. It had happened to French. At the time of the empire, it had happened to English. And today it was happening with a unique form of English—Indian English. I saw what Danish meant when he said that Indians were now not just confident about English. 'They are confident. Period.'

SEVEN

YOUNG GLOBAL DESI

In May 1991, just as Aditya Narayan was about to be delivered, India's foreign reserves were empty. The country had just loaded onto aircrafts sixty-seven tons of gold as collateral for a loan from the International Monetary Fund. Right about the time the newborn was blessed with a name that invoked the sun god, a ray of light emerged for the country's economic future. Barely eight weeks after Aditya arrived, in July, Dr Manmohan Singh, India's then finance minister, cobbled together a budget that lifted the country out of the doldrums and put India on the path to economic liberalization. India opened its gates to international investment. America charged in. Lay's potato chips, Kellogg's cereal and Pampers diapers invaded India's new Western-style supermarkets. American English flooded into Indian living rooms. Oprah became a soul sister to many Indians.

Like children in most middle- and upper-class families, Aditya and his younger brother, Hemanth, grew up on daily doses of *Tom and Jerry*, *The Road Runner Show*, *Looney Tunes*, *Swat Kats*, *The Real Adventures of Jonny Quest*, *Powerpuff Girls*, *Dexter's Laboratory*, *Tintin* and *Heidi*. Aditya soaked up *That '70s Show*, a sitcom set in Wisconsin in the late seventies. He was also hooked on *Jackie Chan Adventures* that he still sometimes watched, even as a grown man. Aditya claims they were all instrumental in honing his tastes in entertainment as well as his sense of humour. The Internet too began to mould his mind after the millennium.

'But I would credit a British woman for most of my formative English years,' the young man told me. 'Two, actually. Enid Blyton and J. K. Rowling. I think Rowling has incurred some wonderful karma for many aeons—by getting an entire generation of kids reading again—after Enid Blyton.' Aditya believed that the standards set by his mother in his early years shaped his vocabulary. Aditya wrote his first poem, 'An Angel in Disguise', when he was ten years old. It was a sappy, maudlin piece on his mother, Viji, whose cheeks glistened like the sides of an Alphonso mango in May.

> But something had fallen into the youngling's mind behind
> 'How much my mother does love me?'
> Was she the star was she the glimmer?
> Was she hiding it in the mind?

An academic star who graduated with a master's degree in Mathematics, Viji was an English aficionado born into a family of Anglophiles in which debates raged over Shakespeare and Milton. At Kala Vidya Mandir, a school in Chennai with Indian and global sensibilities, Aditya found that his teachers always talked about how all good children got 'centum'. That was hardly abnormal for him. Indian parents believed that academic nirvana was getting full marks—or a 'cent percent', as they called it—in all quantitative subjects: math, physics, chemistry, specifically, because it was possible to earn full grades in them as long as the computations were correct. Aditya grew up knowing what he needed to bring home after every exam and he did well in school in both the sciences and in the humanities. 'My dad always used to say "centum vaanganom" and my teachers also used the phrase often.' Still, his parents were not like many Indian parents who were paranoid about grades.

◆

He spoke excellent English, with cadences of Tamil although his choice of words and expressions made it very clear to anyone that he read a lot, wrote a lot and thought one heck of a lot, maybe much too much for his own good. Some of his early poetry was clunky, clearly the work of a young teen mind trying to understand the relationship between the elements of the universe and figure out his place in a world that had grown more intransigent by the minute. At that fragile time, the poem 'Ode to The Monsoons' expressed the chaos in his mind.

> To all this commotion, nature only smiled and only said:
> 'You all
> know that you must give and take that is
> you gave your tears that
> was accepted as an apology for troubling me,
> and I resolved to that
> and brought you Joy by my tears'

The earth was always a source of wonder to him, his interest in astronomy evident both in his writing and in his choice of physics as his major in college. In a poem he titled 'Fulcrum', he wrote about how

> On earth with clanking machinery
> and a hundred jobs to be followed
> lies its fulcrum.

But on one October morning when he stood, clad in a red cotton kurta, a white cotton dhoti, and flip-flops on his feet, on the sands of the Thiruvanmiyur Beach scanning the skies over the Bay of Bengal for the onset of monsoons, he wrote another sort of poetry that he had taken to more recently.

'When you're in front of the infinite ocean, with the

monsoon wind caressing you gently, your mind just empties into pure nothingness.' Aditya had flagged it for his social media readers: #igers #Chennai #meditative #traditionalwear

◆

On a rainy Republic Day morning in the end of January, Vaishali Raghuvanshi, a doctoral student at South Asian University, introduced me to Prateek Joshi and three other 'batchmates', (Kavya Chandra, Syed Murtaza Mushtaq and Johnny Arokiaraj). All five of them were pursuing degrees in international relations. Each spoke with a different accent, depending on the region he or she hailed from and the school they had attended.

The upscale Ambience Mall in Vasant Kunj was a perfect choice given the pelting rain, but the din inside the mall was hardly ideal for conversation. Our voices rose above the cacophony of patriotic Bollywood beats—'Jai Ho' thumped in the background—to talk about life in India, language, the significance of one's English, elitism and the politics of language. Below us, swathes of fabric—in the shades of the tricolour of India's flag—spanned the height and breadth of the mall. Butterflies in the same colours dangled from the ceiling. The spirit of patriotism hung in the air.

I was interested in knowing how the English language had skewed their lives. As they began telling me the stories of their lives, I was drawn to Prateek's particular experience. In his story, I saw the characteristic Indian pluck of making the most of an opportunity. Hair stuffed into a beanie, Prateek sported a scraggly beard and had the air of a struggling poet, although his calling was quite different. His research interests at the university included Indian foreign policy, Pakistan's domestic politics, and historical and contemporary issues of Gilgit-Baltistan.

One particular line had determined his destiny in elementary school: 'Kya aap mujhse fraandship karoge?' Prateek said he'd used that 'cheap' one-liner with people— Hey, will you make friends with me?—when he entered Delhi Public School (DPS) as a student in third grade.

In contrast to Aditya's more privileged background, Prateek was born at the end of 1991 into a poor Kumaoni family from Uttarakhand in the foothills of the Himalayas. Like most people from the region, his family too had sought to make a livelihood in Delhi. Mid-level government jobs were never well paid. For most of his school years, his family lived in a small house allotted by the government. In third grade, his parents enrolled him in the prestigious English-medium school where the price for a dramatic improvement in his English was daily humiliation.

In eighth grade, Prateek had been in a class with a gang of bullies who used to beat up their classmates. His nimble wit saved him many a time. 'I used to joke like anything to escape the beating.' At DPS, he often shared tables with millionaires' children with whom he desperately wanted a 'fraandship'—the stress was on the syllable as in the word 'frank'. Prateek clarified that it was how many of his ilk pronounced the word 'friendship' before they learned how to navigate the 'cool' scene. In his early years, he was always shocked that his classmates at DPS interacted with their parents in English; Prateek said he spoke to his parents only in Hindi. In time, thanks to his buddies, Prateek adopted Indian English expressions and slang that others used in order to belong. Words like 'mugging', 'fundas', 'black money', 'hep', 'mug-pot', 'cool', 'scene', 'dude' and 'cheap' and many other words began to fire up his vocabulary. While his English was still heavily inflected by his bhasha, he spoke good English, often lapsing into Hindi or Urdu, spouting lyrical phrases in the bhasha while his batchmates at South Asian University listened intently, laughing uncontrollably every few minutes. Prateek's sentences sparkled with his gift for irony and self-deprecation. He was a born storyteller. I admired his candour.

As a teenager Prateek learned how to say 'gross' in the way Americans used it, whereas in the past he would say 'gross' with an 'awe' sound. His classmates would correct him: 'Dude, are you talking about a grocery list?' This led to another round of cackling as Prateek talked although I realized that the first syllable of 'grocery' and 'gross' were supposed to be enunciated the same way—at least in the British and American dictionaries. I gathered that Prateek finally attained the markers of acceptance, ascending into the smart clique, he said, from his 'cheap' Indian manner, after about five to seven years 'of trolling'. For a while, he was in the 'catching up' phase before he got comfortable with the accent. He shed his 'cheap' accent, learning not to say 'cassette' with the stress on first syllable as in 'pattern' but as in 'assess' with an 'eh' sound.

Prateek's mother tongues (both Kumauni and Garhwali) were as good as extinct even though there were over two million speakers. The languages were preserved mostly through signs on the mountain roads of Uttarakhand, Prateek said, half-facetiously. But even high up on those mountain passes where few people went, English had been airdropped in. In 2009, a popular number 'Babli Tero mobile' written in Garhwali—with infusions of English words like mobile, smile, and data—topped the charts. The song's greatest selling power was the English language, of course, because it spelt romance and sex appeal for the young.

◆

The British meaning for 'pass out' is to complete one's initial training in the armed forces. That term is still used in India and Pakistan in reference to graduation from the military academy. A 'passing out parade' is conducted for those trainee officers who have successfully completed their training period and received their 'commissioned officer' rank. The expression is now common in every college of advanced education, too. In the summer of 2011, Aditya passed out with a college degree in Physics from the University of Madras.

By the time Aditya graduated, India's economic growth had skyrocketed. Its GDP had risen to 8 per cent and it had bought back 200 tonnes of gold from the IMF.[105] Like the country, Aditya had undergone a seismic shift himself, the politics of the decade affecting him considerably through high school and college. About the time the United States invaded Iraq, in March 2003, Aditya read a poem in his literature textbook that saw life from the perspective of a soldier. At the time, just as many people in the West, he felt that America was unjustified in its actions. The idea of war affected him deeply. He felt that the pain of war was entirely unnecessary in order to modify lines on a political map or secure an energy rich future for just one country. During those weeks, he poured his feelings into a poem he titled 'For Iraq—May 2003'.

> Fiery hues of a hundred days
> with oil burning to smoke and ash
> As if the burning gases were not enough
> Fury and retaliation though hidden
> Confined to the somber sights,
> Of cadavers unclaimed and persons poisoned
>
> Multiple nations aimlessly fight,
> As soul after soul enters heaven's light

There is no meaning now,
All is lost,
Memories burn into vapours

Aditya annotated his poem for me in a message on Facebook. 'The Iraq poem [is] deliberately short as it is from the view of a wounded soldier who finds recollecting it too painful and choking, hence his entire experience flashes quickly. He then gives up the thinking of the events in the poem, resigning [himself] to the fact that those memories are anyway in the past and there is no point in brooding over it. Hence memories burn into vapours.' I was struck by how in a world which rewarded quantitative achievements, Aditya's mother had managed to raise an empathetic teen who could reflect on happenings thousands of miles away. Aditya wrote most of his poems when he was fifteen years old. He believed that there was a link between science and poetry and told me that even Doctor Octopus (Doc Ock), the mad scientist nemesis to Spider-Man, read poetry to impress his wife.

In our interactions I noticed how often Aditya used the word 'befuddled'. It was a word that suited Aditya who was in the audience at all local literature festivals in Chennai and elsewhere to harass panellists and befuddle them. Aditya was always picked for questions at the end of a session because he put up his hands before the panel ended and before the moderator had uttered the standard warning: 'Please ask only a question. No comments, please.' And Aditya, like Scheherazade of the Arabian Nights, held the panellists and audience in his thrall and went about his chain-linked questions cloaked within one large question (which also Trojan-horsed some comments). That was Aditya's style, full-sized in everything.'

At the Hindu Literature Festival, he asked Kanhaiya Kumar, a leader of the All India Students Federation, a left-wing student organization considered to be close to the Communist Party of India, if his revolution was not the devolution of evolution. To that Kanhaiya said, 'I don't even understand your question.' Aditya swiftly switched to Hindi to explain at which point Kanhaiya Kumar snapped back with a platitude: 'If I see unfairness, I want equality.'

In yet another instance at the Hindu Literature Festival, Aditya asked a question, and referred to his own body as having been a challenge for him. He had been ridiculed and marginalized because he was obese. Aditya conveyed his ideas in a thoughtful, nuanced manner, worrying about the tonality of whatever he said, always putting forth his plurality of beliefs and positions. The net of it was that he never asked a question that didn't make the panellists befuddled. The audience clapped even when they didn't understand him. If orotundity was an art in itself Aditya was its uncontested young king. But behind all the verbosity and rhetoric was an authenticity that no one could miss.

One Friday in July, Aditya participated in a TimesNow discussion on television about who was a better political candidate for his state of Tamil Nadu: actor Rajinikanth or actor Kamal Haasan? He was annoyed about the default position of the state. 'Why celebrities again? Can't we have an independent thinking party with well-read people who can lead this state to a better future? Is it that difficult? I cannot choose between Rajinikanth and Kamal Haasan. But haven't we had enough of films stars in Tamil Nadu? I'm in a conundrum because ever since Chief Minister Jayalalithaa died, she has left an inescapable vacuum in Chennai. We're a little disenchanted with the current disposition of MLAs in Chennai. We're always going behind celebrities just because they're popular. When are we going to make the choice and find people who are intelligent enough to take that position and represent the people?' Aditya paused for a few seconds, repeating himself to emphasize his scepticism. 'There has been a history of cine stars in Tamil Nadu. Is it always going to be like this?'[106]

Of course, at least several times a day, much like the trigger-happy forty-fifth president of the United States, Aditya had something to say on Twitter.* To the controversial television anchor Arnab Goswami, Aditya tweeted: 'Congrats [on] calling out these pseudo-secular goondas who continue to wreck India!' To Prime Minister Narendra Modi he sent a tweet to complain about facilities: 'Many stations have non-working lifts & escalators, leaking roofs, urine stench and paan spit. Is this the Railway Metro line we deserve?'

In a nation that had the largest population of young people on the planet, Aditya's courage was, in some ways, emblematic of his entitlement. Like his peers, he was vociferous, eloquent and confident in English, Hindi and at least one other language—and, in the case of Aditya, both Tamil and Kannada, too, although the young man claimed that his fluency in Kannada was not on par with that in the other languages. Like most other Indian youth, Aditya had that multilingual advantage, whose edge, as linguist Graddol put it, would be his innate advantage in the job market of the next many decades.

Aditya Narayan would fit into any writing discussion in Chennai, Kolkata, Singapore, London, Toronto, Sydney and New York. He would blend in at the New Yorker Literature Festival. There too he would be picked for questions at the end of a panel, much to everyone else's chagrin, because Aditya, had such an uncanny intelligence and goodness about his sharp black eyes and his manicured goatee that he seemed ripe with

---

*He tweets at https://twitter.com/iCRAditya.

an engaging question but never rotten with vitriol. When I first began chatting with him, he remarked that he 'quivered with nostalgia' when he began listing for me the sorts of things he had read during his childhood and adolescence. 'I feel like I'm an old soul,' he wrote. I could not argue with that.

When I met Aditya and his mother I could see that while she was proud of him, she was also worried about the more practical aspects of life. When I commended her on raising a thinking child, she told me that she wanted him to do something concrete with his master's degree in Physics. At the moment 'he was simply farting around the house', she said, planting a kiss on Aditya's cheek. I was reminded of my own worries about my son and my daughter. An old Tamil saying slipped into my head—'Oorukku karumbu veetukku vembu'—which means simply that what is considered sugar cane for a village can be bitter as neem for the occupants of a home.

◆

India is poised to grow dramatically to become one of the largest economies by 2050.[107] I sensed the energy and optimism of its young people whenever I attended literature festivals in India. These millennials were moulded by the pressing global issues of the day—political instability, a constant threat of terrorism, feminist cries against patriarchy, the rise of nationalism, and the looming reality of climate change. Perhaps because of that and their sense of urgency they were often intrepid enough to challenge panellists.

Young men like Aditya asked questions that I'd never thought to ask when I was their age. They were opinionated and engaged in the political process. Perhaps because they came of age in a global world and had access to many streams of thought, they also questioned conventional modes of behaviour. Vaishali told me that as part of her curriculum in college, she had travelled to all the nations that made up Southeast Asia. She found the people of Pakistan extremely hospitable and compassionate and she had faced no barriers while reaching out to people who had traditionally been viewed as the enemy. She was frustrated. Why was it that countries couldn't solve their problems with each other when individuals from warring nations could break bread with each other?

The evening of that meeting with Delhi's young people, I had dinner at the home of my host. The gentleman to whom I aired Vaishali's vexations had been in the Indian Army for years. He disagreed with her views and said that while it was easy for civilians to offer armchair diplomacy, on the ground, it was an entirely matter. He warned me to not swallow all that bunkum. Who was I to argue with a man who had fought for my country on the ground? Still, I felt that Vaishali's ideas burned with an audacious hope even though they showed the unnuanced naiveté of youth.

In 2016, following his arrest by the government for alleged sedition, one young student leader took on institutions using hair-raising rhetoric in his Hindi speech at Jawaharlal Nehru University. As I watched Kanhaiya Kumar deliver his fiery speech in Hindi, I was reminded of writer Pavan K. Varma's lament to me the day I met him in his home in the tony suburb of Delhi's Vasant Kunj. Varma decried the pre-eminence of English in a country with its own linguistic and literary traditions and a civilization of many thousand years. 'With such a rich heritage we have reduced ourselves to the lowest common denominator which is English. That pains me.' Varma paused, tapping at the tobacco in his yellow brown pipe. A typewriter sat in the middle of the room that had been packed wall to wall with leather-bound books arranged inside wood-panelled shelves. There was a brooding quality to Varma, one of the most articulate men I'd ever met. With the smoke from his pipe curling around him and rising above his head. it seemed he was blowing off steam on a topic that physically pained him. He was troubled by the way languages had been given short shrift in India.

By lusting after English we had ignored a critical element—what he called the power of original thinking—that had once been India's unique selling proposition. 'If that was not the case, we would not have had a Shankaracharya. Or a Kautilya. We would not have had a Vatsyayana. We've lost that. In the larger globalizing world, we have become happy cogs in somebody else's wheel. And language has a lot to do with it.' Varma saw the irony of his statement even as he spoke to me in English. It was our common link language since I could not speak Hindi and he did not speak Tamil. He had been educated at convent schools and English came effortlessly to him as a result. However, he said he had always made sure to read Hindi and Urdu literature and also write professionally in Hindi. He often lectured in Hindi, and he also translated works from Urdu.

That afternoon, Varma also read a sutra out loud to me. The Brahma Sutras, one of the foundational Sanskrit texts of the Vedanta school of Hindu philosophy, was thought to have been completed between 450 BCE and 200 CE. Each sutra was an aphorism (or a collection of aphorisms) teaching a ritual, some philosophy, or the grammar of a field of knowledge. Varma explained that each sutra was also a demonstration of the clarity of thought and expression of its creator, since each line was compressed until it could be compressed no more. How could one not marvel at the concision of language and expression, he wondered aloud? Entire tomes had been written analysing just one sutra. Varma paused and shook his head, putting the book away back in his organized shelf.

In the annals of writing, it was always said that it was the hardest thing in the world to write a simple, clear sentence. Simplicity didn't translate, however, to simplistic. The importance of concision and simplicity was not lost on me as I too struggled at the craft of writing a meaningful line of prose. I recalled a memorable explanation that Prateek Joshi gave me about poets in the medieval times worrying about simplicity of expression in order to reach the masses. In the thirteenth century, Sufi poet Amir Khusro, Nizamuddin Auliya's disciple, felt that poetry in Farsi would never reach the intended audience. Hence he composed his work with one line in Farsi followed by its translation in Urdu. The popular ghazal 'Zihaal e Miskeen Makun Taghaful' is an example of this. To propagate the message to the lay person, saints created their works in the regional tongue of the people instead of using the more formal Sanskrit, Arabic or Farsi.

After my meeting with Vaishali and friends in Delhi, I came away feeling their passion for the languages they had inherited and for the notion of language as a bearer of our identity. A language could never be its rules of conjugation or merely a skeletal syntax for communication. Between the spaces of the words we spoke was the glue that bound us together, in the form of folklore, rhymes, songs, jokes, adages, beliefs and memories.

Both Aditya Narayan and Prateek Joshi had been humiliated by their classmates—one for speaking English very well, the other for speaking English with a 'cheap' accent. Prateek's predicament in school had been as expected. Impressions counted for a lot. Yet he too conceded that the youth of today did not really care about accent and outwardly conceit. That being true, he also pointed out that a professor in his college who was ultra-smart did not have enough cachet because his

English was not up to snuff.

As an eighteen-year-old, Aditya had seen the stratification caused by English when he enrolled at Loyola, one of Chennai's oldest colleges. He had been raised to love English. He told me that Samuel Coleridge's 'The Rime of the Ancient Mariner' gave him the goosebumps every time he read the poem, but in college, surrounded by classmates, some of whom were not fluent in spoken English, he realized he had been nurtured in a bubble that would put him, at many points in college and beyond, at the receiving end of ridicule. His classmates often accused him of trying to impress others by speaking in an alien tongue, that of the imperial master: 'Yennadaa, Peter-vudraiya?' It was a dig implying that the person was spouting drivel from the stance of a white man.

In a country with so much socio-economic disparity, it was obvious that the relevance of English or the discussions about the way English was spoken mattered a whit. A large number of Indians did not even have a basic level of literacy. The Annual Status of Education Report (*ASER*), the largest NGO-run survey showed that in rural communities, even as the gender gap was shrinking and the out of school numbers were declining, one in four children were completing Class VIII without basic reading skills.[108] Even when money was ploughed into schools, scores did not improve significantly.

Unlike the disadvantaged rural masses of the country, the young people I met in India had all been fortunate enough to have an education. Aditya, Vaishali and their friends had attended English-medium schools for most of their early lives. They had one thing in common. They were writing a lot, casually and professionally, and they were writing with an intent to reach people. I noticed that their expression took many forms, and as writer and translator Arunava Sinha observed to me, the young people of India were writing more than in probably any other generation in history. They were making their feelings heard through many different channels—paper, email, WhatsApp, Facebook, and Instagram.

Almost all the young people I met in India were multilingual, many of them at home in at least three languages. In the foreseeable future, English would likely remain the language of business but beyond that, each region of India would, hopefully, command its lingua franca and guard its unique culture. Pavan Varma put it in perspective when he referred to the nations of Europe: 'English is understood and spoken by an increasing number of Europeans, but the gain for English is not at the cost of the primary language. It is an additional resource, a convenience, a means to facilitate international communication.'[109]

In an ironic playout, English helped some regional languages in India stay in people's consciousness; for instance, the English alphabet was keeping the Kashmiri language alive. Syed Murtaza Mushtaq felt deprived of the opportunity to learn the Kashmiri script, something that few of his people could even read any more. But he managed to communicate with his friends on Facebook in Kashmiri. Over half a century after the fact, Syed still continued to suffer the consequences of India's partition. He had been beaten up for referring to the town of Anantnag in Kashmir valley by its Muslim name of Islamabad. Literacy in the Kashmiri language had been neglected due to various political reasons and a lack of formal education in it. The primary official language of the state of Jammu and Kashmir was now not Kashmiri, but Urdu.

It was clearly important for Syed to learn English for yet another reason. In his eyes and in the opinion of his countrymen—because he believed Kashmir, not India, was his country—English was the language of joy and peace, the language of many unlettered houseboat-wallahs of Kashmir, the tongue redolent of Kashmir Valley's happiest times as a sightseeing paradise. English was thus a symbolic presence. Mastering it was also a political statement. For Kashmiris like him, English was a sweet sound. It felt stable, offering the least controversy in a fraught world defined by an unstable homeland.

◆

The evening in Delhi, as I returned to my Airbnb, I reckoned that while my selection of youth had been random, my discussions had been eye-opening. Every group comes with its biases and its specific constraints, but in the end, I felt that I'd cut through a sliver, however small, of youthful expression. Before we parted company at Ambience mall, Vaishali left me with the following thought, that while she had been exposed to the gems in the canon of Western literature in high school and in college, she had never had any such takeaways from the world of Indian literature. She felt that the same attention had not been given to a work in Hindi, her mother tongue, as in English. The curriculum often did not reflect pride in one's own culture. I suspected that Aditya Narayan had similar misgivings, too. He was frustrated that he was better at expressing himself in English and that he had chosen to write poetry in English, not in Tamil.

From my conversations with them, I noticed how American influence and Western notions of the right way to be had stained not just their language but also their way of life. Despite the invading world, the young people of India had certainly made English their own. A professor of Linguistics and English at Delhi's Indian Institute of Technology, Rukmini Bhaya Nair, observed that English had 'a life of its own' in our country unconstrained by models of American or British English. 'I saw what Nair alluded to. Youngsters like Aditya

Narayan were certainly leading the way in chipping away at the elitism casing the language; they were undaunted by authority and saw through the veneer of people's education and privilege. They also showed an enormous amount of pride in their Indian heritage.

Occasionally, on social media, I watched video posts by Aditya in which he led singers at a devotional music group. Spirituality now occupied a central place in his life. Meditation had helped him battle health challenges. His posts on social media often revolved around religion and spirituality. Given his age (he was around twenty-five when I first met him), it seemed quite at odds with the nature of most young people in India and the world. I was flummoxed by Aditya. He was young and old, liberal and conservative, left and right, English-loving and bhasha-loving. He was, to use one of his own favourite words, a conundrum. To use another of his favourite expressions, that left me befuddled.

In one of the videos, a young man strummed the guitar and an elderly man drummed the tabla while Aditya, mike in hand, was lost in a trance, singing the praise of the blue-bodied Krishna. 'Nand Kishora, navneeta chora' he crooned. The people repeated after him, swaying. A man by the wall danced as he sang. From the extreme corner of the wall, behind Aditya, a guru looked down from a framed picture over Aditya's head, at the congregation. The scene was evocative of a sunset in a poem Aditya wrote a decade ago, 'Calligraphy of a Dying Day'. This poem was his personal favourite.

I too discovered a maturity in its language, thought and execution. He had captured the inanity and transcendence of both the sunset and the written word, observing that both activities could be pedestrian or extraordinary—depending on the orchestra of circumstances. In the closing stanza, he made his reader feel both the dazzling performance of the sunset and the ephemeral nature of it, reflected so perfectly in the arc of the life of a human being.

> The sun bade farewell to the songs of his shift
> And filled the plains with crimson hue
> The night creeping, as this was his cue
> He cloaked the light with his black sift
> And to a pale horizon the indigo sky
> A thousand stars under which I lie
> Sprawled across, as they unevenly wink
> At me, my parchment, and my words of ink.

EIGHT

WHAT ABOUT THE MOTHER TONGUE?

A little space in the durbar of the world,
Would be the real honour to my mother tongue.

—Krairi Mog Choudhury, *Soi Sabud*

When Nabaneeta Dev Sen flew back from London to Calcutta after her marriage crumbled, she re-entered her ancestral house, Bhalo-Basa, in Hindustan Park. After a decade spent accompanying her husband as his career soared, she returned as a single mother with her two daughters, eight and four, in tow, and the memories of two infant sons lost in childbirth. The house into which she had been born was no longer a haven. The town that had once cradled her now rebuked her, casting aspersions on her character. Tongues wagged. Her mother, Radharani, too, was hostile because she was upset about the breakdown of her marriage. 'Divorce was a dirty word,' Nabaneeta wrote later, in a personal narrative about her struggles.[110] In keeping with the mores of the day, if a marriage had failed—even if it was because the man had taken up with another woman—the fault lay with the spurned wife.

The hurt and anguish impelled her to write a poem in Bengali in which she made a plea to her city whose reigning deity symbolized both compassion and vengeance. Nabaneeta translated the poem into English, titling it 'Return of the Dead'.

Receive me then, Calcutta
I am your first love
Your childhood sweetheart
Here I am, an aborted mother,
I have brought the ocean with me instead
My arms are empty, yes, but my breasts
Are heavy, overflowing with wasted milk
Look at the fathomless salt water
Come, look at me, then,
Naked as the setting sun
Touch me, Calcutta, my newborn flesh
Belongs to you now[111]

Nabaneeta began writing again while teaching literature at Jadavpur University. Her mother was against her writing in Bengali. 'Write in English,' she insisted. 'Let the whole world read you.'[112] Radharani believed that success equated to national and international readership. Nabaneeta did not heed her advice because at that time she felt a 'moral and political aversion'[113] for Indians writing in English.

As I sat on a divan inside the drawing room at Bhalo-Basa, inhaling the faint scent of fish and mustard oil, my feet on the cool white-and-black marble floor, I understood how for Nabaneeta the act of writing in her native Bengali was a proclamation of her independence, not just from the trap and the trappings of marriage, but also from success as defined by a parent. It was a statement of defiance, an act to claim her agency.

A fading black-and-white photograph of Nabaneeta's mother flanked by her grandchildren rested inside a cabinet. I sat in a room that had yellowed with age. The drapes were yellow. A fabric in yellow was draped over the divan. In the room was a rocking chair, a desk against one of six wooden cabinets with glass doors that seemed to be fixtures of most Kolkata homes; wooden chairs with braided cane, a common colonial presence; a moda under the wooden desk, worn and darkening; and two Jamini Roy paintings. Through a yellow door curtain that fluttered under the fan, I spotted a large painting propped up on an easel, Raja Ravi Varma's *Shakuntala*. And, everywhere, books. This house was a heritage landmark in Kolkata, a home of decades of reflection and debate—and several showdowns, according to Nabaneeta—and the echoes of that clung to the room, in the fraying spines of books whose names I could not decipher. But their skeletal remains clung together inside many tall bookcases, along low-slung shelves on the wall. Anais Nin. Mayakovsky. Chekhov. James Joyce. Literary criticism. Women poets. I sat in the room, unnerved and wary of the ghosts of the intellects that had once sailed through it. Poet, essayist, short story writer, humourist, satirist, travel writer, novelist, playwright, feminist—many-armed like Kali herself—Nabaneeta was a prolific and beloved writer of Bengali literature and had over eighty books in print and had received almost every lifetime achievement award a writer in India could ever dream of. Naturally, I worried about the meeting. Something else was eating into me, too.

Calcutta gave women a certain power and heft. I always attributed it to the earth itself. Aeons before Job Charnock staked out a plot of land for the East India Company in 1690 and called it Kalikata after one of the three villages, it had been invested with the power of Shakti, the goddess of feminine might, Shiva's consort. Legend has it that Shiva, upon finding his wife Shakti's lifeless body, was overcome with grief and anger. Carrying her body on his shoulders, he began dancing the rudra tandava, the cosmic dance that could destroy the world. Vishnu, the Preserver, launched his weapon, the chakra, which chopped the body of Shakti into fifty-one pieces and quelled Shiva's fury. Each of the pieces fell in a different spot. These places are known as Shakti peeths, where the goddess Shakti is revered and worshipped. The little toe of her right foot is believed to have landed on the river bank around which Calcutta (now Kolkata) was born.

It was in such sacrosanct land, that in the mid-nineteenth century, English-educated Indians like Raja Ram Mohan Roy challenged the practice of sati. Intellectuals like Tagore questioned the treatment of widows and the practice of child marriage. The English language became a weapon to light up the dark corridors of ancient practices and the Brahmo Samaj movement in Bengal ignited a renaissance in thought while kindling a nationalist sprit in the people. A sartorial movement began, too. Gyananandini Das was among the first women to urge women to wear a blouse under the sari.[114] In Kolkata, the emancipation of women became a fight that both women and men participated in, and English was a critical conduit for new ideas. This second city of the British empire also became the fountainhead of literary magazines that fertilized the minds of its hungry readers and the literary life of a town.

Nabaneeta was born in the tumultuous decade before India's independence, in the year 1938 and her name was given to her by Tagore himself. And now, the bearer of that name, meaning 'newly taken one', glided down the staircase in an electro-mechanical contraption that stuttered over a grease-filled banister and delivered her onto the ground with a thud where I stood in astonishment.

'My knees are weak, my dear,' Nabaneeta said, hoisting herself up with the help of her cane. 'I cannot do stairs any more, you see'. She sported a huge red bindi. Her hair was long, although now the strands of white overpowered the black. In her eyes I saw the sparkle of the city's ferocious deity and the inexhaustible energy of someone who renewed herself as if she too were remade yearly at the deity workshops at Kumartuli during the nine-night festival of Durga Puja.

Cupping her hands in mine, I told her I was thrilled to meet her.

'I haven't even begun talking,' she retorted, with a laugh that barely hid her scepticism and yet instantly put me at ease. 'And you're *already* thrilled to meet me?'

These women of Kolkata—whether it was my aunt Samyuktha who had lived in the city for three decades or the historian Reba Som, or crafts council chair Ruby Palchaudhuri or Nabaneeta Dev Sen herself—wielded their words like 'dumdum' bullets. The Dum-Dum foundry in Kolkata once made projectiles designed to expand on impact, increasing in diameter to produce a larger wound for faster incapacitation. But when those puissant women of Kolkata took me under their matronly wings, it seemed they were sweeter than the sugary Bengali rosogulla.

◆

There's a picture in my album from the summer of 2011 when I stayed at The Fairlawn in Calcutta and spent time talking with Mrs Violet Smith, its ninety-year-old proprietor. Every morning, with the help of her staff, she dressed up—pancake make-up on her face and rouge on her cheeks—as if she were attending a party. In the photograph taken with me, she sports a tomato red blouse with white polka dots and a red skirt. Around her neck, she wears a double strand of pearls. Violet Smith was the loveable grand old lady of Calcutta running a small-time hotel that became an institution known for its hospitality and famous guests. With walls and pillars of sea foam green, iron railings in the same shade of green, red floors, shutters of shamrock green, green palms in pots, red lights and green plastic leaves hanging from the ceiling, Fairlawn made me go slightly green the first time I walked about the premises. The dowager seemed unreal too, yet familiar in some way, and it wasn't until I read Geoffrey Moorhouse's *Calcutta* (1971), that I realized why. When Moorhouse wrote about the city's Marble Palace, he called it 'a Chatsworth of a place, muddled up with scenes from an Indian *Great Expectations*; and it would be no surprise at all to encounter Miss Havisham reclining in a corner among the bric-à-brac, the shadows and the cobwebs. This is Calcutta, too.'[115] Like the 200-year-old Fairlawn itself, Calcutta too was caught in a time warp, with its grand, crumbling houses and its many English yearnings from its time as the capital of British India.

Among the things listed in the first newspaper ever published in India—*Hicky's Bengal Gazette* of Calcutta—was a 'Wanted' advertisement—cringeworthy by twenty-first-century (really, any) standards—that was a precursor to India's matrimonial classifieds. A gentleman about town was looking to buy 'three very handsome African Ladies of the true sable hue'.

They must not be younger than fourteen years each.

Nor older than twenty or twenty five
They must be well-grown Girls of their Age
Strait Limbed, and Strait Eyed.
And have a rational use of their Faculties
The better if a little Squeamish.
But beware of spot or blemish
They will be joined in the holy banes of Wedlock,
to three Gentleman of their own Colour, Cast, and Country.
A Dower is not expected with them.
Nor will there be any Jointure settled on them.

As the Master of those African Gentlemen would not

wish to have them disappointed, he hopes no ladies will apply, but those who are really and truly spinsters, for it would be a very disagreeable circumstance to have their passions wound up to their highest pitch of wild desire and then to have their banes forbidden in right to a prior claim.—No matter whether from a Mogul from the East, or from a Hottentot from the West—For in either circumstance, it would be equally distressing. N. B. Any person that has got such ladies to dispose of, let them apply to the Clerk of the Printing Office, and they will be treated with.

From Jamaican bottles of rum to reading glasses, to slaves, nothing was off limits to the consumers of the gazette. The National Library of India in Alipore (where I came across this advertisement) is now a treasure house to the evolution of the Englishman's life in Calcutta. In its modern form, the language—the English of Shakespeare too is considered modern—had been etched, literally, onto the city's daily life in unexpected ways, the Anglophilia soaking also into dessert.

This I discovered when I bit into a ledikeni, a lightly fried reddish-brown sweet ball made of milk solids and flour soaked in molten sugar syrup. 'When the late Lord Canning was the Governor General of India, it was said his Baboo made a present of some native sweetmeats to Lady Canning, who was kindly pleased to accept them.'[116] Writing in 1883, Shib Chunder Bose observed how Bengalis were now so anglicized that they had named a sweetmeat after the illustrious lady and that no grand feast among the Bengalis was considered complete 'unless the "Lady Canning" sort' was offered to the guests.[117]

English names were everywhere on the streets in Calcutta just as in Bangalore. They were six feet under, too, in this city.

The bones of some 1,600 Englishmen had been interred in the city's soil. The life expectancy of Europeans in the East India Company during the early colonial period was so low that in one year, out of the total of 1,200, over a third died between August and December. So common was the annual loss of lives, especially to cholera, dysentery and other tropical ills, that the survivors held thanksgiving banquets towards the end of October 'to celebrate the deliverance'.[118]

One mid-morning in November, I walked past pyramids, obelisks, cairns, shrines, stone urns and fluted columns at the old South Park Cemetery where many of the monuments had been damaged irreparably by roots. The grass yellow, a classic Asian butterfly, that had been greeting me every morning in Chennai as I walked in father's old haunt, Jeeva Park, flew close to the ground before me, guiding me on my course as I ambled about under mango trees and gulmohar branches. Around the moss and whisper of the 250-year-old graveyard, I read couplets and verses from the Romantic period of English literature.

> Sacred To the Memory of John Allen, (Son of Richard Allen, Esq. of Chittagong.) Who died while at Serampore School, December 13th 1804, Aged 10 years.
>
> Why should say 'Tis yet too soon,
> To seek for Heaven or think of Death;
> A flower may fade before 'tis noon.
> And I this day may lose my Breath

The monument that I sought out, however, was the tallest obelisk of them all, competing with the Ashoka trees. It was a grave marked with crossed spades erected in memory of Sir William Jones who died in 1794, the polyglot who studied Sanskrit and its close links with European languages, a scholar, a passionate Indologist and a gifted writer. I was moved by many of the discourses that he gave at the Asiatic Society in Calcutta. When I read a speech he delivered in 1786, I wondered if the course of Indian education may have been rather different had the gentleman not died at forty-seven years of age—four decades before Macaulay formulated his minutes in a speech that undermined the entire body of Indian literature. Jones's masterful discourses seemed appropriate even today: 'The Sanskrit language, whatever be its antiquity, is of a wonderful structure; more perfect than the Greek, more copious than the Latin, and more exquisitely refined than either; yet bearing to both of them a stronger affinity, both in the roots of verbs, and in the forms of grammar, than could possibly have been produced by accident; so strong, indeed, that no philologer could examine them all three without believing them to have sprung from some common source, which, perhaps, no longer exists.'[119]

Both in sight and in sound, the English I witnessed in Calcutta was excellent, even though only a small per cent of the city's five million people actually spoke the language. I noticed fewer spelling mistakes on the city's roads. However, the day I turned from Hungerford Street into Moira Street— right by Sushila Birla Girls's School, Vidya Mandir and La Martiniere For Boys, all English-medium schools catering to the wealthy—a sign on the wall warned 'Commit No Nuisence'. I had read about a much heard criticism in Indian academia—that those who write in English miss some of the registers that regional language accesses and that this naturally means that writing in English doesn't give voice to the marginalized and that the anyone writing in English is innately writing from the vantage point of privilege and missing some of the other perspectives of those in the bhashas. On Kolkata's Moira Street, this observation (although it's more nuanced that this) swam into focus. Next to the euphemistic warning in English, a sign in Hindi cautioned 'Peshab nahi karna', which translated approximately (exactly to the imperative 'Urine no do!') showing that English did indeed not boil down to the elemental or to the specific, crude register of speech in the way that Hindi (or any bhasha) might.

For me, the use of the two languages also highlighted how Bengal, and certainly Kolkata, once fanatical about its Bengali, had changed. It was also a pointer to how it was impossible to orchestrate how a language must or must not permeate a society. Once this Bengali fiefdom had been intimidated by English; now it was slowly being subsumed by Hindi as the tentacles of the city's Marwadi community reached out to the grandest business of them all: English-medium education. A significant transfer of power happened when South Point High School, the bastion of Bengali educators, also passed into the hands of a Marwadi owner.[120] In this power struggle between regional languages, it seemed to me that English was like the familiar guest at the dinner table, privy to all the undercurrents between family members. English was also the guest who'd likely never leave. The avid English readers of Kolkata loved their daily dose of *The Telegraph,* the largest circulated English daily in the eastern region of India.

Sandip Roy Choudhury, a local writer, told me that headlines in *The Telegraph* had a personality, an element of fun. When Bengal's powerful chief minister, Mamata Banerjee (called 'Didi' or elder sister), lost a railway deal, *The Telegraph* carried the headline 'Didirailed', with a graphic of Didi holding a red flag. 'Spinderella', shouted the headlines on another morning when Minister Smriti Irani was downgraded from the Ministry of Human Resource Development to Textiles. The paper, as the city that made it, was seemingly less obsessed with clickbait and search engine optimization. Instead it appreciated involved puns, sardonic wit, and a rather British sense of humour—a very different approach from the stodgier older papers at other metropolises. The paper sometimes stoked the anger of locals with its edgy headlines and mockery.

A women's rights organization went into a tizzy when a photo of the state's top five administrators was photoshopped to show them sporting saris in an attempt to insult them about their ineptitude. Staging a demonstration in front of *The Telegraph* office, the women's organization demanded an apology for the sexist thinking behind the 'liberal façade': 'This is both a demeaning and humiliating stance towards women and we are amazed that a leading English daily holds such regressive attitudes and views.'[121]

It was odd how until a few decades ago, English seemed to be an oppressive subliminal character in Calcutta's social life. I felt its ominousness in the movies made by Calcutta's filmmaker, Satyajit Ray. He showed the aspiration for English as a longing, a promised land that a captain might sight from a ship. It was something that eluded many of Ray's characters. If they mastered English, it was as if they had to compromise something to get there. There's a moment in the movie *Apur Sansar* where Apu helps his wife Aparna with the English sounds—'cat', 'fat' and 'rat'—as she pesters him to teach her the language he seems to know and uses even though he's only 'Intermediate pass'. The importance of English is obvious. Western ways have made inroads into the city. Apu's friend eats with a fork, wears collared Western-style shirts and trousers and goes to work at a local company. Apu, in contrast, lives in a squalid apartment, his undershirt is torn and stretched, and he's always clad in a kurta and dhoti. Yet among his most precious possessions is a small collection of English books on a ramshackle shelf above his bed. I recognized the longing of the Bengali for English in that little detail.

Most Kolkata homes displayed their books around the living rooms, regardless of the size of the house or the income of the owner. Writer Nilanjana Roy described this in an essay about reading. 'The ones large enough to have furniture "sets" and antimacassars ran to full sets of Bengali classics, from Saratchandra to Sharadindu, Jibanananda, Mahasweta, Bankimchandra and co. to Parashuram, Nabarun Bhattacharya, Bani Basu, Moti Nandy.' The homes had the canon of Tagore, of course, and the city's literary magazines. 'The mansions of the boxwallahs, and judges and lawyers' homes, and the Anglicized Brahmos added bound copies of *Time*, *National Geographic* and Nobel Prize winners to their collection.'[122]

By the early twentieth century, Bengali homes read both in the bhasha and in English. In the seventies, Sandip grew up devouring *Anandamela*, a Bengali publication of *Anandabazar Patrika* that was a collection of news, stories and comics for children. Batman, Tintin, and Archie, among many other English comics, appeared translated in Bengali. Nabaneeta's stories for children also appeared in *Anandamela*, her prolific output reaching many age groups through the generations.

Yet, there was the English spoken by Bengalis who had sought education in English-medium schools in the last many decades—Xavier's, La Martiniere, Modern Public School, Lady Brabourne College—that was impeccable. There were armies of other city residents who had attended Bengali-medium schools who would not be literate in the English language as I discovered one day when I asked an Uber driver to drive me to Presidency College, once called Hindoo College.

Daroga Shah, the Uber driver, drove me from Tollygunge Club to College Street that morning and while he tossed out English terms such as 'line by line', 'title', 'strike', 'medical college' he said he hadn't been able to decipher the word

'Presidency' on his phone and hence didn't know where I wanted to go until I got into his car and told him the name of the place. That was my own moment of reckoning about how I looked at the world around me from the vantage point of English. How could I have assumed that everyone in India would be able to read the Roman alphabet even if they knew a smattering of English words?

On College Street, while the fascination for English was obvious, the fascination for college degrees was even more so. Bookstalls distinguished themselves by college degrees and exam acronyms. At one of the stores, Dey Books, the owner, Alik Dey, quickly got me translations of many Bengali books. Even though he didn't read literature in English, he read literature in Bengali and knew what translated works I must read. He began throwing out names. Have you read *Karukku* by Bama? What about U. R. Ananthamurthy's *Samskara: A Rite for a Dead Man*? How about Bankim? And surely you must have heard of Sunil Gangopadhyay's *Those Days*?

While Alik Dey was a rarer breed, Kolkata was filled with English-loving booksellers. These men spoke no English at all but sat in the sun and the rain, cigarette in hand, by their flat bench of plastic-sheathed books and magazines. A staffer at Oxford Bookstore on Park Street told me that his store indulged some of the vendors outside their shop and told them what they could stock for rapid sales and also encouraged their customers to patronize them sometimes.

In this city, I had always noticed a warmth and compassion, an attitude of live and let live, and also an inability to shake off the past. In June 2012 I happened to spend some time in the warehouse of Sabyasachi, a designer from Kolkata who shows his designs in Milan, but still works in a warehouse in a squalid industrial part of town. His words described the ethos of the city. 'In Kolkata we believe that if something works, we don't need to change it.' And so the city has just limped along, its most unforgettable public buildings—some decrepit, some shining—where scavenging dogs scampered around in glee and refugees always found a spot on the footpath to sleep on and subsist on a meal that still cost next to nothing. It was the reason the yellow Ambassador taxi—some painted with the words 'No Refusal'—plied the streets. I discovered, over a period of nine days, how this clunky yellow box on wheels with no air conditioning and rudimentary seats gave the middle finger, again and again, to the Uber or Ola because, unlike them, it was rooted to the din and clank of this town. It spoke its language.

◆

The fight against the English language had been fierce in Calcutta—it coloured and informed the attitudes and lives of those born early in the twentieth century. Naturally, Nabaneeta heard the conflicts bounce off in the walls of her home.

At Jorasanko Thakurbari, the residence on Rabindra Sarani (earlier called Chitpore Road) where Rabindranath Tagore grew up, Western manners and speech were taboo. In the late nineteenth century, Tagore's father once forbade his cousin to address the Brahmo Samaj in English, just as he once refused to accept a letter from a son-in-law because it had been written in English. However, the sons, including Rabindranath, were sent to England to pursue higher studies. Famous for its altruism, the family donated large sums of money for the introduction of Western education and for the study of science and medicine in colleges in the city. Rabindranath's attitude to life was defined by this confluence of eastern tradition and Western progressiveness. He cautioned against following the West mindlessly and loathed the Indian's unctuousness towards the white man thus. 'The moment we feel the slightest handshake of a favor on their part, why immediately are our entire selves transformed into a mass of *jelly*, trembling and wobbling from top to toe?'[123] Gandhi's commentary on this idea was lyrical: 'I want the cultures of all the lands to be blown about my house as freely as possible. But I refuse to be blown off my feet by any.'[124]

In 1867, Bengalis came together to create an organization called Hindu Mela for promoting national feeling and values among the educated natives of Bengal. People were exhorted to speak and write Bengali and not English, to wear dhoti and chadar instead of hats and coats, to boycott British foods and hotels, adopt indigenous activities and choose traditional medicine.

The Indian National Congress was born in the wake of this movement for national pride. Founded in 1885, it was the first modern nationalist movement to emerge in the British empire in Asia and Africa.[125]

But the fight for the choice of language had a history that went back over a hundred years. Calcutta was a hotbed of intellectual activity, resulting in the birth of the Bengal renaissance of which one of the early heroes was Henry Louis Vivian Derozio, then a professor at Hindu College. He was one of the first Indian educators to impart Western education, scientific and rational thinking to his students. This Young Bengal movement brought about the intellectual revolution in Bengal. Young men born into upper-caste Hindu families were attracted to his teachings, becoming anglicized quickly and incurring the wrath of their parents and the college staff. Derozio was fired. Pitted against this was the new awakening in Bengal society. Rabindranath's father, Debendranath, educated during in Ram Mohan Roy's Anglo-Hindu school and influenced by Roy's ideals was dedicated to a reformist

Brahmo Samaj movement in Hinduism to restore the original pristine principles of Hinduism that had been corrupted over time. Debendranath was well versed in European philosophy and, though deeply religious, did not accept all aspects of Hinduism.

As the capital of British India, Calcutta was thus the heart of India's changing ideals, the place of reformation as Derozio encouraged his students to think for themselves. It was where Raja Ram Mohan Roy began a movement called the Brahmo Samaj to reform the archaic practices of Hinduism. Derozio influenced the already anglicized youth to think about atheism; Ram Mohan Roy urged people to think about the ills in Hinduism, to denounce practices like sati and laid the foundation for restoring Bengali pride.

◆

When I met Nabaneeta in November that year, she had already submitted twenty-five different pieces for publication in literary magazines around Bengal. She believed that it was one of the most important things she should do—that such magazines, born out of a village or a region and a social milieu, determined the literary life of a place and kept the bhasha alive.

She experienced some frustrations, too. Sometimes when an editor was pressed for time, they might say to her: 'Okay, Didi, if you don't have time for prose, why not send a poem-shoem or whatever.' In a beautiful essay about her work, Nabaneeta confessed that such words drove her to tears. 'Do they not know that it is forbidden to say "a poem-*shoem* or whatever"? That Saraswati is incensed by such thoughtless remarks?'[126]

As a child Nabaneeta thought everyone wrote when they grew up. Born into a genteel literati upper-crust family, she too was schooled in an English-medium school even though her own literary moorings were different compared to the others. She belonged to the rarefied world where everyone who stopped at Bhalo-Basa already had a book published or was about to be published. She learned European, English and Bengali literature from the poets, essayists and journalists who thronged her home. Very early in life, Nabaneeta gained a reputation as a poet at her school. By the time she was seven years old, she had published two poems in *Sadhana,* the school magazine. While the protagonist of the English poem was a frog, the Bengali poem was called 'Chini O Nun', which translated to 'Sugar and Salt'.

> Chini bole, 'Nun tui durey shorey thak
> ami dami tor cheye bole tule nak.'
> Nun bole, 'Ami bina randhan hoy?'
> Chiniebe kachumachu, nichumukhe roy.

> 'Salt, stay away from me,' Sugar says,
> nose in the air. 'I am dearer than you.'
> Salt says, 'Can food be cooked without me?'
> Defeated, Sugar hangs her head in shame.

Poetry seeped into her soul by osmosis. 'I was lucky enough to closely observe two souls dedicated to the literary world, who believed that staying alive and poetry were indistinguishable. One was my father, Narendra Dev, the other was my teacher, Buddhadeva Bose.'[127]

A luminary who launched the comparative literature department at Jadavpur University, Bose was also a bit of a renegade whose book *Raat Bhor Brishti (It Rained All Night)* found Bose in jail for a night. In it, his protagonist, Maloti, sleeps with a married man and ponders the frailty of her marriage and the significance of the institution of marriage itself. In the late sixties, the idea of sexual frustration, masturbation, sex, marriage and extramarital sex rocked a society in which such discussions didn't leave the bedroom. In the preface to the English translation, Clinton B. Seely vents about how the judge 'not only heaped indignity after indignity upon the sixty-three-year-old writer—such as making him stand in a wire cage, ordering a search for the confiscation and destruction of all copies of his printed book, and destruction of the manuscript—but also refused him leave to appeal'.[128]

Many events in her personal life shaped Nabaneeta's ideas about womanhood. She was the child of a woman from a second marriage; upon losing her husband as a child bride, Radharani defied her parents, eloping to marrying Narayan Dev at a time when widow remarriage was forbidden. Nabaneeta was privy to the English–Bhasha debates over addas at her parents' salon. They shaped her convictions. She was moulded by the struggle for India's independence and the ravages of the Bengal famine and the Second World War. She was raised on the words of Tagore who lamented that India had a lot of work ahead—the improvement in the condition of peasants, wiping out of caste prejudices, repair of Hindu–Muslim relationships and elimination of poverty—before it achieved Independence. Nabaneeta's role models were writers in the regional languages, often professors of English at universities who were fluent in two or more languages including English. She had watched how Buddhadeva Bose and Jibananda Das and many others wrote in the bhasha and refrained from writing in the tongue of their masters. Like them, Nabaneeta stuck to the Bengali tradition of straddling both cultures, using English for academic expression and opting for Bengali in her creative work.

Thus when she returned home and resumed a literary life at Bhalo-Basa in the seventies, she was aghast at the tumult in the world outside. The Englishman had left but India was still, by means of the language and its attendant culture, beholden to the white man. The issues that Tagore raised about the position of women in society continued to dog Bengali life.

In one of her many pieces of non-fiction, she pointed to the social conditioning that she had been subject to, like most women of her time. 'At first I was leading the life my parents wanted me to lead. Luckily, they approved of the man of my choice. Then I was leading the life my husband wanted me to lead. It was only after my marriage broke up that I began leading my own life.'[129]

Nabaneeta became the outspoken matriarch of Calcutta, the one who could not be vanquished by the petty politics of writers who worked in either world. She lashed back at those who decried writers in the bhasha, cried herself hoarse demanding excellence in translation, asked tough questions about the role of English in an India where a majority did not understand the language. While fighting for her language, she also tried to further the cause of women, encouraging them to fight patriarchy, spearheading, as part of this, a magazine featuring the voices of women from all the regions of India. The only way Nabaneeta could empower herself, was in the medium closest to her heart. 'Though I began as a bilingual writer writing poetry and prose, Bengali and English at the same time, it was Bengali poetry that stuck to me.'

I could see why Nabaneeta chafed at an India that had relegated its mother tongue to the status of a second language. Years ago, in the sixties, she had rushed back to the soil to give birth to her children 'to gift them Indian citizenship, so that they would own the land'. Nabaneeta's decision to give her children what she felt was a privilege and a birthright was the same thought process that made her ask me how her fellow Indians could ignore one question as they hankered after the privileges afforded by English: 'What about the mother tongue?'

◆

The evening I met Nabaneeta, she was fatigued. After twelve hours of work over a new website for *Soi*, a platform for women's voices, of which she was the president, she descended from her quarters right above the living room where I waited. In Bengali, the word 'soi' had three meanings: a signature, a woman friend and 'I tolerate' and the magazine published translations of women's prose and poetry and works in English.

While I watched, she turned the pages of *Soi Sabud*, a story collection that *Soi* brought out several times a year. She enlightened me about its storytellers: Bama, Mahasweta Devi, Mridula Garg, Mamta Sagar, Shashi Deshpande...

In a while, setting the magazine down, she began sharing the anxieties uppermost on her mind. She had noticed that a fundamental change in the fabric of families in India had killed the oral tradition of storytelling. Grandmothers once told stories to young children at bedtime. Those stories were often passed down from one generation to another. Listening to stories fired up the imagination. I recalled my own childhood as she talked. In the dark after dinner, my grandmother and I used to sit in the veranda of our Chennai bungalow as she entertained me with tales, many from the Ramayana, the Mahabharata or the *Panchatantra*.

Technology had replaced the storyteller, Nabaneeta said. Children now would rather be entertained by devices. But her bigger concern was the intervention of English, a dam that had altered the flow of the mother tongue even in a state that was proud about its literary heritage. 'We're losing our mother tongue and we're not catching up to the father tongue either,' she said, referring to English as the 'father'—a reference I had not heard from anyone else.

On and off, Nabaneeta would sigh. 'I'm so tired,' she'd say, leaning back against the pillows of the sofa, stating she didn't have an ounce of energy left to talk. When I told her I could leave and come back another day, she shook her head. She was too busy to find me another slot. 'In any event, you look so pretty in that sari,' she said, her voice raspy and gruff. 'How can I not oblige, my dear?' We laughed. 'Can I get you some lime shorbot?' She called out to a maid for sherbet, no ice.

At almost eighty, Nabaneeta was playful and childlike, showing me a side to her that I had glimpsed in her travelogues and writings about the striations of her own life—funny accounts that often turned ideas on their head and aired the contradictions of our lives. When her ex-husband, Amartya Sen, won the Nobel Prize, all of Kolkata went into a tizzy. In a hilarious essay, Nabaneeta vented about how the phone wouldn't stop ringing in her home and everybody, including the chaiwallah outside her home, wanted to tell her how well they knew her ex-husband (and her ex-mother-in-law, Amita, who lived in Shantiniketan nearly 200 kilometres away). Nabaneeta's essay portrayed how her family life was buffeted by waves of adulation after the award was announced. She received calls from strangers.

'"Namaskar. I'm from Batanagar. I used to study with Bablu at St Gregory's in Dhaka. Bablu used to be a close friend."'

'These days I have not come across too many people who were not close friends with Amartya at some point. Of late very few address him as "Amartya"; he is either 'Bablu' or 'Bablu-da' to everybody. His mother is "Amita-di" or "Amita-mashi" to all and sundry. And yet, for the last forty years or so, I have not seen this crowd anywhere near them at all. Intimacy had sprouted suddenly like a magic beanstalk.'[130]

Underlying the humour were harsh truths. For one, a divorce on paper could never sever a past connection. There was the other realization that Nabaneeta's own magnificent accomplishments in the world of poetry and academia were all somehow eclipsed by the biggest 'prize' of them all, that she had once been the wife of a Nobel laureate. Nabaneeta's piece was an incisive commentary, bubble-wrapped in humour, on how even though she might preside over her own endless list of India's literary and lifetime achievement awards, 'a woman's place is in the home'. How could I ever forget those exact words of Satyajit Ray's hero in *Mahanagar*?

For a time, Nabaneeta and I talked about the rising importance of English in an increasingly globalized world. All she wanted was the due respect for the vernacular, equal and fair treatment for those working in the bhasha and pride in the bhasha from the people who spoke it. 'How you use language is how you create literature,' she said.

I had heard the echoes of her feelings in the writings of Ngũgĩ wa Thiong'o. Language as culture was 'the collective memory bank of a people's experience in history', he wrote, lamenting how the colonial empire had decimated the memory of a people, simultaneously robbing them of their self-esteem.[131] Strangely, though, some children of the postcolonial world wished to write in English.

In 1959, one college student at Jadavpur University, Purushottama Lal, decided to start the Writers Workshop, a collective where poets and novelists who dreamed of writing in the English language would review each other's works and support one another. Lal believed that 'English has proved its ability, as a language to play a creative role in Indian literature'.[132]

While Writers Workshop published tightly bound books with bright handloom cloth, handstitched together with P. Lal's signature calligraphy, Buddhadeva Bose, a staunch opponent

of the Writers Workshop, called Indian English poetry 'a blind
alley lined with curio shops leading nowhere'.[133] Incensed,
Lal and the members of the Writers Workshop sent out a
questionnaire to over a hundred writers seeking their response.
Lal compiled the responses and their poetry in a 600-page
tome called *Modern Indian Poetry in English: An Anthology and
a Credo* in 1969.

Lal believed English to be yet another of India's languages,
'a new language with its own worth and pride'.[134] Spearheading
a movement that would spew fire and lava some three decades
afterward, Lal said that he believed that a different English,
whose story had begun over a century ago, was emerging.

One of the earliest adopters of this new English had been
a Bengali officer, Sake Dean Mahomed, the first writer of
Indian origin in English, when he published *The Travels of
Dean Mahomet* in 1794. In 1821, he opened a shampooing cure
treatment centre in Brighton and became the shampooing
surgeon to the king himself. 'Champing' (in Hindi) or
'shampooing' was 'a restorative, luxurious kneading of the
flesh' in warm vapour baths which was essentially an oil
massage and washing of the scalp.

About the same time, in the capital of the Raj, Kasiprasad
Ghosh, a Bengali poet, wrote poems invoking surya (the sun
god) and chandra (the moon) and rhapsodized about India's
singing bird, the koel. These appeared in a volume of poems
he titled *The Shair*. A poet in England, Letitia Landon, in a
memorandum on the poet in *Fisher's Room Scrap Book*, gushed
about the youthful 'Hindoo's' rare gifts observing 'that poetry
is a flower which is born and flourishes on what would seem
its most ungenial soil'.

By the turn of the twentieth century, despite the political
costs of writing in the language of the colonial master, some
were choosing to write, and masterfully too, in English and

flexing their literary muscles. Poets like Kamala Das—just four years senior to Nabaneeta, wrote both in her native Malayalam and in English—were subverting the beliefs of the establishment.

Nabaneeta talked to me about Kamala Das and Mulk Raj Anand and other writers of her generation, many since deceased, who wrote in a particular way that conveyed Indian sensibilities and the life of the common man and middle-class India. They 'were all different somehow,' she said. In the preface to *Kanthapura*, Raja Rao says that Indians 'cannot write like the English... We cannot write only as Indians.'[135] I spotted that unique approach in the 'eye friendship' that Chandran started with Malathi while following her on daily outings on the river in R. K. Narayan's *Bachelor of Arts*. I discovered it also in the oddities, the idioms that seemed perfectly normal to me, raised as I was in India, hearing the way my father and my grandfather spoke English, translating from Tamil into English as they went along. In *A Story-Teller's World*, Narayan writes about life in an Indian village where most of the amenities of the modern world are available. 'Electricity is coming or has come to another village, only three miles away, and water is obtainable from a well open to the skies in the centre of the village.'[136]

But now and then, there was an uproar over authenticity. Since the rise of the literary rock stars from India or of Indian origin, the questions bubbled up in the media. Whose was the authentic voice? Who was the cultural appropriator of the Indian voice? To whom did 'Indianness' actually belong? To the writer of Indian stories in the bhasha? Or to the writer of Indian stories who lived in India? Could someone who was born in India and now lived in the diaspora claim to be an authentic voice of India? Who was an Indian?

Nabaneeta saw the destructive force of these debates on

literature. She witnessed an India being divided on the basis of English and the bhasha. The purveyors of the English world felt they had the right to lord over works in the bhasha because they wrote in the language in which reviews translated to sales.

In 1997, Salman Rushdie made a claim that Indian writing in English coming out of India was far superior in quality to works published in the vernacular. The only person he claimed met the standards he saw in English was the late Saadat Hasan Manto. Marathi writer Kiran Nagarkar's instinctive reaction was similar to mine: 'How could he know?' Surely, Rushdie, of all people, was aware of the paucity of qualified translators in India, especially in the nineties? Nabaneeta's reaction was swift. In July 1997 in a column she titled 'An Open Letter to Salman Rushdie', Nabaneeta chided him for his dismissiveness. 'A familiar voice, Mr Rushdie, we have heard it before. Remember Lord Macaulay. We always bow to the supreme wisdom of one who reads no Indian language.'[137]

Nabaneeta continued the fight for recognition of bhasha. She had several questions for all the literature festivals being held in India: At last count there were about seventy festivals across South East Asia. 'We think India is becoming more and more aware of literature with all its many festivals. We are not thinking about which literatures? Which languages? Why do literature festivals feature young aspiring writers in English in place of senior experienced writers in the regional languages?' In Nabaneeta's opinion, regional writers had become second-class citizens and people in the world of English had become a coterie. Kolkata's famous Oxford Bookstore did not stock a single work by Nabaneeta Dev Sen while the latest English writers crowded the shelves.

Nabaneeta had been repeatedly asking for a translation unit in India with trained translators who are paid well. She felt that India was ignoring a treasure trove of bhasha literature.

'Just because someone can read a newspaper in a language does not mean they are translators of that language,' Nabaneeta said. 'Translation is harder than creative writing. You must pour your heart and soul into it. In translation you're enslaved.'

As I left Bhalo-Basa that night, Nabaneeta stood by the landing of her home, cautioning me. 'Watch out, my dear, stay clear of the railing or you'll ruin your pretty Kerala sari.' And I saw something that I had missed earlier when I trundled up the stairs. A sticky white gel coated the stone hand rail all the way down so that Nabaneeta's chair could transport her downstairs into the cacophony of Calcutta where she had once returned to gather the shards of her shattered soul.

> Why, then, this stunned silence?
> Lift up your chin, don't shift your eyes, speak to me
> here she is, returned from the dead
> just as you had wished
> yes, look at me, I am her,
> your world of passion, your old flame
> your very own
> Nabaneeta.

◆

At a lecture on the topic of translation and multilingualism in Hyderabad a few years ago, Nabaneeta had paused before saying: 'You cannot be global without being rooted in your culture.' I felt my breath catch in my chest. It was a grain of wisdom cradling the world within it: If I were secure in myself, I would be generous and tolerant towards the world.

I thought then of Nabaneeta's sprawling canopy of work and of her ability to connect several worlds with her knowledge of Hindi, Odia, Assamese, French, German, Sanskrit and Hebrew, in addition to Bengali and English. Nabaneeta was driving towards that oneness we could all achieve as Indians, as human beings, really, if only we would harness our ability to feel, to imagine, to recognize and to know, that through 'that mirror of translation', as Nabaneeta so lyrically said to a roomful of students and professors at the university, one could see one's own head on another's shoulder.

I left Kolkata that week, my soul deflated, that somewhere, somehow, what had seemed as a gain in the short term for India had perhaps amounted to a loss over the long term. While English had become a necessary evil uniting a nation in a common goal, several generations of Indians had also had their brains altered in a way—that our regional languages, the tongues we were born into, would survive without our active, concerted effort in keeping them alive through the medium of daily speech, literature and art. As I end this journey chasing a topic that is vast and hairy, I'm convinced I must read Tamil literature to know more about where I come from and to appreciate the ideas that shaped the minds of the people who went before me.

The world is shaped by new forces every day. No one nation can predict the creation of a language. In his brilliant essay 'Hindi or Urdu?', Saadat Hasan Manto ridiculed the dispute over the official language of India and parlayed his derision into an argument between a Muslim and a Hindu over which one was better, a lemon soft drink or a bottle of soda. I felt that Manto's conclusion was prescient not only for the journey of Indian English but also for the trajectory of any language in the world: 'Languages are not created, they make themselves and no human effort can destroy one already made.'[138] No one could alter the course of a language or lord over the creation of it. But we had one solemn duty: The task to keep our mother tongue alive.

In India, English is here to stay. Indian English is young,

dynamic and different. It's found as food. It's seen in spelling mistakes inside India's government museums. I see it in the masterful strokes of literature by droves of Indians writing in English. As Crystal maintains, India's English will continue to be powerful because of the number of people who speak it and because of India's global forays in technology. But he writes that India certainly must strike a balance between its 'language of empowerment' and its 'language of identity'.[139]

As human beings, we come into this world with a rich treasure trove of experiences and memories handed down to us from several generations of our ancestors. We must leave the world with at least as much as we came in with, not less. We must tell our children and our grandchildren this immutable truth that a word contains the world inside it and that if only we cared enough, we could have the best of many worlds.

NOTES

1 Derek Walcott, 'Tropic Zone', *Midsummer: Poems by Derek Walcott*, New York: Farrar, Straus & Giroux, 1984.

2 P. G. Wodehouse, *The World of Jeeves*, London: Arrow Books, 2008.

3 William Dalrymple, *City of Djinns: A Year in Delhi*, London: HarperCollins Publishers, 1993.

4 George Bernard Shaw, *Pygmalion*, Clayton: Prestwick House Literary Touchstone Classics, 2005.

5 'More than 19,500 mother tongues spoken in India: Census', *Indian Express*, 1 July 2018.

6 Gurcharan Das, *India Unbound: From Independence to the Global Information Age*, New Delhi, Penguin Books India, 2000.

7 Kiran Nagarkar, *Ravan and Eddie*, New York: New York Review Books, 1995.

8 Thomas Babington Macaulay,' Minute by the Hon'ble T. B. Macaulay, dated the 2nd February 1835' <http://www.columbia.edu/itc/mealac/pritchett/00generallinks/macaulay/txt_minute_education_1835.html> [accessed: 20 May 2019].

9 R. K. Narayan, *A Writer's Nightmare: Selected Essays 1958–1988*, New Delhi: Penguin Books India, 1988.

10 Quoted in Shefali Chandra, *The Sexual Life of English: Languages of Caste and Desire in Colonial India (Next Wave: New Directions in Women's Studies)*,Durham: Duke University Press, 2012.

11 Kunwar Narain, 'A strange problem', Pratik Kanjilal trans., *Little Magazine*, Vol. IV, issue 5 and 6.

12 R. K. Narayan, 'Toasted English', *A Story-Teller's World: Essays, Sketches*, New Delhi: Penguin Books India, 1989.

13 E. M. Forster, *A Passage to India*, Harcourt, Brace & World, Inc., 1924.

14 Rohinton Mistry, 'The ghost of Firozsha Baag', *Swimming Lessons and Other Stories from Firozsha Baag*, New York: Vintage International, 1987.

15 Mistry, 'The ghost of Firozsha Baag'.

16 Steven R. Weisman, 'On Language; Doing The Needful', *New York Times*, 12 July 1987.

17 Nissim Ezekiel, 'The Professor', *All Poetry* <https://allpoetry.com/poem/8592069-The-Professor-by-Nissim-Ezekiel> [accessed: 3 May 2019].

18 Amar Nath Prasad, 'Foreign foliage on native root', *Critical Essays: Indian Writing In English*, New Delhi: Sarup & Sons, 2002

19 David Graddol, 'The future of language', *Science*, Vol. 333, Issue 5662, 27

February 2004, <https://science.sciencemag.org/content/303/5662/1329.full> [accessed: 3 May 2019].

20   Nina Strochlic, 'The race to save the world's disappearing languages', *National Geographic*, 16 April 2018 < https://news.nationalgeographic.com/2018/04/saving-dying-disappearing-languages-wikitongues-culture/> [accessed: 3 May 2019].

21   Graddol, 'The future of language'.

22   Dick Leith and David Graddol with contributions by Liz Jackson, 'Modernity and English as a national language', Changing English, Routledge in association with the Open University, 2007.

23   Kory Stamper, *Word by Word: The Secret Life of Dictionaries*, New York: Pantheon Books, 2017.

24   Mihir Sharma, 'Half of its population is under the age of 25. Two-thirds are less than 35', *Livemint*, 8 September 2017.

25   Harveen Ahluwalia, 'Print media publications grew at a slower rate of 3.58% in 2016-17', *Livemint*, 18 December 2017.

26   Shaw, *Pygmalion*.

27   Arundhathi Subramaniam, 'To The Welsh critic who doesn't find me identifiably Indian', *Indian Literature*, Vol. 47, No. 3, New Delhi: Sahitya Akademi, May–June 2003

28   Quoted in Braj Kachru, 'The *Indianness* in Indian English', *Word*, 21:3, 391-410, DOI: 10.1080/00437956.1965.11435436, p. 397 <https://www.tandfonline.com/doi/pdf/10.1080/00437956.1965.11435436> [accessed: 3 May 2019]

29   Macaulay, 'Minute by the Hon'ble T. B. Macaulay, dated the 2nd February 1835'.

30   'Inequality being cynically constructed: Sainath', *Assam Tribune*, 4 September 2017.

31   Mark Tully, 'The only way to save government schools is to improve them', *Hindustan Times*, 10 December 2016.

32   Mohandas Karamchand Gandhi, *The Collected Works of Mahatma Gandhi, Volume 44 (July-December 1930)*, New Delhi: The Publications Division, Ministry of Information and Broadcasting, Government of India

33   Ibid.

34   Narayan, 'English in India', *A Story-teller's World*.

35   Rev. Samuel Mateer, *The Land of Charity: A Descriptive Account of Travancore and its People, with Especial Reference to Missionary Labour*, London: John Snow and Co., 1871.

36   Thakazhi S. Pillai, *Chemmeen*, Narayana Menon trans., Bombay: Jaico Publishing House, 1962.

37   Aubrey Menen, 'My grandmother and the dirty English', *New Yorker*, 26 June 1953

38   Ibid.

39   'C.M.S College, Kottayam: a peep into the past', *CMS College Kottayam* <http://cmscollege.ac.in/history.html> [accessed: 13 May 2019].

40   Achuthsankar S. Nair, 'Swathi Thirunal: Historicity of the person and

Authenticity of his compositions', PhD Thesis, University of Kerala, Thiruvananthapuram, 2016.

41 M. M. Kaye, *The Sun in the Morning: My Early Years in India and England*, New York: St. Martin's Press, 1990.

42 Ibid.

43 Menen, 'My grandmother and the dirty English'.

44 Ibid.

45 Mohandas Karamchand Gandhi, *The Collected Works of Mahatma Gandhi*, Volume 31: 22 March 1925-15 June 1925, *Gandhiserve.org* < http://gandhiserve. org/cwmg/VOL031.PDF> [accessed: 13 May 2019].

46 Thiruvathira Tirunal Lakshmi Bayi, 'For us, the aroma of nearness', *Outlook*, 18 July 2011.

47 Mark Tully, *No Full Stops in India*, London: Penguin Books, 1991.

48 Mark Tully, 'My father's Raj', *Granta 57: India! The Golden Jubilee*, Spring 1997.

49 Ibid.

50 Ibid.

51 Forster, *A Passage to India*.

52 Tom Wintringham, 'Better history and better English', *Nehru Abhinandan Granth: A Birthday Book*, New Delhi: Nehru Abhinandan Granth Committee,1949.

53 Ibid.

54 Ibid.

55 Mir Taqi Mir, quoted in Dalrymple, *City of Djinns* and 'Mirza Ghalib, his love for mangoes and lesser known facts', *Asian Age*, 27 December 2017.

56 Mark Tully, *The Heart of India*, New Delhi: Penguin Books India, 1996

57 Tully, 'My father's Raj'.

58 Ahmed Ali, *Twilight in Delhi*, London: Hogarth Press, 1940

59 Ibid.

60 Ibid.

61 Tully, *No Full Stops in India*.

62 Ibid.

63 Tully, *The Heart of India*.

64 R. K. Narayan, *The Guide*, New York: Viking Press, 1958.

65 Tully, *No Full Stops in India*.

66 Ibid.

67 Ved Mehta, *Walking the Indian Streets*, Boston: Little, Brown, 1960.

68 Tully, 'The only way to save government schools is to improve them'.

69 Mayank Austen Soofi, 'Delhi's Belly | Dial M for Mithilesh', *Livemint*, 2 October 2014.

70 Rao Bahadur R. Krishna Rao Bhonsle, I.S.O, 'Origin of the word "Madras"', *The Madras Tercentenary Commemoration Volume*, Madras: Humphrey Milford Oxford University Press, 1939.

71 Henry Davison Love, *Vestiges of Old Madras: 1640–1800*, Vol. 1, London: John Murray, 1913.

72 Rao Saheb C. S. Srinivasachari, 'A history of the mayoralty of Madras', *The*

Madras Tercentenary Commemoration Volume, London, Bombay, Calcutta, Madras: Humphrey Milford Oxford University Press, 1939

73   'Andrew Bell: priest', *Westminster Abbey* <https://www.westminster-abbey.org/abbey-commemorations/commemorations/andrew-bell> [accessed: 15 May 2019].

74   Glyn Barlow, *The Story of Madras*, Madras: Humphrey Milford, Oxford University Press, 1921.

75   Rangaswami Parthasarthi, *A Hundred Years Of The Hindu*, Madras: Kasturi & Sons, 1902.

76   G. Subramania Aiyer, quoted in C. Paramarthalingam, *Religion and Social Reform in Tamil Nadu*, Rajakumari Publications, 1997.

77   'Looking back: Willing to strike and not reluctant to wound', *The Hindu*, 13 September 2003.

78   Quoted in 'Looking back: Developing a paper for a new reader', *The Hindu*, 13 September 2003.

79   For more on this, see 'Robert L. Hardgrave, Jr., 'The riots in Tamilnad: problems and prospects of India's language crisis', *Asian Survey*, Vol. 5, No. 8, Berkeley: University of California Press, Aug. 1965; 'Part 2: Language issue in India: anti Hindi agitations', *Guruprasad's Portal* <http://guruprasad.net/posts/part-2-language-issue-in-india-anti-hindi-agitations/> [accessed: 15 May 2019]; and R. Kannan, *Anna: The Life and Times of C. N. Annadurai*, New Delhi: Penguin Books India, 2010.

80   C. Rajagopalachari, 'Why we need English', Ramachandra Guha ed., *Makers of Modern India*, Viking, Penguin Books India, 2010.

81   SVK, 'Innovation, but at what cost?', *The Hindu*, 12 December 2013.

82   See Ken Auletta, 'Citizens Jain', *New Yorker*, 1 October 2012.

83   Jerry Pinto, *Em and the Big Hoom*, New Delhi: Aleph Book Company, 2012.

84   Binoo John, *Entry from Backside Only: Hazaar Fundas of Indian English*, New Delhi: Rupa Publications, 2013.

85   Nissim Ezekiel, 'The patriot', *Poem Hunter* <https://www.poemhunter.com/poem/the-patriot-10/> [accessed: 15 May 2019].

86   Sharmila Ganesan Ram, 'Hot pooris and a hanging: The legends of Pancham Puriwala', *Times of India*, 4 February 2017.

87   Mistry, 'Lend me your light', *Swimming Lessons and Other Stories from Firozsha Baag*.

88   Bachi Karkaria, 'Why is Infia's wealthy Parsi community vanishing?', *BBC*, 9 January 2016.

89   Mistry, 'The ghost of Firozsha Baag'.

90   *Report of the Indian Cinematograph Committee, 1927–1928*, Calcutta: Central Publications Branch. Government of India, 1928.

91   Ibid.

92   Devyani Chaubal, 'Ace gossip columnist Devyani Chaubal writes on Raj Kapoor's leading ladies', *India Today*, 5 September 2014.

93   N. Ramakrishnan, 'Is radio relevant in the 21st century?', *The Hindu*, 11 January 2018.

94 Ibid.

95 Melville de Mellow, *Remembered Glory*, New Delhi: Publications Division, Ministry of Information and Broadcasting, Government of India, October 1972.

96 Ibid.

97 Barbara Wallraff, 'What global language?', *The Atlantic*, November 2000.

98 'Future faces of Indian science and technology', *India Today*, 27 December 1999.

99 David Arnold, 'Nehruvian science and postcolonial India', David Arnold, Nehruvian Science and Postcolonial India, Vol. 104, No. 2 (June 2013), The University of Chicago Press on behalf of The History of Science Society, Vol. 104, No. 2, June 2013.

100 'New GSMA study projects almost one billion mobile subscribers in India by 2020', *GSMA*, 26 October 2016 <https://www.gsma.com/newsroom/press-release/new-gsma-study-projects-almost-one-billion-mobile-subscribers-india-2020/> [accessed: 23 May 2019].

101 Girish Karnad, *Boiled Beans on Toast: A Play*, Oxford University Press, 2014.

102 T. J. S. George, *Askew: A Short Biography of Bangalore*, New Delhi: Aleph Book Company, 2016.

103 B. Lewis Rice, Mysore: A Gazetteer Compiled For Government, Archibald Constable and Company, 1897.

104 Danish Sait, 'Episode 16 - Nograj Sir is deeply hurt by banning of 500 and 1000 notes', *YouTube*, 14 November 2016 <https://www.youtube.com/watch?v=vQbkp0ML0Tc> [accessed: 23 May 2019].

105 Abhrajit Gangopadhyay and Elisabeth Behrmann, 'India buys 200 tons of IMF's gold allotment', *Wall Street Journal*, 4 November 2009.

106 Aditya Narayan <https://www.facebook.com/cradityanarayan/videos/10154926627998473/> [accessed: 23 May 2019].

107 Justin Kuepper, 'What Will Be the World's Largest Economies By 2050?', *The Balance*, 28 December 2018 <https://www.thebalance.com/largest-world-economies-in-2050-4153858> [accessed: 23 May 2019].

108 'Main findings: All India rural report', Annual Status of Education Report 2018 <http://img.asercentre.org/docs/ASER%202018/Release%20Material/aser2018nationalfindingsppt.pdf> [accessed: 23 May 2019].

109 Pavan Varma, *Becoming Indian: The Unfinished Revolution of Culture and Identity*, New Delhi: Penguin Books India, 2012.

110 Nabaneeta Dev Sen, 'The wind beneath my wings', Leela Gulati and Jasodhara Bagchi, eds., *A Space of Her Own: Personal Narratives of Twelve Women*, New Delhi: Sage Publications, 2005

111 Sen, 'Receive me, then, Calcutta', the *Hindu Literary Review*, 5 May 2002.

112 Sen, 'From *My Life, My Work*', Meena Alexander, ed., *Name Me A Word: Indian Writers Reflect on Writing*, New Haven: Yale University Press, 2018.

113 Ibid.

114 Mukulika Banerjee, Daniel Miller, *The Sari*, London: Bloomsbury Publishing, 2008.

115   Geoffrey Moorhouse, *Calcutta*, London: Weidenfeld & Nicolson, 1971

116   Shib Chunder Bose, *The Hindoos As They Are: A Description of the Manners, Customs and Inner Life of Hindoo Society in Bengal*, Calcutta and London: W. Newman & Co., 1881.

117   Ibid.

118   Theon Wilkinson, *Two Monsoons: The Life and Death of Europeans in India*, London: Gerald Duckworth & Co Ltd., 1976.

119   Sir William Jones, *Discourses delivered before the Asiatic Society: and Miscellaneous Papers, on the Religion, Poetry, Literature, etc. of the Nations of India*, London: Printed for Charles S. Arnold, 1824.

120   Sandip Roy, 'Marwari City: Stories of Kolkata's heritage often exclude its prominent community, *Firstpost*, 11 May 2016.

121   'Protests against Telegraph visual', *The Telegraph*, 18 July 2009.

122   Nilanjana Roy, *The Girl Who Ate Books: Adventures in Reading*, New Delhi: Fourth Estate, HarperCollins Publishers, 2016.

123   Fakrul Alam and Radha Chakravarty eds., *The Essential Tagore*, Cambridge (Mass.): Belknap Press, 2014.

124   Gandhi, *Young India*, Vol. 23, No. 215, 1 June 1921.

125   P. J. Marshall, ed., Cambridge: *The Cambridge Illustrated History of the British Empire*, 1996.

126   Sen, 'Name me a word', Meena Alexander, ed., *Name Me A Word: Indian Writers Reflect on Writing*.

127   Ibid.

128   Clinton B. Seely, 'Translator's note', Buddhadeva Bose, *'t Rained All Night*, New Delhi: Penguin Books India, 2010.

129   Sen, 'Ours was a family of strong women', *The Telegraph*, 8 March 2013.

130   Sen, 'Stand back, please, it's the Nobel!', Indira Chowdhury, trans., *Indian Literature*, Vol. 50, No. 6, New Delhi: Sahitya Akademi, November-December 2006.

131   Ngũgĩ wa Thiong'o, *Decolonizing the Mind*, Nairobi: East African Educational Publishers, 1986.

132   'Meet the author: P. Lal', New Delhi: Sahitya Akademi, 8 March 1996.

133   Buddhadeva Bose, qtd. in M. K. Naik, 'Indian pride and Indian prejudice: reflections on the relationship between regional Indian languages and Indian writing in English', New Delhi: *Indian Literature*, Vol. 47, No. 4 (216), July–August 2003, pp. 168–180.

134   'P. Lal', *The Economist*, 11 November 2010.

135   Raja Rao, *Kanthapura*, George Allen & Unwin, 1938.

136   Narayan, *A Story-Teller's World*.

137   Sen, 'An open petter to Salman Rushdie', *Indian Express Magazine*, 13 July 1997.

138   Saadat Hasan Manto, 'Hindi or Urdu?', Aakar Patel, ed. and trans., *Why I Write: Essays by Saadat Hasan Manto*, Chennai: Tranquebar Press, 2014.

139   David Crystal, 'Mother-tongue India', Talk for Lingua Franca, ABC Australia, January 2005.